THE BEGINNING OF US

HILARI T. COHEN

vinci
BOOKS

Vinci Books

vinci-books.com

Published by Vinci Books Ltd in 2026

1

This work is a work of fiction. Names, characters, places and incidents are the product of the author's imagination or are used fictitiously. Any resemblance to actual persons, living or dead, places and incidents is entirely coincidental.

A CIP catalogue record for this book is available from the British Library.

Paperback ISBN: 9781036712648

The EU GPSR authorised representative is Logos Europe, 9 rue Nicolas Poussion, 17000 La Rochelle, France contact@logoseurope.eu

By Hilari T. Cohen

The Seasons of Us

The Beginning of Us

Almost Us

Still Us

Always Us

Forever Us

Also by Hilari T. Cohen

The Lyric of Memory

Adjusting the Rear View

Perfectly Polite

Fabulously Flirty

The Wick and the Flame

The Woodcarver's Secret

Question Everything

Quarantined by Love

Chapter One

Ruby needed a job. She needed one fast. It wasn't even like it had been an active decision for her to get into her car and drive, but that's where she was--on the highway, racing against the approaching sunset, pushing her old, grey, dented Kia to its maximum potential as she merged onto the 495 toward the Bourne Bridge. The car ride, which she could have done eyes closed, used to give her the ultimate rush. As a child, she had spent many happy hours playing I Spy in the backseat of her parents' latest model SUV, headed to their summer home in Bluff's Cove, a small outpost almost at Provincetown, near the end of Cape Cod. Right now, hands clenched tightly to the wheel, those safe and happy times seemed to be a distant memory of someone else's life. Her world was upended when her father had made the poor decision to invest every penny of his personal and business wealth into what turned out to be a Ponzi scheme, and lost it all. Their lives had been thrown into turmoil, their Park Avenue condo and possessions sold, their futures uncertain. And it all happened right after

Ruby's acceptance into Harvard Law School, which now she'd need to fund herself if she still had the inner fortitude to attend. Her father's words were ringing in her ears as she drove.

"You have to go, Ruby. Don't let my mistakes change the course of your life."

"But dad. Wouldn't it be better if I just got a job and helped you and mom?" she asked as she looked around the tiny apartment in Queens where her parents had moved, a far come-down from the pricey digs she'd grown up in.

"Absolutely not!" shouted the man who'd not raised his voice to her once in all the years she'd lived at home. "You will not suffer from my misfortune, not on my watch. Take the loans and go to Harvard. Invest in yourself, Ruby. You're worth it!"

An ivy league education might be priceless, Ruby considered as she made her way to the Cape, but it didn't come without a huge cost. And when she reviewed her options, there seemed to be only one clear solution, the one her father suggested. She'd need a summer job that would cover her living expenses for the year, and she'd borrow the tuition from a bank. She'd be in debt for quite a while after graduation, but she was counting on that old "crimson tie" connection to land her a career that would earn her a considerable salary. It was her only hope, and she was putting all of her eggs into that one basket. Now she just needed the job that would net her enough cash to safely tuck away and live on when summer ended and school began, and she knew just the place to go. The Hut.

The Hut was a beachside bar that just happened to serve enough of a menu to call itself a restaurant. Tucked away at the end of one of the most popular beaches on the National Seashore, it opened on Memorial Day and closed on Labor Day, netting the employees a ton of cash in the short but busy summer season. It was mostly staffed by a tightly knit group of locals, but it was Ruby's intention to apply for a waitressing job there nonetheless. Getting hired would be an almost impossible task, because there was a core group who always seemed to secure the most prime positions, but she didn't plan on giving up until she completed her mission. She knew that the employees were given free housing and she was counting on that, because the summer home she'd grown up in had been sold as well. The new owners had bought the house with everything still in it, almost down to the picture frames on the end tables and the decorative pillows that her mother had spent hours needlepointing, with whimsical sea creatures and colorful sunsets scattered on the comfortable couches throughout the living room. Ruby was counting on the fact that these new people weren't up on the Cape as yet, because she needed a place to sleep tonight, and she knew where the spare key was hidden. She had been the one to suggest the hiding place once she could drive a car and didn't want to carry a big bulky keyring in her little designer dress pockets. She let out a breath. That all seemed so long ago.

It was now early May, and Ruby could see signs of life beginning to emerge as she drove deeper onto the Cape. Towns like Orleans stayed open and operational all year round, but Bluff's Cove was a true summer destination, with most of the homes situated on a craggy piece of shore perched on a natural sand shelf high above the ocean. Very few stalwart souls managed to survive the harsh winters there. Most of the locals who worked at The Hut packed up by late autumn and head off to wherever the surf was warm, in tropical locations all over the world. If they were able to take their earnings from the three months of back-breaking restaurant work on the Cape and lived on it for the rest of the year, so could she. Or at least that's what she kept telling herself.

The sun was setting in the distance as she pulled off Route 6 and into the neighborhood where her former house stood. There was no sign of life in any of the homes on Sea Cliff Road, but she cut off her headlights just in case. Ruby really didn't want to draw any attention to the fact that she was about to break into the massively large house at the end of the lane, the one she'd grown up in. She pulled the car up the driveway and parked it behind the three-car garage, out of sight. She very quietly opened her door, stepped out onto the cold, hard ground and latched it shut again without a sound. Ruby walked into the outdoor shower and felt around under the shelf that they used in the summertime for shampoo and soap and there it was – the magnetic key holder, still attached to the little metal strip her dad had installed just for this purpose. For a brief moment, Ruby considered the thought that the new owners would have changed the locks, but that would be so strange here on the Cape. Most of the time, residents didn't lock their doors at all, only doing so if they were to be away for an extended amount of time. She held her breath as she shook the silver key out of the box and made her way to the back door. Sending up a quick silent prayer, she pushed it into the lock, turned the tumbler, and the door opened. She hoped it was a sign that she would be this lucky when she applied for a job in the morning.

Stepping into the kitchen, Ruby shuddered. It was cold inside the dark house. She didn't dare dial up the heat or turn on any lights, she just silently padded up the steps and down the hall into what used to be her room. It was exactly as she'd left it. A pale, pink comforter sat on the bed with pillows of various sizes and shapes stacked up against the light green wrought iron headboard. The poster she'd framed of an old map of New York City still hung on one wall. It was eerie, being there all alone, knowing that it was no longer hers. Ruby could feel tears prick the back of her eyes, but she fought off a full-on crying jag. She pulled back the blanket, shook off her shoes and clothing and climbed into the bed. She set the alarm on her phone for sunrise, and closed her eyes. Surprisingly, sleep came quickly, and she had no time to dream.

The next morning dawned brightly, with the sun peeking through her window on the wall opposite her bed, warming her face. She'd burrowed under the thick comforter during the night and had created a little pocket of cozy heat for herself, one that she really didn't want to have to leave anytime soon. Ruby allowed herself a few moments to luxuriate in the familiar feel of her childhood bed before dealing with the inevitable. With sheer will and determination, she pushed herself out from beneath the soft sheets and stood in the chilly morning air, hopping from foot to foot in a failing effort to keep warm. Running into the bathroom, she braced herself for the freezing water that she knew would flow from the faucet – even when the heater was on, it took a while for the warmth to work its way through the pipes and up toward the second floor of the old house. As she quickly washed her face and brushed her teeth as best as she could manage with the small stash of toiletry supplies she'd crammed into her backpack for this trip, she thought about getting out of the house in the pale morning light without notice. She'd gotten away with her scheme this far and she most certainly didn't want to throw a wrench in her plans by getting arrested for breaking and entering. The brief image of a fictitious headline on the front page of the Cape Cod Herald flashed before her eyes: *Poor Little Former Rich Girl Arrested Inside Home Lost in Huge Financial Downturn, Shaming Family Once and For All.* She shuddered more at the thought than the imagery. Now finished in the bathroom, she grabbed her bag, went back into the bedroom to put on the same clothes she'd worn the day before, smoothed the comforter back over the bed and replaced all the pillows. Satisfied that it all looked as it did before she arrived, Ruby turned to leave, but hesitated at the doorway to her old room. She looked around one last time before heading to the stairs, but stopped again before she got there and turned back. She had almost forgotten why she had made the effort to sneak into the house in the first place. She returned to her room and walked over to the high window on the wall across from the bed. Standing on her tiptoes, she reached up and was rewarded with the prize she'd come for – her seashell collection. As a child, she'd sourced the precious mementoes as she'd walk the beach with her dad and secret them away, standing on a chair to get them into their hiding place. While she no longer needed any help reaching them, seeing the time-worn shells resting now in her palm brought her right back to that happy place, the long afternoons she'd spent here without a care in the world. And although years had passed, and although her life was entirely different on this morning than it had once been, she wanted the shells as a talisman. She'd find that kind of inner peace again, the comfort in knowing that all would be well in her world. She just wasn't sure how long that would take.

Ruby made her way down the stairs, avoiding the big

picture window in the front of the house. She really didn't think that any of her former summer neighbors were there, but she took no chances. She quietly closed the back door behind her, replaced the key in its hiding place in the outdoor shower and opened the Kia's door, throwing the backpack on the passenger seat next to hers. Still standing outside, she reached in, released the parking brake, shifted the car into neutral, and began to push the small vehicle slowly down the sloping driveway, jumping in only when it began to gain some momentum. As the car cleared the property, she turned the key in the ignition and the engine roared to life. She was halfway down the block before she looked back in her rearview mirror, relieved to find no one on the street. She had made it out unseen. Releasing the deep breath she'd been unaware that she'd been holding in the whole time, Ruby pointed her car toward the only place she knew was open year-round for coffee – Le Petit Gateau – the French bakery on the edge of town. Pierre, the owner, had known Ruby since she was a child. He used to give her little buttery madeleines when she'd come in with her mother for his freshly baked baguettes on weekday mornings. She pulled the car into the nearly empty parking lot and sprinted through the cold morning air into the shop.

Once inside, she was happy to see that while not as busy as it would be in just a few weeks from now, the bakery was alive with activity. The open kitchen was practically humming. There were two bakers clearly tasked with rolling out dough and cutting the buttery confections into smaller pieces to be placed in the greased brioche pans in front of them. A large rack with giant loaves of cooling sourdough bread sat off to one corner and the display cases were full of pastries, croissants and delicate cookies. The combination of smells--yeast and butter and sugar-- were enough to make Ruby's stomach come to life. She was hungry. She reached into her bag for her wallet and stepped up to the counter and got the attention of the young girl working behind it.

"May I please have an almond croissant and an extra-large café au lait?" she asked.

As the clerk turned to assemble her order, she heard a deep voice rumble her name. "Ruby? Is that you?" Pierre stepped out from behind one of the massive ovens, broom in hand. He rested it against one wall and came to where she stood, grabbing her into a warm embrace. As he let her go, a small puff of flour was released into the air, and when Ruby looked down, she saw the remains of Pierre's hand-prints on each of the sleeves of her jacket.

"Pierre. How are you? It's been so long…"

"Yes, cherie, it has been. We all heard about what happened to your family, and that your parents sold the house. I'm so sorry, ma petite, I truly am." He gave her a telling glance, both of them acknowledging the speed with which gossip traveled in this very small and insular town.

For the second time in less than twelve hours, Ruby fought the tears she felt forming and blinked them away. "Thank you, Pierre," she murmured softly.

"So, what brings you up here, and so early in the season at that. No one is here yet. C'est un um, um, how you say… ghost town?"

Despite herself, Ruby smiled. "I came up to try and get a summer job, Pierre."

"You can always work here, you know that," the baker said sincerely.

"Thank you so much, but I really need to make up for the shortfall in my living expenses. I start law school in the fall."

"Ah, but of course. You were always the smart one in the family, n'est pas?"

"I'm thinking of applying at The Hut."

The color drained from Pierre's face. "Are you sure, ma petite? You know how wild it can get there in the summertime. And besides, the locals pretty much run wild there. Very few outsiders get jobs."

"I know, but the tips are supposed to be substantial. And the housing's free."

"You mean that barn that they consider fit for their employees? Ha! I wouldn't let them shelter a cow of mine!"

"I've got to try, Pierre. I mean it. I can't afford school if I don't get this job."

He shrugged his shoulders and said, "Well, okay Ruby, okay." He swiftly turned to the counter and took her now ready coffee and pastry, handing the delicious breakfast to her. "But if all else fails, come back! I'll teach you the fine art of French macarons! You can make money on the side with your baking once I'm done with you!"

Ruby smiled for what felt like the first time in days. "You are too kind to me Pierre. How much do I…"

"Non! This is on me. And if you are hungry this summer, you know where to turn. Your mother was always so generous to me. All those parties, all the cakes I made for her! Non. Your money is no good here. Just eat! You are way too thin."

Ruby leaned in and kissed the older man on the cheek, smelling the sweet, sugary scent that clung to his skin. "Thank you so much. I will let you know what happens…" She turned to leave, but her reached out and put a hand on her arm, stopping her.

"But of course, you must! And say hello to your parents for me. Tell them I think about them both and only wish them well. I don't believe those rumors about your father and his business dealings. Okay? Good." He turned back to bark an order out to one of his bakers, immersing himself back into the details of his day.

Ruby hesitated, almost ready to ask him what he meant about her dad's business dealings, but thought better of it. If she got the job at The Hut, she'd be here all summer, and was sure she'd get the opportunity to speak with Pierre again. For now, she just wanted to take a few minutes to gather her thoughts before applying for work.

The rising sun still had not sufficiently heated the air, and as soon as she sat back down in her car and opened her steaming coffee, the windows began to get foggy. She turned on the engine and put on the defroster, giving it a minute to work before heading away from the bakery. She took a deep gulp of her drink and immediately felt warmer as the rich liquid made its way down her throat. It was still too early to go over to apply for a job, so Ruby decided to drive to the beach and eat her breakfast there. At this time of year, there would be no crowd in the parking lot, so she figured she'd just sit in her car until The Hut was open. As she made her way along the familiar streets she could really sense the emerging spring. There were buds on the trees, but no open leaves yet, and the grass was still short on the lawns that met the sidewalks of the homes in the center of town. She could not recall ever being up on the Cape at this time of year before, so each and every turn of the road brought a new surprise. Yet even without the usual summertime landmarks, Ruby knew her way. This was the one place where she'd never need a map… it was all so familiar.

Once at the beach parking lot, she was stunned to see a number of flatbed trucks parked along the fence that separated the sand from the paved road. As far as she could tell, there were no occupants in the trucks, but as she drove closer to the edge of the dune, she could see them. Surfers. There were dozens of them dotting the horizon, sitting on their boards, waiting for the next big wave to crest and take them to shore for a ride. She was cold just looking at them. *The water must be just above freezing at this time of year*, she thought to herself. Despite their winter weight wet suits, it still had to be unbearable sitting out there in the middle of that icy ocean. But surfers were a patient lot. They waited, watching the horizon until the deep sea churned up enough energy to cause a wall of water to form behind them. Once the wave formed they moved, almost as one, paddling furiously and then standing on their narrow boards, navigating the course that pulled them along to the shoreline.

Ruby had taken surfing lessons once, when she was twelve. She had gotten the hang of it quickly enough, but found herself too distracted by her instructor to ever really master the sport. Steamroller was his nickname—she'd never known his given one, and he had been the first man she'd ever developed a crush on – tall, tan, muscular, with piercing hazel eyes and sun bleached dreadlocks that brushed against his shoulders. He called her Bumblebee, a simple play on her name as well as a reference to how her blonde hair and black wet suit reminded him of the pesky bugs that flew around the trash cans at the entrance to the beach where they surfed. She leaned back against the car seat's headrest for a minute and closed her eyes. She had been all long legs and lanky arms back then, having not really grown into her body yet, before filling out some and developing a soft curve to her hip and round, full breasts. It was almost embarrassing to remember just how boy-crazed she was that summer. All she did was think about Steamroller, planning on the day when she was older and he might notice her. Now, all she could do was hope that he didn't recognize her as that long ago little girl. *She could most certainly avoid that happening today*, Ruby thought to herself. She snapped her eyes open and went to turn the car on to make a quick exit from the parking lot when she noticed that there was no one left in the water. Instead, the whole group of surfers were already making their way up the dune that led to their trucks. She quickly downed what was left in her coffee cup and looked over to reach for the gear shift when she heard a soft tapping on the hood of her car. *Oh no*, was all she could think as she saw Steamroller standing right outside her door. She pushed the button and her window rolled down.

"Hi," he said. "Are you lost?"

She considered a snarky reply, one that had more to do with the existential aspects of that sort of open-ended question, but knew that he was being completely literal.

"Not really. I know my way around the beach here."

"Huh. That's funny. You don't look familiar. Do you live in Bluff's Cove or are you from Truro, or Brewster or somewhere else on the Cape?"

Oh, my God, he doesn't recognize me, was Ruby's immediate thought. *Wow. Think fast!* she told herself. She cleared her throat. "I've been here before," she said in as matter-of-fact a tone as she could muster. "I was just having some breakfast before I head over to try and apply for a job at The Hut." She reflexively brushed some croissant crumbs off of her lap and onto the floor mat.

He let out a little laugh. "The Hut? Good luck with that. Terry doesn't often hire off-Islanders. But I guess there's always a first time for everything!"

"Who said I was an off-Islander?" she shot back. He just smiled broadly and started walking away, his words lifting on the wind, "I hope you get it so that you can hang around this summer. Love to buy you a drink sometime!" Once he reached the old, beat-up blue Ford 150 that she assumed was his, he unlatched the tail gate and hoisted his board into the truck's bed in one smooth and practiced motion. It was all Ruby could do to stop her hand from shaking as she placed it on the steering wheel and slowly drove out of the lot in the direction of what she hoped would be her salvation.

In a matter of minutes, she was parked outside of The Hut, rehearsing her story over again in her mind. She had no real restaurant experience, but was a firm believer in the theory that with a healthy amount of confidence, you could convince anyone of anything. You just had to have the right air of authority about you, enough poise to pull the wool over the other person's eyes. She had decided to say that she had two years of prior experience at a restaurant in Manhattan that she knew recently went out of business. If she needed to give the name of a reference, her best friend Mimi was set to pretend to be the owner of the place she'd last worked. They'd spun a whole story about just how great Ruby was at waitressing, how she never got flustered and could manage a large, loud crowd, no matter how much they'd had to drink at the bar before being seated at a table. She had to sell the fairytale she'd created. Her whole future depended on it.

Ruby squared her shoulders, stood up to her full 5'3" and started walking down the path of crushed sea shells toward the entrance to the restaurant. This place did have the most prime location, that she had to admit to herself. A former lifesaving station from the 1890's, the original portion of the building sat at the top of the dune, both an American flag and a pirate flag flying in the cold wind whipping around and chilling Ruby down to her bones. Over time, more had been added on to the original structure so that it was now a series of buildings that could be seen for miles around the shoreline. It was only when you were close up to The Hut that you could see it for what it really was… a flimsily constructed bar on the beach with a rickety flight of stairs that led to the outdoor seating area of a restaurant comprised of picnic tables and benches, and a large indoor concert space with yet another bar that took up one entire wall. It just proved the theory about confidence to Ruby. If there was ever a shabby venue posing as the place to be, this was it. And it was go time.

She made her way past a dumpster and saw two men unloading what appeared to be keg after keg of beer from an unmarked truck. "Excuse me. Can you tell me where the manager of the restaurant might be?" she asked.

One of the men paused and just pointed toward the indoor space. She kept walking until she found an open door. It took a moment for her eyes to adjust to the semi-darkness, but once her vision cleared, she could see the flurry of activity. It was still three weeks until Memorial Day, but the work toward that date had begun. There were plastic chairs and tables stacked on each other haphazardly off to the side opposite the large bar, and a crew of workers were using a sanding machine on the ancient wood floor. Old posters adorned every available inch of the walls, advertising concerts from previous summers and despite the open windows to the bracing wind, there was a distinct smell of old, stale alcohol in the space, a reminder of what had been and a harbinger for the summer still to come. Ruby caught a glimpse of a middle-aged man with a clipboard coming out of what she assumed was the kitchen and made her way over to him.

"Good morning. Are you the manager here?" she asked politely.

"No."

He made to move past her when she continued. "Well, is the manager here today?"

He looked up at her. Ruby could see that he was hassled, and that he didn't want to be wasting his time talking to her.

"The manager's in, but let me tell you, she's not in a good mood."

Well this is an unexpected twist, Ruby thought, at the same time chastising herself for assuming that the manager would be male. "Can I speak with her?" she continued with her questioning of the man in front of her. "I'd like to apply for a job." There. She'd said it out loud, of that she was sure, because all the activity around her came to a halt.

"I think she's done all the hiring she needs to do for the season," was the man's reply. He put his head back down and continued to consult the papers on his clipboard.

Ruby was not to be so easily dismissed. "I'd like to speak with her myself, if that's okay."

"You sure about that?" a female voice from behind her inquired.

When she whirled herself around, she found herself face to face with her own personal moment of truth.

Chapter Two

Ruby pulled herself up to her full height as she faced the diminutive woman in front of her. She had jet black hair with a large streak of white framing both sides of her face. All Ruby could think was that the lady in front of her looked like the Disney villainess, Cruella de Ville. Putting on her most confident smile, she blurted, "I'd like to apply for a waitressing job."

"I'm done hiring for the season," the other woman said with a gruff voice, one that sounded like it had been the victim of one too many cigarettes over the course of its lifetime. "Cruella" turned her attention to the crew sanding the floor. "Watch the corners. Make sure you buff it all, even if you need to get on your hands and knees to get it done." The men seemed to freeze in place for a moment. "MOVE," was all she added before the frenzy of activity increased once more. The woman turned away from Ruby and began to walk across the room. Reflexively, Ruby reached out and touched the manager's arm.

"Please. I really need the work. I'll pick up any shift, any shift at all." She reached into her bag, attempting to pull out the falsified resume she'd stored there, knocking her wallet to the freshly sanded floor, pennies, dimes and quarters making their way free from the unzipped change compartment, skittering haphazardly around her feet. She immediately bent down to try to retrieve the errant money.

"You're really lucky that these idiots have not put down the fresh coat of varnish yet. If they had, I'd have been really pissed off at you right about now."

Ruby looked up from her position crouched on the floor, one hand full of change. "I'm sorry, but I'm more nervous than I thought I'd be." She stood up, threw the coins into her open purse and thrust her hand out toward the woman in the attempt to offer a handshake, which was fully ignored. "I'm Ruby. I know that you tend to hire locals, but my family has been living up here in the summertime for as long as I can remember. I know my way around and…"

The older woman cut her off with a narrowing glance. "Well, I'm Terry. I own this place. And the last person I want to hire is a summer resident. You're all the same. You won't make it for an hour here. I know your type. You're used to be served, not to doing the serving."

"No, not me. I've waitressed before." She thrust the now crumpled resume toward the gap between them.

Terry looked Ruby up and down, taking in the slim cut jeans and merino wool fisherman's sweater she was wearing. She walked closer, and in a low, menacing whisper said, "do much waitressing in those boots?"

Ruby felt a rush of heat move up her legs toward her face. She had worn a pair of old Prada boots, left over from a time when she spent money as if there was a tree sprouting dollar bills in the backyard of her former Bluff's

Cove home. She said, "Well, this isn't exactly what I wear when I work…"

"You can parade around in whatever you'd like to wear my dear, wherever you end up working. You just won't be waitressing here." She turned to leave.

"Please Terry. I really need this job. My dad lost everything in a bad business deal and we had to sell our house here. I'm just trying to make enough money to go to law school."

The older woman stopped in her tracks and shook her head before she turned back. For a brief moment, Ruby thought she saw Terry's face soften the slightest bit before the mask she'd worn earlier was restored. Time seemed frozen until Terry seemed to loosen her stance a bit and said, "The world doesn't need any more lawyers, but I do need a tee shirt girl." She stood straighter as she looked Ruby up and down. "You might be able to handle that."

"A tee shirt girl?"

"Yup. Got a concession out front where the bouncer sits. We sell shirts and beer mugs and a variety of other… paraphernalia. I usually hire a younger kid for that job, but you can give it a try for a night." She looked Ruby up and down. "Yeah. Put that blonde hair of yours up in pigtails and bat those big green eyes at the customers, and you might make a living. Let's see if you can keep up the pace, though."

"Does that job include lodging in the Barn?"

Terry looked back in surprise. "You want to live in the Barn? How do you know about the Barn anyway?"

"I told you. I'm very familiar with this place. I grew up here… I just, I mean, as I said earlier, my family doesn't live here anymore."

Just then, a look of awareness crossed Terry's face, her

eyes widening slightly. Ruby realized that the woman had made the connection and now knew exactly who she was and who her father was. "Well, I must be in a real generous mood today. You can go over and see if there's an open bunk on the girl's side. Ask for Cindy. Tell her I sent you. And be back here in an hour. If you want the work, you can start today. We have a whole lot of cleaning up to do before the season starts and everyone needs to pitch in. But from what I see here standing in front of me, you'll probably go running off before nightfall. It's real work, you know? Physical, back-bending work. What did you say your name was again?"

Ruby smiled for the first time since entering the building. "Ruby. It's Ruby. And I'm ready to work, you'll see. I'll be fine."

"Sure you will," Terry's tone was sarcastic once again, her earlier kindness vanished as she glanced at her watch and then looked directly into Ruby's stare. "Well then. What's the hold-up? Get going!" she demanded before turning her attention back to the men sanding the floor, each one having slowed their pace to pay careful attention to the conversation between these two women. "What the hell are you looking at?" she shouted. "Get back to work! We need the floor done before the tables can get scrubbed down. Go!"

Ruby didn't wait for Terry to change her mind. She scurried out into the parking lot and back to her car, heading off to the Barn before the tough old bird could reconsider and send her packing.

Cindy must have learned at the foot of the master, because she, too, gave Ruby a proper interrogation before begrudgingly opening the door to a shabby room, a bunk bed on each wall. "You can take that empty top one," she said, pointing to the well-worn mattress on the unsteady looking frame. There are some sheets in the closet at the end of the hall, might be a blanket or a pillow there as well. But I'd hurry. If Terry gave you an hour, you can bet she'll be looking for you at minute fifty- nine. Good luck."

"Thanks," was all Ruby could say. She threw her knapsack on the bed as if to mark it as her own and went off looking for the sheets. She would bring her larger duffle bag out of the trunk of her car later, but for now she wanted to get back over to The Hut. Once she found the linens, she hastily made up her bed. She grabbed the remaining threadbare blanket, and made a mental note to go into Hyannis when she got a moment. She knew there was a Sears in the Cape's only mall – she remembered going there with her mom once or twice -- she'd have to splurge and buy her own pillow as there were none in the closet. The Barn was relatively quiet. Aside from Cindy, Ruby hadn't seen another soul, but figured that every other resident was hard at work. She rummaged through her knapsack and pulled out her sneakers. Kicking off her boots, she slipped her well-worn Nikes on, knowing that she'd fit in better without a designer label so blatantly displayed anywhere on her body. It didn't matter that the clothes she wore, the clothes she had with her, were a few seasons old – no one would notice that. They wouldn't know that she could barely afford food and did her best to survive each and every day. Ruby knew that first impressions were all that mattered. She drew in a deep breath, head out the door of the room and back down the hallway, to the staircase that would bring her to the entrance. Once outside, she squinted in the sunlight. She might not have gotten the waitressing job she'd come for. *Not yet*, she told herself. She had every intention of working her way up the ladder before the season officially started. It was a personal challenge, one she fully expected to meet and conquer.

Once back at The Hut, one of the men showed her where they stored the tee shirts and told her to start to fill the shelves of the concession stand with some of each different design. It was mindless work. The shelves were clearly marked with little stickers for size and gender. There were sample shirts already hanging above each cubby, so Ruby knew exactly where to place each new one. Taking some initiative, she washed down the entire stand, buffed up each shelf and rehung the samples. Her hair was damp from exertion and her face was streaked with dirt. Just as she was in the middle of lugging yet another very heavy box across the parking lot from the storage unit, the now familiar blue truck pulled in, shells popping and spraying out behind the oversized tires. She looked up in time to see Steamroller and a beautiful shapely blonde woman step out.

"You again," he shouted, a large smile plastered across his face. "Looks like you did the impossible!"

Ruby stopped pulling on the box and wiped her grimy hands on the legs of her jeans. "Told you. I never doubted it," she answered a bit smugly.

"So, Terry's got her waitresses stocking the concession now?" he smirked.

"Not exactly a waitress yet. But just give me some more time. I'll get what I want!"

"Something tells me you always do." He turned to the woman he was with and pointed. "This is my sister, Jenny. She works here. As a waitress."

"Hi," Ruby said, knowing that with the hierarchy of this place, being a waitress meant you had made it to the top of the food chain.

"I didn't catch your name, but you look a little familiar. Have we met before?" the other woman asked, her critical eyes looking Ruby up and down.

"My name's Ruby." She reached out her hand in the common gesture of acknowledgment, but Jenny ignored her. Ruby continued, "I don't think we've met. I just got into town last night." She could feel the inevitable coming.

"Really? Wow. I have a thing for faces, I remember the people I meet. Helps me at work, you know, sorting out the orders when we're getting slammed here on a concert night. Wait. Let me try and place you…"

"I used to live up here every summer with my family," Ruby offered, trying to stall the uncomfortable moment she knew was only seconds away now. "Maybe you recognize me from that, you know, when we'd come into the restaurant for dinner."

Jenny narrowed her gaze and Ruby could pinpoint the exact moment when the lightbulb went off. "Wait a sec. Did my dumbass brother ever give you surfing lessons?"

If the ground would just open up and swallow me whole, Ruby thought to herself. *That's about all I could ask for right now…* She looked the other woman straight in the eye. "Well now that you mention it, I do believe that he did."

"I did?" Steamroller broke in. "I'm not sure I remember," he said, searching her eyes for a glimmer of recognition.

"Ha!" Jenny laughed out loud. "Maybe you should smoke a little less weed, brother. It might help jog your memory. Or at least keep you from erasing any new ones you might get the chance to make!" She rolled her eyes skyward.

Undeterred, Steamroller continued. "We didn't sleep together, did we? How long ago was that anyway?" he then asked earnestly.

"Ten summers ago. I was twelve."

Awareness dawned on his face and he turned to his sister. "I do remember, Jenny. Stop hassling me for once." He then reached out for Ruby, drawing her into a clumsy embrace. "Bumblebee? Is that you? You've sure filled out some…"

"It's Ruby. Just Ruby. And yeah, that's me."

"Why the hell didn't you say so? I can't believe it."

Just then Jenny cut in. She'd connected all the dots. "Isn't your dad the one who lost all his money in some weird illegal business deal? I read something about it last winter. Kind of a scandal, no?"

"It's not important," she said quickly, trying to change the path of the conversation. "I'm just me, here trying to make enough money to go to school in the fall." Ruby hoped that would put an end to this line of questioning, but she pretty much knew it wouldn't. She steeled herself for whatever was to come next.

"Did you have to pull out of some fancy university or something?" Jenny challenged.

"No. It's grad school. I have a BA already," Ruby said barely above a whisper.

"Hear that big bro? She's done with college. Gonna get more of a fancy education."

"C'mon Jenny. Give the kid a break. She's just trying to get a leg up on life," he said, smiling genuinely at Ruby.

"Right. And she thinks she's better than us." Jenny

turned away, starting to walk toward the entrance to The Hut. "Don't waste your time, Steamroller. She won't last here. Not even selling those crappy tee shirts Terry keeps hawking to the tourists." She slipped inside, leaving Ruby feeling deflated with her former crush standing in front of her.

Steamroller grimaced. "Don't listen to Jenny. She's got a tough outer layer, but believe me, she's not so bad. She'll warm up to you once she sees that you're not stealing her customers. It's very territorial here. People come back year after year, so the staff knows who the whales are. They fight over who gets to serve them."

"The whales?"

"Yeah. The big tippers. That's the reason so many locals work here. They really make a huge bankroll in a short amount of time."

"That's sure why I'm here." She turned to resume lugging the heavy box to her post when two more pick-up trucks pulled into the lot and came to a screeching stop inches from where they stood.

"Hey Nick, what's up?" she heard Steamroller say.

"Yo, dude. I was just about to ask you the same thing," a deep voice replied. A tall, thin guy stepped out of his truck. "And who is this? Moving in on the new blood already, man?" He smiled at Ruby, but she could barely see his face for the overgrown, shaggy mane of dark hair that obscured her view.

"Cut it out, Nick. She's just getting the feel of the place. This is Ruby."

"Well, baby, nice to meet you," he came to stand so close to her that she could smell the musky male scent of him. It felt like an assault.

"My name's not Baby," she replied tersely. "It's Ruby.'

"Well, I think you've got a pretty little baby face, no matter what your real name is," Nick replied, "so I'm just gonna call you Baby!"

"Cut the shit and stop hassling the woman," the third man said as he stepped out of his truck. He walked toward Ruby, reaching his hand out to offer to shake hers. "Hey. I'm Cooper. Nice to meet you." When she looked up her gaze was met by his dark blue twinkling eyes. Her breath caught in her throat when their hands touched, and her knees went a little weak when she felt the genuine warmth of his palm as his long fingers grasped hers. The others continued their conversations around her, but she couldn't really pay any attention to what was being said, other than to try and muster up something to say back to him.

"Hi," was her barely mumbled response. "I'm Ruby."

"Right," he smiled, adding, "so I've heard. Where're you from?"

"Um, Manhattan." She had to get back some control. He was making her tongue-tied.

"That's great. Haven't been there in years. I'm not the big city type!"

"Yeah, well, it's certainly a whole different sort of vibe, I guess."

She could feel herself start to sweat despite the fact that the sun had disappeared behind a menacing dark rain cloud. Searching for words, she spat out, "So, Cooper. What do you do all summer?"

"I bartend. Here. At The Hut."

"Of course you do. Why else would you be," she stumbled over the words. "I mean, we're all here for the same reason. To get the place together for opening day…" She crossed her arms in front of her chest trying to regain some control even as she felt as though she was spiraling out into the universe. "How's that work out for you?" She watched his thinly veiled amusement at her discomfort and felt flushed.

"Can't complain. I mix drinks for a living, get great tips and make people happy on hot summer nights. It's a good gig, you know?"

"If you say so…"

He turned to walk into the restaurant, then stopped. "Do you need help with that box?"

She looked up at him, her work forgotten for the time that they stood together in the parking lot. It was a tempting offer. His broad shoulders and muscular forearms strained against the fabric of his worn flannel shirt. It would have been no problem for him to lift one of the boxes and carry it inside for her. But Ruby couldn't let that happen. She had to do this job herself.

"No. I've got this," she smiled, hoping to convince him that she really did have everything under control.

"Ok." Taking another step closer to her, he asked, "What are you doing later? I could show you around town, you know, help you get acquainted with the area."

"Oh, I'm familiar with Bluff's Cove. I've been here before." Just then it dawned on Ruby that Cooper had no idea who her family was, and maybe didn't know about her father and the scandal that had clearly made news all the way up here.

"Cool. Then have a drink with me later? We could go over to the Underground, get to know each other better."

Ruby felt her nerves begin to really overwhelm her. She said quickly, "I don't know what time I'll be done here. I'm not sure."

He smiled warmly. "No worries. I'll come find you once Terry lets us all knock off for the night." He leaned in and whispered in her ear, his warm breath tickling her neck, "Just so you know. Her bark is a whole lot worse than her bite." He then moved past her, whistling all the way into the restaurant and out of sight.

In that moment, Ruby's only thought was that it was going to be one hell of a summer.

Chapter Three

After the day's back-breaking work was done, Ruby sat on the floor of her room at the Barn, her duffle bag full of clothing unzipped in front of her, feeling both exhausted and wired at the same time. She had much more in the bag than would fit in the small cubby allotted to her in the shared space, and she certainly did not want to have more available to wear than the other women living there. She pulled out a few simple tee shirts, her oversized blue sweater, two pair of shorts, two pair of jeans and some underwear and sweat pants. She rummaged around on the bottom of the bag for her flip flops and one pair of wedged sandals before zipping the bag back up and shoving it far underneath the bed. She had the thought that she'd put the duffle back in the trunk of her car, but a full day of lifting and moving boxes made her arms feel like rubber. The bag would have to wait. She was refolding her clothing into the smallest possible little packages she could to maximize the shelf space she had when the door pushed open. A tall woman entered the room, her burnished cocoa skin damp from the shower, her curly dark hair poking out from underneath the towel precariously balanced on her head.

"Oh hey," she said. "You must be the new girl everyone's talking about. Is that your stuff on that top bunk?"

Ruby looked up. She had left her clean, folded towels and toiletry bag on her bed. "Yeah, that's the bed Cindy told me to take," she said a little defensively. "I was going to take a shower, but I wanted to unpack first. I'm Ruby."

"So I've heard. I'm CeCe. And if you want to shower, you'd better hurry. The bathroom's coed, and most of the guys give us the first hour after quitting time at to get in there before they go. It sorta works out before the season starts when everybody's hours are basically the same. Once summer comes, it's mayhem in there."

"Thanks for the warning. I really appreciate the help." She stood to grab her towel and looked shyly at the other woman.

CeCe smiled. "Just so you know, I like to decide for myself how I feel about people. I try to keep above the fray. There's a lot of talk about how Terry hired a tourist to work the concessions in there." She tilted her head toward the door, and added, "Just keep to yourself. Let them come to you."

"Them?"

"Yeah. The other girls. It can be a little rough being the newbie. Especially when you're different. Trust me, I know."

Ruby smiled back. "Oh, you mean you're not a local either?"

"Oh no, honey. I'm a local. Bluff's Cove born and bred. I'm just black."

Ruby shook her head, not knowing how to answer. "I guess I'm going to grab that shower now." Pulling her essentials down off of her bed, she stepped into her flip flops, wrapped herself tightly in her towel, threw her bra and underwear on her bed and walked out of the room down the hall to the communal bathroom. It was a sight. There were four sinks against a wall that had some tiles missing, a similar number of toilet stalls with old banged up doors hanging precariously on rusty hinges and three showers, two of them occupied at the moment. She could hear singing coming from behind one of the muddy colored curtains, steam from the hot water filling the room. The voice was both pleasant and powerful.

"Sing out, Louise!" a voice rose from the doorway to the bathroom. Ruby turned, startled to find a woman standing there, hair still wet from a recent washing. "And move it along, you two. The new girl is here and she wants to say hello," The woman stepped closer. "You are the new girl, right?" she asked, crowding Ruby's personal space.

"I am."

"Tourist," she said in a low voice, and then louder for the others to hear, "I mean, you're not from the Cape." She turned to the mirror and started to brush out her long brown hair.

This whole "tourist" thing was starting to get old for Ruby, but she was careful not to let her real feelings show. She'd have to endure the initial hazing, of that she was certain.

"Right. But I'm here now. And I can't wait to meet everyone," she said with a forced cheerfulness that she truly did not feel.

At that moment, she heard the showers turn off in unison. The two women behind the curtains emerged – one naked, one wrapped in her towel. All Ruby could think was that this was just like freshman year at college. She'd have to try and blend in as best she could.

"It's Ruby, right?" the naked girl asked, making her way over to the sink. She took her towel and wiped away the built-up steam before wrapping her body in the now somewhat wet terrycloth.

"I am."

"I'm Patti. This is Ronnie," she said, pointing at the woman in the doorway. "And this one," she pointed at the towel-clad redhead, "is our resident American Idol, Louise," she joked at the expense of her co-worker.

"Oh, I thought you were making a joke about 'Gypsy'..."

"Who's a gypsy?" Louise asked, stepping forward, looking somewhat insulted.

"No, it's a line from a Broadway show," Ruby began to explain, but thought better of it. "Never mind. I better take a quick shower before the guys show up and want to get in here."

"Hold on," Patti, clearly emerging as the leader of the group, inquired, stepping between Ruby and the available shower stall. "You've got a minute. Who'd you know? How'd you get Terry to hire you?"

"I don't know anyone. She decided to give me a chance."

"That old bird doesn't give anyone a break. You must be special, then, huh?" Ronnie challenged. The other women remained silent, but clearly were interested in hearing her response.

"I can't tell you why she decided to hire me, but I can promise you that I'll work my ass off."

"I don't need your empty promises, and I don't care

what you do, just as long as you don't come near any of my regulars. I've built up quite a following and I don't need you and your kind stepping in on my turf. Understand me?"

"Loud and clear," was Ruby's response as she pushed her way between the other women and stepped into the shower, pulling the curtain closed behind her, effectively shutting down the conversation.

Hanging her towel on the rusty hook, she turned the water on as hot as she could bear it and dived under the soothing spray. It had been a long time since sunrise that morning and she really just wanted to wash off the effects of the day and go to sleep. She didn't feel at all hungry. She was just overwhelmingly tired. She washed her hair, taking a quick minute to throw on some conditioner, but hyper-aware of the time. She could barely deal with the naked women. She most certainly didn't want to run into any unclothed men. At least not yet.

Ruby's mind turned to Cooper and she wondered if he was living in the Barn as well. She hadn't asked earlier, too afraid to know the answer. Tipping her head back and rinsing the shampoo from her hair, she shut off the water, grabbed her towel and wrapped it tightly around her body. She wanted to get out of that bathroom before she was confronted with any more questions. Thankfully the hallway was blissfully empty and she was able to step back into her room unseen, only to find out that both Patti and Ronnie were her other roommates. *Fantastic,* was all she could think. *The hits just keep on coming…"*

CeCe was sitting on the top bunk across from hers, applying make-up to her face with a small, lighted magnifying mirror balanced precariously on the top of the bedframe. "I'm going to get a burger at Benny's out on Route 6. Wanna join?"

Ruby looked up at CeCe, not sure if the other woman had been addressing her. "Are you asking me?" she questioned.

CeCe held her kohl eye pencil up in the air. "Hell yeah. I'm asking you." She smirked. "Long day?"

As tired as she was, Ruby knew that she shouldn't turn down this offer. She had to try and make some friends here, and the sooner the better.

"Sure. I'll just dry my hair and throw on some jeans…"

"Don't bother with anything too fancy," Patti chimed in. "We're all Levis and Old Navy types. We don't have rich daddies backing us up."

"Knock it off, Patti, please. You know that Ruby's got nothing anymore," CeCe turned. "You should just set the record straight, honey, once and for all. We've all heard the rumors. Just tell it like it is and we can be done with this whole thing."

Ruby looked around. The other three women faced her, expectantly. She drew in a breath. "Ok. I used to come up to Bluff's Creek in the summers with my family. But a year ago my dad lost all of our money in a business transaction. I really don't know the details, and I don't want to. My parents sold our home here, and our apartment in Manhattan as well. I was accepted into law school this fall, and I'd like to attend, but know that's only possible if I make enough money this summer. I have no other plan, no one funding my life anymore. It's just me." The words came out in a rush and when she was done, Ruby silently held her breath waiting for the response.

"Oh boo-hoo girls. She doesn't know the particulars, you see. C'mon. You think we should believe that, really?" Patti insisted.

In a moment of exhaustion and exasperation, Ruby

threw her towel onto her bed, pulled a tee shirt over her head and tucked it into her jeans. "No, I don't. I didn't ask my parents as we were being evicted from our home, everything we owned either sold or repossessed or just put out on the street. You can believe me or not, I really don't care. I am here to work. It would be nice to make a few friends, but I've found out in the last few months that I'm fine alone. I guess it's your choice." She looked around at the other women, hoping that the line of questioning had come to an end.

"It's been my experience that stuff just doesn't get repossessed. Hell, when my old man's truck got picked up by the repo man it was after he ignored the payment letters for months. You must have had some clue," Patti demanded.

Ruby just shook her head. "I wasn't really privy to my parent's financial life."

"Financial life? What the hell is that," Patti gave a knowing smile to the other women. "You mean your folks had money in the bank? They didn't live paycheck to paycheck like the rest of us?" She laughed. "Financial life. That's a good one."

"Enough already Patti. Give the girl a break. You asked her to explain herself and I think she just did. Back off," CeCe challenged, jumping down from her top bunk. She turned to Ruby. "Are you coming out for a burger, or what?"

"I'm ready," was Ruby's response. She quickly threw her still wet hair into a high ponytail, put some lip gloss on and grabbed a blue sweater from her cubby. She slipped her feet into her wedged sandals. "Let's go."

"Are you guys heading to the Underground later?" CeCe asked over her shoulder as they walked to the door.

"Probably," Patti replied.

"See you there," CeCe said, leading Ruby into the hallway.

The two women walked to the parking lot in silence, but once outside, CeCe turned to Ruby and said, "You're driving."

Ruby motioned to the Kia. "That one's mine."

CeCe smiled. "Well, it sure ain't fancy, that's for sure."

All Ruby felt was relief. She pressed the button on the remote and the locks opened. They got inside and CeCe began to give directions to the little roadside shack that she swore served the best burgers anywhere in the state of Massachusetts.

For all the years Ruby had been coming up to the Cape, Benny's Burgers had gone unnoticed. Barely visible from the road, it was little more than a permanent food truck with two picnic tables set off to one side. They parked just off of Route 6 under a small cluster of trees. The sun was almost completely gone from the horizon and Ruby was glad she had her sweater on. It was much chillier now in the encroaching darkness. They stepped up to the window and CeCe ordered for both of them – the classic burger, fries and onion rings. Once the food was cooked, they took their dinner on red plastic trays to one of the tables. After one bite of the juicy burger, Ruby knew that CeCe had been right – it was the best she'd ever tasted.

"This is so good!" she exclaimed, taking another napkin to wipe her face. "Or I didn't realize that I was actually hungry!"

"Oh no, it's that good. I come here a lot on my days off. The food is fresh and the price is right."

"Does Terry allow you to eat at the restaurant?"

"Yeah. There's a family meal each day at 4:30, before

the dinner rush. Nothing fancy, a lot of pasta. But it's decent, and best of all, it's free."

"How long have you been working at the Hut?" Ruby asked as she dipped a fry into the pool of ketchup on her plate.

"This is my second summer. The girls weren't so nice to me either at first, and I've known them most of my life. They don't like new or different, I guess you can say."

"But you grew up here, right?"

"Yeah, I did. My folks don't live here anymore though. The winters got too tough."

"I don't get it. If the others have known you forever, why…"

"There aren't too many black families in Bluff's Cove. I was never part of their crowd in high school. I stuck to myself mostly."

"You must have been lonely."

"Not really. I was pretty active in our church when I was younger. It's not too far from here. And I made some friends once I moved to Boston and started college."

"Oh, so you're in school too!"

"Yeah, but keep that to yourself. Most natives think that getting a higher education is only for people like you." She held her burger mid-air. "Wait. That came out wrong. Sorry." She stopped talking for a minute before saying, "Most of the people from Bluff's Cove never leave here, you know? They don't ever think beyond what they know. And actually, I'd rather you didn't share the fact that I'm a student with anyone. I'd just get a lot of shit for it. Kinda like what they did to you before."

"Okay. But how much more of that do you think I'm going to get? Are they done yet?"

"Oh no, honey, not by a long shot! They live to feed on

people like you. You're fresh meat!" She laughed. "But I've got your back. And they'll get bored sooner or later anyway."

"Great."

"Don't let it bother you. They can't help themselves."

Ruby chewed on her burger before asking, "what's your major?"

"Nursing. I really want to be a trauma nurse. I like the adrenaline rush."

"Wow. That's a tough career."

"My mama always said that nothing's worth doing if it's not a challenge," CeCe replied.

"Huh," Ruby answered. "Then I guess I've got my work cut out for me this summer."

"Oh yeah. We all do!" CeCe answered.

The two women ate their meal and talked until the sky was completely dark. With no moon above there was nothing to light their path, so they held on to each other's arm and walked carefully. Once back in the car, CeCe said, "Just pull out onto the road. I'll get my bearings in a minute."

"Twice today I've heard mention of the Underground. What is it?" Ruby asked as she maneuvered in the darkness.

"It's one of the few places that the tourists haven't discovered yet. It used to be a bomb shelter back in the day. You know, up here in the Cape during the Cold War in the '60's, folks truly believed that we might be attacked by Russia because the coast is right here. And they might have been right, who really knows? They built a series of shelters in the woods, away from the water. Most of them were knocked down when developers started to build all those big houses." She paused. "No offense, but we locals really hate those homes. All those mega-mansions just don't belong here. We were a community of small cottages until someone discovered just how beautiful it is here."

"I'm sure," Ruby murmured with growing self-awareness.

"Anyway, one of the remaining shelters was turned into a bar. After the Hut closes most of us head there to count our tips and lick our wounds."

"Lick your wounds?"

"Don't kid yourself, Ruby. It's back-breaking work to bring people their overpriced seafood dinners. And then you get the idiots who get drunk and try to grab your ass. Ugh."

"Does that happen a lot?" Ruby's eyes widened.

"More often than I'd like to admit." She looked at the road ahead. "Our turn is coming up. Make a left."

Ruby signaled even though there was no other car in sight and pulled onto what seemed to be a dirt path, overgrown with low hanging branches that almost engulfed her small car. "Are you sure I can drive on this?"

"Yeah. You'll see it in a minute."

A little further ahead, in a clearing of trees, sat the Underground. A small concrete structure with a flimsy tin roof, it was surrounded by at least a dozen other trucks and motorcycles.

"Told ya. We're here."

The Underground was true to CeCe's description. Barely a building, the cement, windowless walls were covered in graffiti. On the far side of the room away from the entrance was a foosball table and behind that, a well-worn dart board hung precariously from a silver nail. The bar took up one end of the place, wobbly stools pulled close to the well-worn wooden countertop. There was an old juke box in the corner. As soon as they walked in, the bartender called out to CeCe, "Well look who's here! I haven't seen you yet this season!"

"Hey Ned," CeCe replied affectionately to the beefy, balding man in the red plaid flannel shirt behind the bar. "How was your winter?"

"Can't complain. Was only snowed in once, and I didn't even kill the wife!"

"Ha!" CeCe responded. "Glad to hear it! By the way, this is Ruby. She's new."

"An Underground virgin? That calls for a drink, doesn't it?" He smiled and lifted two icy bottles of Pabst Blue Ribbon beer onto the counter. "The first one's one me, sweetheart!" He winked at Ruby.

"I was hoping you'd say that!" CeCe kidded. "Thanks!" She lifted both bottles and passing one to her new friend. "Ned's the best. He owns this place. Built it up from scratch. The wood on the bar was reclaimed from an old fishing boat. Very cool."

Ruby looked at the bottle in her hand. The iconic label, with its silver foil paper and distinctive blue ribbon was something she'd only seen in pictures. It certainly wasn't the artisanal beer she was used to being served in Manhattan, but *when in Rome*, she thought. She lifted the bottle to her lips and took a long swallow, letting the cold liquid swim down her throat. It tasted good. She had about three quarters of the bottle finished when CeCe grabbed her hand and dragged her over to the juke box. Fishing around in her pockets, she had come up one quarter short.

"Do you have any change?" she asked.

"Um, let's see." Ruby reached into the bottom of the little purse she'd been wearing across her body. Success.

"Here's fifty cents," she said, putting the two silver coins into her new friend's palm.

"Perfect, thanks." As CeCe leaned over the machine to make her selection, Ruby lifted the bottle to her lips, only to stop before taking another drink. The door to the Underground opened again, and the cool night air rushed in, bringing Cooper along with it.

Chapter Four

Ruby was frozen to the floor in front of the juke box as music started to play, swirling around the room and surrounding her in a cocoon of sound. It felt like everything was moving in some sort of weird slow motion…Bill Medley's voice rose from the ancient machine and she watched as Cooper looked around, finally settling on her gaze. He smiled broadly and walked toward her.

"Looks like we can have that drink together after all," he said.

"Seems to me that I'm ahead of you on that," she motioned to the nearly empty bottle in her hand. She had finished most of the contents a bit too quickly and was feeling looser and more relaxed than she had when they first met.

"Easy enough to rectify," he responded as he stepped up to the bar, returning in a quick minute with two fresh drinks.

"If only all life's problems were that easy to fix," she joked, looking at the colorful label on the new bottle he handed her. "Thanks," she said admiring the artwork that surrounded the logo. "Satan's Satin. I don't think I've ever had this beer before," she took a sip, tasting a smooth combination of cherries and hops. "Wow. It's good."

"Glad you like it. It's a local brew," he said offhandedly. "It might help chase your problems," he said, stepping closer to her. "But you can't drink them away. Take it from me, I learned the hard way. You've got to deal with them head on. Adjust your attitude. It's the first line of defense." He smiled broadly before taking a long pull on his beer.

"Wow. A barroom philosopher. How unique," she said with a large dose of sarcasm.

"That's cynical," he said, pulling back with a mock expression of surprise.

"Well, I have heard a lot of different types of advice over the last few months from people who think they know me when they don't. Besides, you may have your experience, but I have mine. There are some problems you can't fix with… how'd you put it? 'The proper attitude'?"

"First of all, I think you might have misunderstood me. It's not that you can fix it. It's the way you approach whatever the conflict is that counts."

"How's that?" she countered.

"I'll give you an example. "Let's say that, oh, I don't know. You meet a girl, and she seems really different. You offer to buy her a drink and she tells you she's unavailable, but you walk into your favorite bar, and there she is, drinking without you. Now, you could be offended, or you could try to put that aside and talk to her anyway, pick up where you left off and move forward."

Ruby felt herself flush. "Um, I really didn't plan on being here tonight, so please don't think that I turned you down with the intention of…"

"No worries, Ruby, really. I've learned to adjust my attitude on the fly." He winked at her. "And I would like to get to know you better."

Ruby looked down at the floor and pushed aside some of the accumulated sawdust with one toe. She drew in a deep breath and centered herself. She was most definitely intrigued. She switched the beer bottle from her right to her left and thrust the now available hand out into the space between them. She looked up and said, "Let's start over. My name's Ruby. It's nice to meet you."

His smile reached up to his eyes, softening his face and making him even more appealing. "And apparently, a quick learner, as well." He took her hand in his, but instead of shaking it, he lifted it onto his chest and whispered, "be still my heart."

Ruby could feel the strong beat behind the soft, well-worn fabric of his denim shirt. Her fingers tingled at the feel of the blood coursing through his muscular torso and she was surprised to find herself wanting to know the heat of his skin beneath the thin layer of cotton there. The brief connection was so unfamiliar, so unlike anything she'd known before that she actually felt the warmth of him pass between them. She jumped back, pulling her hand away. She couldn't let this happen. She had no time for a summer romance, and this particular type of man wasn't in her life plan. She had a responsibility, she reminded herself, to make enough money to attend school. That's why she was there. No other reason, plain and simple. There was no way she could allow herself this diversion, to fall into the depths of his deep, dark blue eyes. But, for as much as she tried to be strong, his smile, the way his mouth turned up so appealingly made it difficult to be strong enough to resist continuing their conversation. "You must have bigger problems than me," Ruby said, trying to steer clear of any more physical contact with the man in front of her.

"Not today," he said cheerfully. "For right now, you're it."

"Wow," she responded. "That's amazing. I have a whole long list of obstacles in my life right now."

"Anything you want to talk about?" he asked earnestly.

For Ruby, it seemed as though the rest of the room receded a bit and that they were in a small, private bubble that no one else could see or penetrate. And for as much as she could fight against it, she liked this newfound sensation, the connection she felt with him. She told him about school and shared both her excitement and trepidation about attending in the fall.

"Let me understand this," he said an hour later, after bringing two fresh beers over to where they now sat at a small table opposite the bar. "You spend three years breaking your back to learn everything you can about the law, you study and pass a two-day test to get your license and then you work eighteen hour days inside some cubicle in a big tall office building? That's just crazy talk. I mean, when do you get outside? When do you get to experience the world?"

"After I establish myself. It will take some time…"

"Yeah, and you'll be old and grey. You'll have missed your life."

Ruby stared back at him. "No I won't. I'll have a whole career, I'll make a decent living, have nice things again."

"Oh, I see," he replied. "What kind of 'things' are important to you?"

"Well for starters, I'd love to have a home to live in, which, right now I don't."He lifted his eyebrows in noticeable confusion.

Oh, I'm sorry, I thought the gossip mill had worked its way all around the island by now. I'm *that* girl. You know, the uppity one, whose father lost it all and now needs to work to afford to eat."He frowned at her words. "Sorry. I hadn't heard. But, so what? We all have to work.""Yeah, well some of my new roommates think that I won't make it here. As if I don't know how to sell tee shirts. What a joke."

"I'm sure you'll do fine. But go back to your life plan. What will you do once you're a big, fancy lawyer? But a mega mansion? A penthouse apartment? You'll never be there. You'll be working your eighteen hour days, won't you?"

She chose to ignore his sarcastic tone and continued. "Only at the beginning. But law partners in big firms have little henchmen like me to do their grudge work for them. Then once I have a home, I'd like to fill it with art and pretty pieces of odds and ends that I pick up along the way. And I dream about having an actual bank account again, one that has a positive balance…"

"Those are just material things, Ruby. I'm talking about living a life without encumbrance."

"Is that so? And you don't like to have little luxuries?" She sat back in her chair and thought for a minute. "What kind of surfboard do you have? I bet it cost you a pretty penny – those things aren't cheap. And your truck? It must have set you back some."

He smiled and looked down at his beer. "You could call those necessities. I surf because it helps me balance out my life. I've solved a whole lot of issues up on that board. And I use that truck for my work."

"I'm not doubting you, or that you need to have those items, if that's what floats your boat. That's actually my point. I just don't think you're so different than me in that way."

He leaned in and spoke in a low voice, "The difference between us is this – I've got a few possessions, that's true. But I could leave them behind right now and not miss them. I'm done collecting 'things'. You seem to have a longer list of the stuff you can't do without. Spend some time with me and see how little you really need to make you happy. You need to identify your personal passion. It might be a game-changer for you."

She looked at him and did her best not to fall into his deepening dark blue gaze. "Is that so? I think it's all just a line you use on women. You're just trying to get me to sleep with you."

"Here's the thing," he whispered, moving in even closer. "I don't plan that far ahead. I just let my life unfold as it does. I don't fight it, though. It's a good lesson to learn." He planted a soft kiss behind her ear. "You might want to take that one little piece of advice." He paused and then added, "but I doubt we'd get much sleep anyway."

Ruby felt a warm spark of sensation as his soft lips touched her now overly sensitized skin. She willed herself to stay calm in the moment, but it was a battle she could feel herself losing. "*Oh no*," she thought. *"Be strong. No distractions."*Cooper let his mouth linger for a moment longer than necessary before he sat back in his chair, his blue eyes locked on her green ones. "I can tell you feel it too." The heat and electricity between them was palpable and Ruby knew that if she didn't do something to break this connection and soon, she'd end up in his bed, and she was sure that she wasn't ready for that. She abruptly stood up, awkwardly knocking the chair she had been sitting on to the scuffed wooden floor. "I need some air," she said, walking quickly toward the door. She pushed through the crowd of people that had gathered outside by the entrance into a small clear spot in the parking lot, drawing in big gulps of the now cooled night air. She could see her breath as she exhaled and she drew her arms in closer to her body. Her pulse rate was returning to a more normal speed and her brain was beginning to clear. Just then CeCe came walking toward her.

"Hey. Are you okay? Did Cooper say something to upset you? One minute it looked like the two of you were trying to solve the question of world peace, and in the next second you throw a chair to the ground and leave the bar. What the hell is going on?"

"Nothing, CeCe. Nothing," she replied, not wanting to let on how Cooper's nearness affected her. I just got really tired all of a sudden. I want to go back to the Barn and go to sleep. Are you coming with me?"

"Yeah. Just give me a second. I ran out without my jacket. I'll go back and get it," she said as she ducked through the doorway and back into the bar. Ruby stared up at the night sky full of stars until she sensed someone was standing behind her. When she turned around, she came face to face with Cooper.

"I didn't mean to make you leave," he said, his blue eyes flashing concern.

"Look, Cooper, the truth is, I just don't need any more complications to my life right now."

He looked bewildered. "What does that mean, Ruby?"

"It just means that I have a pretty full plate of problems. I need to focus on myself this summer. I can't get involved with you, or with anyone for that matter. I have to figure out how to move myself into a waitressing job at the Hut and I've got to save up every penny I possibly can to afford school. I don't think I'll be going out much. It's best if we don't start this... whatever it is."

"Why do I feel like I'm being dismissed?" he asked.

"I wouldn't say it that way. If circumstances were different, well..."

A smile crossed his lips. "And you think I'm going to give up this easily?"

"It's not about 'giving up'. It's about understanding that I just have no time for a summer fling."

He put his hand over his heart. "You wound me!" he teased.

"I'm serious Cooper." Out of the corner of her eye, Ruby saw CeCe step into the parking lot. "I'm heading out now. Thanks for the beer."

Just then CeCe reached where they were standing. "Ready?" she asked.

Cooper reached up and touched Ruby's arm before she stepped out of his reach. His touch seared her skin and she drew in a deep breath. She pulled back."Don't work too hard. All things in moderation, you know," he said into the widening distance between them.

But she didn't hear him. She was already walking away.

After a fitful night of trying to sleep, Ruby woke with the sunrise. She quietly slipped into the empty hallway bathroom, thankful for the solitude. She hadn't had three other roommates since freshman year at college and in her wakefulness felt as though she heard every breath the other women took in the hours she'd spent tossing and turning in her bed. Every time she closed her eyes, Cooper's face appeared. In the darkest part of night, she had admitted to herself that she was drawn to him in a way that she'd not felt about any of the men she'd dated in the past. She realized that it would be a true challenge to stay away from him, to not allow herself to fall into a summer romance, the kind where you fully submerge yourself in the other person, and where a few short weeks felt like a lifetime compressed. Ruby splashed cold water on her face and looked in the chipped mirror that hung over the sink. She was pale, and dark circles were forming underneath her eyes. *Real attractive,* she thought. She took a quick shower and organized her thoughts. Keeping focused, she started to devise a timeline in her head for when she could broach the subject of waitressing with Terry again. She hadn't seen the other woman again since they'd met, but she'd gotten some praise from a few of the other staff members on the progress she'd made already in getting the concession stand set up. She had moved a few things around, trying to put the items she thought would sell fast up front. Aside from tees and sweatshirts, there was an assortment of other paraphernalia – beer glasses with the bar's logo across the front, shot glasses as well – and keychains, hats and towels. It just made sense to Ruby that some of the smaller things were impulse buys, especially to those with the right amount of alcohol in their systems. She'd been guilty of just that type of behavior in her younger days. She'd come home from a shopping spree with things she'd end up hanging in her closet and never wearing, eventually donating the items to Goodwill with the price tags still hanging on them. Money had absolutely no meaning to her then. It seemed to be readily available, always in large supply; all she had to do was ask her father, and magically her pockets were filled. She stepped out of the shower, wrapping a towel around herself and straightened her posture to stand at her full height. She had no room for self-pity. She just had to get on with her life. She tiptoed back into her room and dressed in the semi-darkness amid the soft sounds of sleep from the other beds. Then she silently walked outside and to her car, feeling the call of the beach and the tide to help soothe her soul.

Ruby drove the short distance to her favorite spot, the same parking lot she'd been to the day before. She stopped her car short of the big dune that met the pavement and hopped out. There were no other cars there, the ocean flat and calm against a brightening horizon, ribbons of pink, purple and a faint layer of yellow along the bottom where the sky met the sea. It was a blissfully serene sight. She drank in the peacefulness of the moment, as if she could store it away and call upon it later when she knew she'd need it most. She crawled up onto the hood of her car and leaned back against the dusty windshield. The warmth of the rising sun bathed her face and she closed her eyes and felt herself drift off into that state of semi-wakefulness; not really sleeping, but certainly not fully conscious, the place between thinking and dreaming. It was there that she sat, and twenty minutes later, feeling much better, was back in her car, heading to the Hut, prepared for whatever calamity today might bring, even if it meant seeing Cooper again. She'd stored some strength, and she knew she'd have it if she really needed it. She had no other choice.

After a quick stop at the local convenience store for a large coffee, she pulled into the parking lot of the Hut. Sipping at her hot drink, she stepped into her little area, the concession stand, and surveyed her work. She'd still need to grab more tee shirts out of the storage unit, but she was pleased with what she'd accomplished so far. She was sure that by the time the season began, she'd have all the prices memorized and a good system in place for refilling her inventory during what she had been told could be some pretty busy and wild nights during the summer months.

There wasn't too much activity yet this morning. She could hear the loud clatter of pots and pans from inside the building, and she decided to take a look to see just what was happening in there before dragging those heavy boxes of shirts across the parking lot. She stepped into the dim bar area and waited for her eyes to adjust before pushing through the double doors that led into the industrial sized kitchen. There were three huge men washing large stock pots and two others scrubbing down the grill, speaking to one another in heavily accented English. All but one had their long dreadlocks pulled up into ponytails; the other man was completely bald. They turned to greet her.

"Good morning, Miss Sunshine. How might you be on this glorious day?" one of the men asked.

"I'm okay. How are you?" She smiled shyly.

The bald man stepped forward. "We're giving glory up to the Lord. Getting this ship to be top shape, you know? Happy to be alive!" He laughed with a deep, resonating sound that made her feel happy for the first time in days.

"Where you be from?" one of the men asked.

"Um, New York. And you?"

"We are all from the island of Jamaica, mam. The finest place on this whole, wide world." He stopped for a moment, wiping his massive hand on his apron before offering it out to her. "I am Louie," the bald man continued. "And this here is James, Raffi, Smith and Big Red."

"I'm Ruby," she said, offering her hand in return timidly, afraid that he might crush it. Instead, he gave it a gentle shake.

"And what might it be that you do here, Miss Ruby?"

"Terry hired me to work the concession stand," she said, quickly adding, "but I'd really like to be a waitress."

"You?" Louie laughed deeply, the others joining in. "We'll see little darling, time will tell," he said, wiping a tear from his eye.

"Is that funny?" she asked, feeling like the target of a joke that she didn't get.

"You be too little," Raffi said. "Those are heavy plates, mam. You need to eat some Wheaties!"

"I'm stronger than I look," Ruby replied defensively.

"Ok then, little one. We'll see," Big Red flexed his arms to show off his muscles. He walked across the room and picked up a serving tray, piling it high with dishes and glassware. With one hand, he lifted it up over his head and walked across the room and back, setting it down on long countertop. "When we slammed in here, this is what you'd need to carry." He stepped back. "Well? Waiting for a bus or someting? Let's see what you've got."

Ruby hesitated a minute. She doubted that she could lift that heavy tray, but she didn't want these men to know it. Drawing in a deep breath, she approached the challenge, bent her knees and slid her hand beneath the cool metal. As she lifted the impossibly weighty server, she paused to ground herself. More assured that she felt balanced, Ruby began to walk slowly across the kitchen. Just then the door swung open, revealing a non-too-pleased Terry, a frightening scowl plastered across her face.

"Just what do you think you're doing?" she boomed.

That was all it took. Ruby crumbled under the strain, and the tray slipped from her hands, glassware shattering around her feet.

"Sorry. That was my fault," she said in a voice barely above a whisper.

Terry's eyes shrank to small slits. "And now you owe me money. Tally up my losses, boys. Ruby here needs to know how many hours she's working for free.

Chapter Five

Nightmare was all Ruby could think. *Her worst nightmare.* She put the tray on one of the counters and began to pick up the broken shards of glass.

"I'm sorry Terry, really. I was just trying to prove…" She stopped herself when she looked up and saw the scowl on her boss's face.

"I don't want to see you back in this kitchen again. And if you want to keep your job at the concession stand, I suggest you get there now." Terry spoke in a tone that left no room for a response. She turned toward the men, who Ruby thought were now just standing there, probably wishing to be invisible. "And you all know better. I should take the damage out of your salaries too! Now get back to work!" With that, she turned and angrily pushed the door open, and left in a huff.

Smith pulled an industrial sized metal garbage can toward the mess and Big Red began sweeping up the glass with the oversized broom he'd grabbed from one corner.

"You best do what the boss lady says. Get yourself outside and in that concession space before she fires you." Louie made a gesture with his arms, shooing her out of the kitchen.

"Okay," she replied quietly. "I'm going. I really thought…" She stopped talking when she realized the men were hard at work cleaning up her mess and not listening anyway. She walked out of the building and into the bright sunlight of the morning. This was not the way she wanted to start her day. Walking over to the storage unit, she pulled a big box of extra-large men's tee shirts off of one shelf and dragged it across the parking lot to the concession stand. She had a job to do, and she knew she was hanging on to it by a thread. She put her head down and began to work.

It was nearly noon when Ruby looked up, satisfied that she'd done as well as possible at pulling together an attractive retail environment for Terry's goods. If there was one thing she did know, it was shopping. She was a champion at it, and she knew that if a store looked appealing, more sales were bound to happen. Every shirt was neatly folded and stacked by size and color; there was one of each design hanging decoratively on a large peg board behind her. The glasses and beer cozies were displayed on shelves under the shirts, and she'd hand written prices on stickers in colorful markers beneath them. It was a bright and cheerful space now, one she knew was eye-catching and accessible.

Ruby had her back to the parking lot, straightening the last pile of shirts when she heard a car door slam. She turned in time to see Cooper walk around to the back of his truck and effortlessly lift a beat-up cardboard box onto his shoulder. With a few long strides, he stood in front of her, placing his cargo on her counter.

"Hey," she quietly, trying to cover the nervousness she felt by his close proximity. "I just polished that wood. Don't put your garbage up here!" She stood on her toes to try and see what was underneath the closed flaps.

"Good afternoon to you too, Ruby," he replied. "And I'll have you know that I would never put trash on your counter."

"Really? What's in the box?"

"Something I've been working on." He pulled back the top of the worn cardboard and pulled out a bottle of the Satan's Satin beer they'd been drinking last night.

"What do you mean? Are you working on drinking those?"

He smirked. "Not exactly. I brew this stuff. The Dive serves it. I'm trying to expand and get Terry to put it on the menu as well."

Ruby was stunned. "*You make beer*?"

"I do. In small batches, so far, but I'm trying to start a real business with it, and getting it served here this summer will really be a true test of the market."

"I thought you said you were a bartender…"

"I am. Bartending pays my bills. I've been working here forever it seems. I just think it's time to live my dream, you know, do something I'm passionate about."

"Beer?"

"Not just any beer. This beer." He lifted up the bottle, bringing it closer to her face. "You drank it last night…"

"Yeah. You've said that already. Besides, I remember."

"Well, did you like it? You left in such a hurry, I didn't get to ask." He looked at her expectantly.

"I did," Ruby responded quickly, glad to have something concrete to talk about with him. "It was really good."

"And that's surprising?"

"I guess it's only surprising now that I know you made it."

"Ouch," he teased. "You really know how to hurt a guy!"

"No, it's not that. It's just…"

"You thought I was a merely a surfer with no ambition for anything but chase the waves, huh?"

Ruby didn't want to admit to him that he was right. More importantly, she didn't want him to know that she had felt an uneasy sense of longing for him before she knew about his beer business. It didn't matter that she had not known about Satin's Satin being his creation. She was undeniably attracted to him one way or another. She pulled herself back into the present. "No, seriously. Bartending is a fine career choice if that's what makes you happy."

"Not like being some elite corporate lawyer, though, is it Ruby?" His tone had a sarcastic, cutting edge.

"Is that what you think?" she challenged back.

"I guess the better question is whether or not you believe it. You ran away pretty quickly last night."

"Look, Cooper, I told you the truth. I have to work this summer to be able to afford school. Any distraction could blow up my life at this point," she said, feeling her mouth go dry, knowing that the words she'd just said were true to a point, however, she couldn't deny the quaking of her knees at the moment. She was attracted to him. It hung unspoken in the air, the high counter the only physical barrier between them.

"I hear what you're saying, Ruby. I was just hoping

you'd reconsider. I know I'm not crazy. This doesn't happen to me a lot, this crazy mixed-up feeling. This isn't a line. It's real."

Then he reached over and gently lay his palm on her hand which had been resting on the wooden bar of the concession stand. It was undeniable… the current of electricity that raced between them, the heat of desire. It was all there. She pulled her hand back, hoping to snuff out the longing she had felt. He was making her dizzy. All she could do was offer a weak smile, which he jumped on. Reaching into the box, he pulled out a bottle with its colorful label boldly displayed.

"Hang on to this one. Maybe I'll convince you to share it with me later."

She shyly lifted the bottle and said, "Well, I do like this particular beer."

"Then let me take you out to dinner and tell you all about how I came up with the whole idea. I promise not to make a move on you. I won't even kiss you… you have my word. We'll keep it strictly business." He smiled and she was lost.

"Business? Maybe."

"Great. I'll take that as a yes. See you later. I'll pick you up at the Barn at six." He lifted the box and winked at her, walking toward the building and through the door to the inside, giving her no chance to turn him down.

An hour later, all Ruby could still think about was that he promised not to kiss her and that for her false bravado, for all that she wanted it to be different, to be immune to his charm and unabashed sex appeal, she wasn't sure if she could deal with the disappointment of his lips not touching her own in what she was sure would be the start of something spectacular. *Shake it off. You've got work to do,* she admonished herself. She let herself out of the side door of the stand and went off to look for Terry. Ruby hoped that all of her hard work today would go a far way to have her boss forgive her earlier transgression. Taking a deep breath, she stepped inside the building to look for the other woman.

Once her eyes were acclimated to the dim interior, she found her target. Terry was sitting on a stool next to Cooper, an open bottle of Satan's Satin and a half-filled glass beside it on the bar. They looked to be deep in conversation and she decided to come back later, but when Cooper's head lifted just the slightest bit, their eyes locked. It was almost as if he sensed her presence before he made actual visual contact with her. He smiled broadly.

"Hey there Ruby, come on over," he offered.

"Um, no, I can wait. I don't want to interrupt your meeting."

"The meeting's over. And Terry's agreed to take on a small order of my brew. Isn't that awesome?"

"Don't get overexcited," Terry deadpanned. "If you don't move that stuff out quick, or if I hear a complaint, our business is done."

"I know. You've made your feelings very clear." He smiled. "I'm honored to have the opportunity."

"Yeah, yeah," Terry said slipping off the barstool to stand in front of Ruby. "And what can I do for you? Break anything else today?"

Ruby could feel color rising to her cheeks. This tough broad really got under her skin. "Um, no. I just wanted to show you the concession stand. I've got it all ready to go."

"Well bully for you. This isn't school, and I'm not the teacher you need to impress. We'll know how well you did during the soft open this weekend. Sell some merchandise and all will be forgiven."

"If I sell a lot, will you reconsider and not dock my pay for those dishes?" Ruby asked with a hopeful tone.

"Nope. I'm taking my losses out of your first check. But sell some stuff and I'll let you stick around."

"Yes ma'am." Ruby looked down at her feet, totally humiliated in front of Cooper.

The older woman turned her attention to a vendor who walked in through the kitchen, leaving Ruby and Cooper alone at the bar.

"She may be gruff on the outside, but she's a mushy mess on the inside," Cooper started. "She agreed to let me push my beer this summer. That could really be the start of something for me." His smile stretched from ear to ear.

"Yeah, well, congrats on that! I just think she tolerates me so she'll have someone to vent at. We'll see how long I last here."

"You'll do fine! And now we really have something fun to celebrate tonight."

Ruby smiled back at him. "So, I'm a foregone conclusion, then?"

"I wouldn't dare say that. I'm just hoping I can coax you to dinner. Do you like homemade pasta? I know just the spot."

"Love it. But I find it hard to believe that you can get homemade pasta this far from Boston's North End."

"Shows what you know!"

"Really? Where is this great restaurant?"

"Who said anything about a restaurant? I'm talking about my house. I make a mean linguine with white clams."

"Your house?" she asked somewhat cautiously.

"Oh, don't worry. I promised not to kiss you… but after you taste my cooking, you may just want to kiss me first."

"We'll see about that," was all she could muster as an answer, already dreaming about touching her lips to his.

Ruby spent a good hour deciding what to wear. She had her head still buried in her duffle bag which she'd dragged out from under the bed when CeCe came into their shared room. There were clothes strewn all over the floor, along with lacy scraps of lingerie sprinkled among them.

"Planning some sort of tag sale?" CeCe teased.

"Nope. I've got a date."

"Really?" CeCe said somewhat sarcastically. "Let me guess. Big Red."

"You're funny, but you already know that, don't you?"

"Well, I would have said Cooper but you ran out on him real fast last night."

"I did. But I am seeing him tonight." She took a white cotton camisole with a scalloped edge out of her bag and shook out the wrinkles. Satisfied that it would look good under the cornflower blue cotton blouse she'd chosen to wear with her faded jeans, she began to fold the other items and replace them in her luggage.

"He's a free agent right now,"

"What does that mean?" Ruby looked at her new friend. "And how does it matter anyway?"

"Oh, it doesn't, but you know, the whole summer romance thing. It gets a little crazy here. Girls tend to get passed around."

"Passed around? I don't understand what you're saying."

CeCe sat down on the floor with Ruby and started to

help her put her clothing away. "For instance, Patti was with Cooper last summer. And the summer before that, she was with Brett. I don't think you've met him yet, he's a lifeguard. He's not up here right now, but he'll be back."

Ruby was still stuck on the nugget of information about Patti having been Cooper's girlfriend. "Patti and Cooper were an item, but they broke up after last summer?"

"That's pretty much how it works. May through Labor Day, then done. That's why they call it a summer romance, duh?" She rolled her eyes.

"And everyone here knows that?"

"Yeah. Once the summer's over, most people go off and travel somewhere warm. For instance, Steamroller was all over Australia this past winter, surfing. He said it was crazy surf there. Why else would we work at this backbreaking pace? The money's good. I mean, I use it for tuition, but most everyone else gave up on school a long time ago. It's a lifestyle choice, that's what it is," she said matter-of-factly.

Awareness was beginning to dawn on Ruby. "So, you think Cooper is just trying to make his mark on me? Just setting out the boundaries for everyone else this summer?"

"You say that as if it's a bad thing! He clearly likes you enough to want to pursue this. Why not have some fun? It's only until September…"

Ruby sat back on her heels, contemplating what CeCe had said. She hadn't had fun in so long, not since her family's financial troubles began. It had been one obstacle in front of another, a weight that sat heavily in her chest, a sinking feeling in her stomach, a constant ache. Maybe she should try and adopt the attitude everyone else seemed to live by here. And if she did, perhaps she'd fit in better.

"Just for the summer, you say?"

CeCe smiled. "Yup."

Ruby finished folding her clothes, took CeCe's neatly stacked pile and put everything except what she'd picked out to wear tonight back in her luggage before stowing it under the bed once again. Then she stood up and reached for her toiletries.

"Are you any good with a curling iron?" Ruby asked the other woman.

"I'm not bad. Patti's better. She almost completed her cosmetology degree, but there was an incident with some eyelashes…"

"Well, I have a feeling that I'm not one of her favorite people, even before Cooper showed any interest in me." She paused to pick up the beauty tool in question and found a plug near her bed. "Will you help me with my hair?"

"Oh yeah. This should be fun."

"I'll be back in a flash. Just gonna rinse off in the shower."

"Let me go get a chair for you to sit on from the common room so that I have some leverage!" she winked and was gone.

Ruby looked around the room, grabbed a towel and head off to the shower. She took the time to moisturize her body and shave her legs, all the while questioning to herself if these actions were premature. She hardly knew Cooper. Did she really want to jump into his bed?

As she rinsed the final suds from her scalp and applied conditioner to the ends of her long blonde hair, she couldn't keep her thoughts straight. On the one hand, she didn't want to be another notch in his belt. *But then*, she thought, *why shouldn't she consider adding a notch to her own?* Ruby knew all the reasons why going to Cooper's house tonight was a terrible idea. There was a world of trouble on her doorstep and he might be more grief in the long run, and she most certainly didn't need any more of that. She drew in a deep breath as she shut off the water, wrapped a towel closely around her body, and for the first time in what felt like forever, smiled. It was summer. She had a job. She'd be leaving in September. If she could keep things light with Cooper, just have a fling and not lose her heart, why the hell not? Didn't she deserve to have a little fun?

Chapter Six

Ruby stepped out of the Barn and into the parking lot. The sun was setting in the distance, its straw-colored light scattered everywhere, softening the horizon and casting an eerie halo over Cooper's head. She silently gasped. Clearly, he was no angel. But neither was she. As she walked toward him, she willed herself to put her lustful thoughts out of her head, at least for the time being.

"Hi. You look lovely," he said as he smiled before coming around to open the door on the passenger side of his truck.

"Thank you," she replied. CeCe had proved to be very adept with the curling iron, and Ruby's waist length blonde hair was now set in soft waves that framed her face the shorter layers skimming the collar of her shirt. Her roommate had also applied a thick coat of mascara to Ruby's lashes after rimming her lids with an emerald toned eye pencil, making her green eyes seem even more luminous and larger than usual. She took his offered hand and stepped up into the truck, buckling her seat belt as he closed the door and came back around to the driver's seat.

"I'm so glad you decided to let me cook for you. It's one of my favorite hobbies."

"What else do you like to do?" she asked.

He smirked. "Well, you know about the surfing. And now the cooking. I do have a few other ways I like to blow off steam, but I think we should get to know each other better first."

Ruby felt a wave of heat rise from her toes to her face. "I'm sure you do," was all she managed to say. She watched as the sun continued to set as he turned the truck into a tidy neighborhood off the main road. They drove for a few more minutes before he pulled his car into a driveway in front of a small garage. To the left of that sat a well-maintained cottage. To Ruby, it looked like a dollhouse, with its neat green trim and shutters and pale yellow siding. There was no real lawn, but instead it looked as though the house was surrounded by some sort of beach grass. Wildflowers were beginning to sprout up on the well-worn stone path to the front door. He answered the question in her head before she even asked.

"This house belonged to my grandmother. She left it to me in her will. I used to spend all of my time here, with her when my parents divorced. After my dad split and my mom went back to work, this was my safe haven. I don't know what would have happened if my grandmother hadn't been there, watching out for me."

"Do you have any siblings?"

"Nope. Only child."

"Wow," she remarked, adding, "me too."

"Just another piece of common ground," he said with a smile. He reached over and unlatched the door. "Welcome to my home," he murmured as he stepped aside to let her enter first.

Ruby's eyes opened wide once inside. She hadn't expected Cooper's place to be so put-together. There were two low black leather couches set across from each other in the common room, with a glass coffee table between them. On the far wall, there was a massive fireplace carved out of what seemed like enormous river rocks. A piece of recycled wood served as a mantel. Beyond that was an open concept kitchen with stainless steel appliances light blue cabinets. A gleaming white granite countertop ran the length of the space, extending into the great room with dark blue leather covering the stools set out to define the dining area. That portion of the counter had been set with small votive candles in colorful stained glass holders, two plates, red linen napkins, silverware and wine goblets. It took Ruby's breath away. She murmured, "So much for you making fun of my desire to own a home…"

Sensing her surprise, Cooper said, "My grandmother left me the house and a bit of money. I worked on the remodel with a buddy of mine, spent most of my bartending tips on furniture. And with what was left, combined with what I make at the Hut, I started the beer brewing business." He walked over to the fireplace and lit the kindling that sat underneath some logs. She watched his graceful spare movements as within moments, flames appeared to catch the dry wood, and a cozy warmth was released into the room, chasing the cool spring night air away.

"You must be a really good bartender," was all she could think to say.

He laughed out loud. "Well, I like to think so. But that's

not all I do well." Taking her hand, he led her to a barstool. "Have a seat."

Ruby did as she was told, never taking her eyes off of Cooper's efficient motions. He pulled a bottle of red wine out of the built-in cooler and quickly opened it. He poured two glasses and then raised his. "Here's to the beginning of a great summer," he said.

She lifted her own glass and touched it briefly to his before taking a sip. It was spicy and delicious. "That's good. Do you make your own wine, as well?"

He raised an eyebrow. "Nope. Just the Satan's Satin for now. I don't think the grapes would survive a winter up here. But if you're interested, I'll show you where the beer-making magic happens after dinner."

"I'd love to see that!" Ruby responded. She didn't know if it was the wine or the fact that she found Cooper to be easy company, but she began to relax. She watched as he pulled a large stock pot out of a cabinet, filled it with water to boil for the pasta and then began to chop what seemed to be a whole head of garlic for their dinner.

"I would offer to help you, but I'm not that great in the kitchen."

"Done much cooking?" he asked.

"Hardly. In Manhattan, you don't need to prepare your own meals. There's so much take-out. And when I was a kid, my nanny cooked for me."

"Your nanny?"

"My parents were out almost every night. And my mom doesn't exactly know a spatula from a salad spinner. I've come to understand that my life then was very different from my reality today. My past is actually starting to feel like a dream, like it happened to someone else."

"Where are your parents now?" he asked.

"In a crappy one bedroom rental in Queens. It's a furnished sublet. All of our stuff was sold."

"That's pretty awful, Ruby."

"I just wish I knew more about what happened. Even though I was there during the entire thing, my parents always sheltered me from the truth. I didn't have any idea of how bad it was for my father until we were about to be evicted. Everything I have is either under my bed at the Barn or in the trunk of my car."

He put down the small knife he'd been using and came around to sit next to her, and turned her barstool to face him, their knees touching. "But you're going to school in the fall, right?"

"That's the plan. Of course, assuming I make the money I need to live on."

"No chance of getting a student loan?"

"Nope. I have no credit, and my dad's ruined. No one would lend him a dime. If it wasn't for the academic scholarship, well…"

"How are your parents surviving?"

"Unbelievably, they both went back to work. Well, my dad did, but he was always the money-maker. My mom never held a job in her life before this."

"Wow."

"Yeah. My dad drives an Uber. Mom works at a boutique she used to shop in. It's so humiliating."

"I disagree. They're doing what they have to do, Ruby. It may not be ideal, but at least they have each other."

"That's true. Throughout it all, they've been each other's salvation."

"I think that's pretty special," he said, taking a sip of his wine. "My parents certainly didn't have that kind of relationship. My dad cheated on my mom with our next-door neighbor. That kind of juicy gossip spreads like wildfire when you live in a small town and with my mom at work, I was home alone a lot. That's why I spent so much time here with my grandmother. It was bad enough to hear the taunts in school, I didn't want to listen to that crap when I didn't have to, you know? And I was a terrible student. I hated sitting in a classroom. I never could follow along with the lesson at the front of the room. I was always better off when I worked with my own hands, and my grandmother always seemed to need me to fix something for her. So, I spent every free minute right here," he said looking around.

"You were lucky to have a place to run to," Ruby said quietly.

"It seems like you've found a soft-landing spot as well," he replied, keeping his gaze locked with hers, replacing his glass on the counter. "Now, I better get cooking, or we'll never eat dinner tonight!"

Cooper walked back to his cutting board and completed the garlic preparation. He then grabbed a large skillet from underneath the six-burner stovetop and poured olive oil into it, turning up the heat. "Do me a favor, Ruby?" he asked. "Open the refrigerator and pull out the clams."

She jumped off of the stool and followed his directions. When she opened the stainless-steel door, she found the shellfish resting in a glass bowl set into a tray of crushed ice. She carefully carried the entire thing over to Cooper, not wanting a repeat of this morning's experience in Terry's kitchen. As she put it down on the counter he came up behind her, reaching over her head for the red pepper chili flakes in the spice rack above the stove. She could feel his brisk motions, the heat of his strength as he flexed his muscles so naturally. He made this innocent space feel decadent, and she scurried back to her bar stool to drink more wine, keeping her eyes on his every motion. He threw the garlic in the pan and said, "As long as we're both eating this, I'm not sparing the spice!"

She was feeling the heat build within her as she watched him add salt, pepper and the red pepper flakes to the slightly browned garlic. When he was satisfied that the flavors had blended in the hot oil, he added the clams, a plastic container of fresh clam juice and covered the pan. He added a large handful of sea salt to the pot with the now boiling water, waiting a few seconds and then dropped a pile of homemade linguine into it.

"I made this pasta earlier today," he said. "Maybe next time I'll teach you how…" he looked at her expectantly.

"I think I'd like that," she said softly.

He then checked the skillet full of clams. "Once they're open, we're good to go. About another minute." He quickly lit the votive candles and turned back to the pasta. Satisfied that it was sufficiently cooked, he turned the flame off the pot, pulled a very large bowl out of an upper cabinet and began to place the strands of linguine into the pan with the clams. He stirred in some of the used pasta water and Ruby watched with surprise as the sauce thickened just a bit before he turned the flame off the skillet as well. Then he poured the whole thing into the bowl, sprinkled fresh parsley over the top and pulled two large serving utensils out of a drawer and said, "Dinner is ready!"

"It smells delicious," she smiled.

"Let's hope it tastes as good then!"

He put a large serving in a dish for her, and sat back waiting for her to taste it.

Ruby sensed his anticipation of her response, and she didn't want to disappoint him. The fragrance of the food made her sure that she wouldn't have to. She twirled some pasta onto her fork and took a bite. It had a briny bite and was truly wonderful.

"This is spectacular!" she exclaimed once she'd taken a bite. "Who needs the North End of Boston? You're a really good cook!"

He smiled, his shoulders visibly relaxing at her positive response. "I'm so glad you like it!" He shifted around the counter and came to sit down on the stool next to hers.

"I do! And I guess I didn't realize just how hungry I was," she said before devouring a claim. "These are so fresh!"

"I know. I went shelling for them this morning."

She paused mid-chew. "What?"

"I have a shelling license. You know, for oysters and clams," was his matter-of-fact response.

"You make your own pasta and you farm your own fish?"

"Don't forget that I brew my own beer," he added in a kidding tone.

"What are you? Some sort of survivalist? Do you have a fall-out shelter underneath the house as well?"

He nearly choked on the wine he'd just sipped in laughter.

"No. I'm just a New Englander. We're resourceful up here. The winters can be very long…"

"Well I guess I know where to come if the end is near," she deadpanned.

"Umm," he murmured, looking directly into her eyes. "You, me and the end of the world. Now that has its possibilities…" "There are probably some things we could do to comfort one another before that last moment."

Ruby's gaze never wavered from his face, as all at once she felt her hunger shift downward. She took a large sip of wine for courage. "Thanks for making me this really special meal." She leaned in closer and kissed him, softly at first, giving into the connection she felt between them. He put down his fork and placed his arms around her waist, lifting her onto his lap, never once losing contact with her lips. She was emboldened by his immediate response to her touch. She sat there, her legs now wrapped around the back of his barstool, taking it all in: the shockwaves of electricity she could feel passing between them; the firmness of his mouth on hers, his tongue invading the inner recesses of her mouth; the desire to forget everything and slip out of her clothing and into his bed. As though he could read her mind, he reached for the hem of the shirt she was wearing and pulled it off over her head, leaving the thin cotton camisole on as he slowly kissed his way down from her neck to the top of her breasts.

She was awash in awareness as he stood up and carried her over to the couch, laying her down gently. She could see into his eyes, a mirror of her own emotions as he took off his shirt, exposing his strong chest and muscular arms. She reached up to softly caress his skin before pulling him down on top of her, softly nipping his neck with her teeth then exploring his mouth with her tongue. It was what she needed, all of this pure sensation, to free her mind from worry and trouble, this man, this moment. When she felt his growing erection against her leg, she shifted and they both paused, staring at each other, silent for a moment.

"Ruby…" he whispered in her ear. "I want…"

"Me too," was all she said before lifting her hips up off the cushions and unzipping her jeans. Standing, he finished the job for her. Grabbing the hem of each leg, he pulled them off until she lay on the couch in just her camisole and panties. He then undid the buttons of his jeans and without breaking eye contact with her, took them off and threw them on the ground, pausing only long enough to remove a condom from the back pocket. He stepped out of his boxers and stood naked and strong in front of her for a minute, his desire apparent, before reaching down to shed her of her remaining clothing.

"Do you know how beautiful you are?" Cooper whispered before lying down next to her once more, caressing her with the lightest of kisses, his fingers softly exploring all of her until she could stand the teasing torture no more. It was only when he entered her did she feel whole, with each rhythmic thrust bringing her closer to forgetting the world of trouble that lay outside of Cooper's door. And then, in a mind-blowing moment of release, she called out his name, pulling him closer to her, reveling in pure sensation, never wanting to let him go.

When Ruby awoke, it was dark inside the house, and for a brief moment, she was disoriented. The candles on the bar had long burned down and none of the lamps had been turned on. Cooper rested on her chest, sleeping. It was the most peaceful feeling she'd experienced in months, and she released a silent sigh. His eyelids fluttered, then opened.

"Hey there," was all he said.

"Hi," she responded, shifting on the couch, suddenly aware of his weight pressing her down into the cushions.

"I think we should take this into my bedroom. We'll be more comfortable there." He stood up in all of his naked glory. "Unless you want me to drive you back to the Barn. I mean, I want you to stay, but if you want to go…"

She shook out her arm, which was full of pins and needles from having him laying on her for so long. The logs had burned down and were almost extinguished, and without him on top of her she felt the chill in the air. Cooper reached for her, pulling her up into his embrace. His skin was heated and judging from the state of his arousal, he was in no mind to have her leave. "Why would I want to do that?" she whispered, taking his hand. "Is the bedroom this way?" she nodded to a hallway to the left of where they stood.

He smiled and pulled her along with him, both of them stepping over their previously discarding clothing still on the floor. On the way through the small house, she couldn't help but notice the framed pictures in small, neat wooden frames hung in a row. In the near-darkness, she couldn't really see the details, but they all looked like pictures of the beach in different seasons. Once in his room, Cooper turned on the small lamp on the night table next to his bed. Pulling back the comforter, he motioned for her to get in. The sheets felt cool against her heated skin, the anticipation of Cooper's touch causing her heart to beat more quickly in her chest. He lay down next to her and whispered in her ear.

"I'm glad you decided to stay."

"Me too."

"I'm going to kiss you now," was all he said, as his lips grazed her own, then traveled down her body, touching her intimately, caressing her everywhere. They made love more slowly this time, but with no less urgency and she felt as though she had found a connection with him that she'd not shared with anyone before. Satiated, the last thought Ruby had as her eyelids fluttered shut was that she felt safe, warm and protected. And despite knowing that the summer was short, ignoring the history that CeCe had explained, that this type of relationship would not withstand the cold and barren months ahead, she slept.

Dawn crept underneath the corners of the curtains of Cooper's bedroom, bathing them in weak sunlight. For as much as she didn't want to leave the warmth and comfort of his bed, Ruby had to pee. She pushed back the blanket, careful not to wake him as she made her way into the bathroom. Quietly opening the door, she was struck by just how masculine the space was, done in dark blue tile with black accents. There was a huge jetted tub on one end, a large clear jar with some sort of bath beads off to the side of it and glass enclosed shower next to it, easily big enough to hold two people at once. There was an enormous wide fixture above, which provided a rain-like effect for those inside. The toilet was off to one side and a double sink was sunk into a blue and black specked granite countertop. Twin mirrors hung above that, both framed in silver. Thick, fluffy navy blue towels hung from a warming rack. As she sat down on the toilet, all she could think about was taking a hot shower. It was more than inviting – it was exactly what she needed.

Finishing and flushing, she couldn't resist. She opened the glass door and turned on the water. It heated up quickly, causing deep clouds of steam to rise around the room. She stepped inside. It felt heavenly. She lifted the soap and was struck by the musky scent; it smelled like Cooper. Eyes closed, she was about to lather up her body when she heard him slip into the stall beside her.

"Can I help you with that?" he asked.

Relinquishing the slippery bar to him, she whispered, "please…"

He took the soap from her hand and made quite the show of lathering her from head to toe, kneeling down before her and trailing kisses down from her navel to the soft sensitive spot between her legs. Her knees felt weak and sensing her unsteadiness, he grabbed her hips for a moment before rising up again and slipping himself inside of her. Rocking together under the steamy water made every single fiber of her being aware of the moment they were sharing, the intimacy of the act, the strong and immediate feelings she was experiencing. This connection to someone else, so quick and so true, had never happened to her before. Cooper was lifting her to a place she'd never known existed, a mind-blowing space of sensory overload. She heard a moan, and barely recognizing her own voice, finished in an explosion that swept all of the air out of her lungs.

A few moments passed before either of them spoke, the hot water still raining down, doing nothing to cool off their bodies. Finally, he said, "Good morning."

"You could call it that," was her response.

"Well, that might be my favorite way to start the day."

"I'll keep that in mind," she replied with a smile.

He reached behind her and turned off the shower, then opened the glass door into the cloudy room. Cooper took a towel off the rack and wrapped it around her, pulling a second one around his own waist. He then opened the bathroom door, releasing the built-up steam into the bedroom.

"I'll be right back," she said, ducking down the hallway to find the clothing she'd discarded in the living room the night before. She had to look to find her panties -- they had found their way under the couch somehow – and scooped up the rest of her things to bring them back to the bedroom. On the way, she stopped for a moment to get a closer look at the four framed photographs on the wall. One was more beautiful than the next, all sunsets on the beach. It was apparent that they were taken at different times of year and that they were meant to be displayed together.

Walking into the bedroom she said, "I love those beach scenes. They're beautiful."

He smiled. "Yeah. They were a house gift from Patti."

She felt her heart slow for a minute and turned away from him to try and compose herself. Objectively she realized that it shouldn't matter, that he had a whole life before they'd met, as had she. But emotionally it was a whole different ballgame. That woman didn't like her, and she had been Cooper's girlfriend before Ruby ever decided to come up to the Cape. How was Patti going to feel knowing that she was now involved with Cooper? Ruby shuddered.

"Are you cold?" he asked. I'll turn up the heat."

"No. I'm going to get dressed and then I should get back to the Barn. I've got to get ready for work." She watched as awareness dawned on his face.

"And here I was going to tempt you to stay with my famous blueberry pancakes."

She hesitated for a minute, but then choked out, "I need to get back."

"What's the rush, Ruby? It's early." He threw the wet towel down on the bed and stood naked in front of her. She turned away, unwilling to allow him to distract her.

"Listen, Cooper. Really, it's okay. I just want to go back now. That's all."

He put his hands on his head in defeat. "Okay. But only if you promise to try my pancakes next time."

It took all of her inner strength to hold back the tears she felt forming. She didn't want to cry. "That would be great."

They finished dressing in silence. He took her hand and led her out of his room to the front door. Looking back, she realized they hadn't cleaned up from their dinner the night before. "I'm sorry to be leaving such a mess for you to handle. I hope that's okay."

He shrugged. "It's fine. I'll take care of it later." He opened the door and she walked to his truck, climbing inside. They drove the entire way in an uncomfortable silence until he got to the Barn.

"Thanks for the ride," she said adding, "and for an amazing evening." She unlatched the lock and was about to step out when he pulled her back.

"Wait."

"Cooper…" she began.

"No, Ruby, listen. I know what you've heard about this place, and all the crazy summer romance shit that goes on. But last night was different. It was…" he hesitated and then added, "please believe me."

"I don't need it to be different, Cooper. I just don't want to feel attached to anything right now. I'm here for a purpose. And as special as last night was, I shouldn't have let it happen like that. I don't want to lead you on. Let's just forget it." She could hear her own words, but knew that they rang hollow in her heart. Crazy though it was, she did feel connected to him.

He grabbed onto her hand and she felt that sudden jolt of electricity again. She looked up at him and saw the raw honesty in his eyes. "Ruby… please. Have dinner with me tonight."

For as much as she wanted to be back in his arms, back in his bed, she said, "No. I don't think that's a good idea."

"We can eat in public, in a restaurant. I promise that I won't take you home at the end of the night, if that's what you're afraid of."

"I'm not afraid, Cooper. I'm just, just…"

"Just what, Ruby?" he countered.

"Uncomfortable."

"With me?"

"With this." With her free hand, she gestured in the air between them. "Of not wanting to ever leave here."

"Don't get ahead of yourself," he said. "Let's just take it slow and see what happens. But you've got to know that I feel it too…"

She snapped her head up and fixed her green gaze on his deep blue one. "But how…"

"I don't know, Ruby. I can't explain it either. I just think that we owe it to each other to try and see where this goes. C'mon. At least think about it before you answer."

She drew in a deep breath, leaned over and lightly kissed his cheek. "No promises," she said, withdrawing her hand from his and finally stepping out of the truck.

"I'll take that as a definite maybe," he smiled, once again with confidence. "And I'll check in with you later, okay?"

She nodded, closed the door and turned toward the building so that she did not have to watch him drive away. She made her way up to her room, hoping to sneak in and change out of yesterday's clothing while everyone was still asleep. When opened the door, however, she realized that she'd have no such luck.

Chapter Seven

As soon as she stepped into the room, Ruby found herself to be the center of attention.

"Well look who's doing the walk of shame this morning girls," said Patti to the others, as she crossed her arms over her chest, "Miss Fancy Pants herself!"

Ruby said nothing as she pulled out her duffle bag to choose some clean clothing to change into.

"I sure hope you don't fall too hard for Cooper," Patti taunted. "He isn't the type of guy who can manage a relationship. He's got that beer business to launch, you know. He's no trust fund baby anyhow."

She spoke with such stunning authority that Ruby steadied herself against the bedframe. "I'm not discussing this with you Patti," she countered, turning to look from one woman to the next. "I'm not discussing my life with any of you." She grabbed a tee shirt and jeans, clean underwear and her make-up bag. "So, if you'll excuse me, I'm going to get ready for work." She pushed past Patti and made her way to the door, swinging it open wide and then letting it slam loudly behind her. She already regretted showing her anger to the group. *This day keeps getting better,* was all she could think.

Ruby quickly moved to the sink in the bathroom and splashed cold water on her face. It felt good and helped to cool down the rage she felt.

"Are you okay?"

Ruby heard CeCe's voice behind her.

"You don't need to look after me. I'll be fine if everyone just leaves me alone."

"Don't let her get under your skin."

"Easier said than done. He's got her photos hanging on the wall in his house, you know."

"Pictures of Patti?"

"No. Pictures she took of the beach." Ruby paused for a minute to catch her breath, hearing her own words and immediately realizing how petty she sounded. It wasn't her place to judge what art Cooper chose to hang in his home. *She'd spent one night there,* she reminded herself. *And it was meaningless*. "He framed them beautifully," she softly added, "they must be special to him."

"But he's not with her anymore, Ruby. Besides, he seems really interested in you."

Ruby turned from the sink to look at CeCe. "What ended it between them?"

She was immediately sorry that she asked and did not want to let on the truth, that her immediate attraction to Cooper terrified her. Quickly, she said, "Wait. Don't answer that. The larger problem for me is that I just can't do this. I thought for about thirty seconds that I could try to leave things light, but I just can't have this big a distraction in my life."

CeCe shook her head. "You're crazy, Ruby. We're only

young once. It's about to be summer. If ever there was a time to be distracted, this is it."

"I wish it were that easy."

"It can be." CeCe stepped forward and put her arm around Ruby. "Give yourself a break, have some fun."

"Fun? What's that?" she asked. "I feel as though the whole world is crashing down around me."

"Wow. And that's from just one night with the man? He must be something else in the bedroom!" she kidded.

"It has nothing to do with last night." She paused, regretting the lie, wishing that she could tell CeCe the truth, knowing that she could never share what she felt about Cooper with anyone but him. She sighed. "I mean, it has a lot to do with last night, but it's my finances, mostly. I'm really scared."

"Let's work out a way to wrangle you a waitressing job then."

"Really? After yesterday's fiasco, I'm lucky to still be the concession girl."

"One thing at a time. Sell some merchandise at the soft open this weekend. If that goes well, maybe Terry will give you a shot."

"Do you think so?"

"Look, I've known Terry for a long time. She's all about the bottom line. Money talks to her. Sell the shit out of that concession stand, then we'll see what we can do to change her mind." CeCe smiled. "Now get dressed. You don't want to be late for work, and neither do I. Terry values punctuality."

"Right," Ruby said.

"I'm just a step behind you. I'll meet you outside in ten minutes." She threw off her robe and jumped into the shower.

"Okay," Ruby responded somewhat dully, changing into her clean clothing.

"I need coffee. Do you need coffee? We can stop at get some," CeCe shouted above the sound of the shower.

"I do." Ruby pulled herself up and weakly smiled into the mirror. At least she'd made a friend in CeCe. Picking up her eyeliner, she began to think about what she could do to boost sales and get noticed. Her financial life depended on it. Then a moment of extreme clarity dawned.

"Hey, CeCe," she yelled over the sound of the water. "Does the wait staff wear a uniform?"

"Kind of. White shirt, black pants."

"Not a specific shirt, just a generic white shirt?"

"Yeah. I buy them by the dozen at Wal-Mart. They get pretty gross. I mean, we're serving fried seafood."

"Interesting," Ruby said, her mind racing.

"Why do you ask?" CeCe inquired, stepping out of the shower stall and reaching for her towel.

"Because I just had an idea that could help me move more merchandise. What if every server was wearing a different Hut logo shirt? You know, show off what we sell at the stand, but in real time?"

"Terry would never give us shirts to wear. She's too cheap."

"Maybe I can convince her."

CeCe laughed. "That's a good one, but if you want to try…"

"Meet me at my car. I have a legal pad there. I'm going to organize my thoughts so I can make a presentation to Terry," Ruby said, stuffing her make-up back into her cosmetic bag. "I'll wait for you there."

Ten minutes later, Ruby had two sides of the first sheet of paper filled with sketches and ideas. If she made the product less static, it could fly off the shelves. She could try to convince Terry that approaching the tired, old point of sale approach wasn't the best way to make money. *And maybe pigs could fly*, she thought, self-doubt shrouding her like a scratchy blanket. Just then CeCe opened the passenger door.

"Coffee. I need coffee."

"I need a lot more than a little caffeine," Ruby replied. She put the papers on CeCe's lap and backed the car out of the Barn's parking lot.

CeCe turned the sheets over, looked at the sketches and said, "Maybe law school's the wrong choice. Maybe you should have applied to business school."

"No. I'm just a class A shopper. I know what people want to see when they look at this stuff. I apply my own experience to it, you know? Most clothes look crappy on the hanger, but once you put something on, well…"

"Hold on. This isn't some designer dress we're talking about. It's a tee shirt, or maybe a sweatshirt."

"I know. But the same principle applies. Let's say everyone in the place is walking around wearing a different shirt. That way the customer sees the designs displayed in real-life. And maybe if they like their server, they want the shirt. Or they see one of the other designs on a bartender and they think he's cute, so they buy one for their boyfriend, or girlfriend, who knows?"

"I get it," CeCe said, awareness dawning.

"And take it a step further. You, the server, add the shirt onto the tab, effectively making the payment easier and the sale secure. I mean, there's no buyer's remorse after the dinner bill is paid, because the merchandise is on that check. The sale is made. It might even net a larger tip, but to make it more appealing to the staff and to maybe get them on board with the idea, I'll give up a piece of my commission to the server who sells the most."

"Well, that's one way to make some friends...and some enemies."

"I'm not looking for friends, and let's face it," she said pausing for effect. "And we both know I've got at least one enemy."

CeCe laughed. "That's true... but I'd also like to think that you've got at least one friend."

Ruby looked the other woman and continued, "I'm so grateful for you, CeCe. You've got to know that. But this is just all theoretical. I've got to get the idea past Terry first." She pulled up to the door of the convenience store so they could get coffee.

"It's a really good idea, Ruby. You never know what the old bird will say. I do know one thing, however. She loves to make money."

"That's what I've got at the front of my mind, believe me." They both silently stepped up to the self-serve counter and poured hot coffee into to-go cups, pausing to add milk before walking over to the cashier to pay.

"Well," CeCe said once they were back in the car. "At least you dream big."

"Not always," Ruby replied, Cooper's face flashing through her mind.

"Hey," CeCe remarked. "That's the thing that sets you apart. Don't diminish how important it is for you to be you."

"If I'm me, I'll never fit in here. If I'm me, I'll run so far from Cooper that we'll never have a shot..."

"Whoa," the other woman exclaimed. "One thing at a

time. Just for now, let's deal with Terry. Save the Cooper discussion for drinks later, okay?"

Ruby smiled weakly and turned the car in the direction of the Hut. Once there, CeCe ran inside to help set up all of the serving stations. The soft open was only two days away and there was a lot of work that still needed to be done. Ruby straightened up the concession stand one final time before going inside the building to look for Terry. She found her berating one of the busboys.

"Are you serious?" Ruby overheard part of the conversation. "You call this station clean? Well, it's not by any standard, let alone mine! Do it again!"

The busboy scampered over to the offending tabletop and began to vigorously scrub it with a towel.

"No, no, no! Go get a fresh sponge!" Terry yelled. "Do it now!"

The offender ran off to do his boss's bidding. While the timing wasn't ideal, Ruby saw the opportunity to grab Terry's attention and took it.

"Excuse me, Terry. Can I talk to you for a minute?"

"What is it?" the older woman asked gruffly.

"I have an idea I'd like to run by you. I think I can sell more merchandise if we change the way we display what we've got."

"I've done just fine with the concession stand. Those are impulse items. It's not like choosing fine art, you know. We're talking about tee shirts and shot glasses."

"I realize that, but um…" she hesitated. Maybe drawing this kind of attention to herself was a bad idea.

"I don't have a lot of time. Just spit it out," Terry said impatiently.

"I was thinking that the wait staff should be wearing the logo branded shirts," Ruby said in a rush. "That way, the customers see the gear in action. They can buy one from their server, or if they don't, I can still grab their attention on their way out the door. We'd increase our sales potential that way."

"You want me to give free shirts to the staff?" Terry asked, immediately understanding where Ruby was going with this concept.

"Just the first one," Ruby said and continued in a rush of words, "if they need more, they'll have to provide them on their own."

"No way. I don't think they'll like that idea at all. They won't buy themselves the additional gear and a dirty, grimy tee shirt sends the message that my place is substandard. It's too risky."

"But look at the upside. I really think you'll sell more merchandise if you give this a try."

Terry took a moment, and Ruby was pretty sure that her boss was calculating the cost of this scheme in her head. The older woman's eyes narrowed. "Okay, hot shot. You can bring this to the staff tonight at the team meeting. I think it will die a quick death, but, if they're good with it, I'll give it a go."

"Me? Present my concept to everyone? Don't you want to…"

"Yeah. You. Your idea. You pitch it and we'll see what happens." She turned and walked away.

Ruby stood still for a long moment, not knowing how to feel – exhilarated or terrified. She might have just unlocked a great sales technique that could net her a larger share of the profits through her commissions, eliminating the need to switch roles and waitress. But she may just alienate the entire staff as well, and she was well aware that the odds of her finding success with this group were really small. One way or another, she'd committed to the idea by offering it up to Terry, and now she'd just have to follow through with it. For the rest of the day Ruby practiced the presentation she planned on making to the staff over and over again in her head. At lunch time, she tried it on CeCe.

"I don't know about everyone else, Ruby, but I like it. Especially since I might make more in the long run, I mean, I'll buy one more shirt if Terry's giving us one for free. I'll just do a lot of laundry and alternate wearing them."

"Let's hope everyone else sees it that way," Ruby replied. Her leg was shaking under the table with nervous energy. Then she asked, "Do you think I'm being set up to fail? By Terry, I mean? It could be her way of getting rid of me, you know, by throwing me to the sharks."

Her friend looked back at her thoughtfully and said, "Anything is possible, and Terry's pretty shrewd. But you make a compelling argument, and don't worry. I'll back you up."

"Thanks, CeCe. I appreciate it, I do."

"That's what friends are for!" the other woman replied, taking the last bite of her tuna sandwich and polishing off a Diet Coke. She stood and walked back toward the kitchen entrance to the building, turning once to shout out, "Just look at me when you speak to everyone. You'll do just fine." And then she was gone from sight.

Ruby returned to her post at the concession stand and chose a shirt to wear to the meeting. Looking around and seeing no one, she ducked down, removed her own top and threw on the branded one. Then, on the spur of the moment, she took the rubber band that had been holding her hair back off of her face and gathered the bottom of the shirt, fastening it to one side. It gave shape to the otherwise boxy tee shirt, hugging her curves and shortening the length of the fabric to sit right above the waistband of her jeans. She quickly brushed out her hair and threw on some clear lip gloss. She was ready. Or at least as ready as she was ever going to be.

At the appointed time, she went inside to join the rest of the staff to hear Terry's final instructions for the soft open. Mostly everyone had already gathered in the dining room and she quickly glanced around for Cooper. Not seeing him, she took a seat next to CeCe and waited for Terry to call on her to speak. When Terry shouted her name, she froze. CeCe had to nudge her to stand.

"Hi, everyone," Ruby began, and as briefly as possible, she outlined her idea for the staff.

"Let me get this straight," Patti exclaimed. "You want us to buy tee shirts from you? And you make a commission on each one you sell? How the hell is that fair? I bust my ass hauling oysters and chowder all night, and if I sell this merchandise, you get a cut?"

"As I said," Ruby repeated part of her earlier presentation, "I'd been willing to share my profit with the person who sells the most. We can have a weekly tally sheet. The person at the top of the leaderboard gets a percentage of what I make."

"That sucks. What if the people I serve don't want a damned shirt or shot glass?"

"It's up to you to make them want it," Cooper's voice rung out from somewhere in the back of the room. Ruby hadn't seen him come in, but she was very glad that he was there now.

"Right. Add that to the list of what I need to do to make a living around here," was Patti's sarcastic retort.

"It sounds like a fine idea to me," he replied. "And I'm

most certainly willing to give it a go." He smiled at Ruby and she felt his warmth from across the room.

"Me too," CeCe added. "Any chance that I can add to my income sounds good. When can I pick up my shirt?"

"Well, if we're going to do this, she can distribute the shirts tonight," Terry said authoritatively, taking over. She turned to Ruby. "I want a strict accounting on this. I want to know who gets which shirt, and there better be no funny business – or else. One free shirt per worker. You can buy your additional gear for cost, people, but be aware that I've got my eyes on this little project."

"Ok, Terry, got it," Ruby said, breathing a sigh of relief, as the crowd dispersed. Looking up, she saw Cooper walking toward her.

"Pretty impressive. You never mentioned this brainstorm of yours last night…"

"I sort of came up with it this morning. I never expected this to come together so fast."

"What about dinner? Now we have something cool to celebrate."

"I have to go distribute those shirts, and then I promised CeCe that I'd grab a drink with her." She heard her friend's words from earlier that day about it being summer and giving herself a break. "But if you want to have a late dinner – out somewhere, that is – I would too."

He smiled and she felt herself melting into a puddle of desire on the spot where she stood. "Well, I know just the place."

"No funny business, Cooper. Just dinner."

"I heard you. I promise."

"Hey, Ruby," Patti shouted from the door of the dining room. "Are you going to talk to Cooper all night or are you going to give out those shirts?"

"I'll be there in a minute," she yelled back.

"I won't keep you from your customers," he winked. I'll wait a bit to get my shirt. Put aside the one you think suits me best," he said pausing briefly and resting one hand lightly on her back. "And I'll pick you up later. Where will you be?"

"The Dive," she said as she walked in the direction of the concession stand, already devising a quick inventory system in her head.

What felt like hours later, she'd given out the shirts, letting each employee choose their favorite, keeping a strict list of sizes and designs so that she'd be able to restock the next morning. She'd also had every person sign next to their printed name, insuring that no one who already had been given their merchandise could later make a claim that they hadn't received one. Finally, she pulled down the grate and locked the stand. She had told CeCe that she'd catch up with her for that drink at the Dive when she was done, so Ruby drove herself to the bar. Once there, she bought a Satan's Satin and found CeCe at a small table near the juke box. It was crowded in the small space, with everyone from the Hut there looking to get in one of the last nights of freedom before work started in earnest.

"Got your drink of choice I see," her friend teased.

"I have to admit, it's pretty good," Ruby smiled back.

"A little pricey, but yeah. It's good." She clinked her own bottle of Pabst to Ruby's drink. "Well bottom's up. You're gonna need to take the edge off. Patti's been talking some nasty crap already."

"She made her feelings known at the meeting. And I

can't say I'm surprised. Even if she thought I had a good idea she'd smack it down, just because it was mine."

CeCe tipped her own bottle back and took a long swallow before answering. "You may be right. But when you're fighting for every dollar, sometimes you don't see the forest for the trees. She'll catch on once this plan of yours takes effect. I really think it could work. It's simple, but it makes a whole lot of sense."

"Thanks, CeCe. It means a lot to hear you say that."

"Take the small victories where you can. This is a tough culture to crack, believe me, I know."

"And then there was last night," Ruby said, about to open up about the strong pull she had toward a man she'd just met, when she sensed a subtle change in the air. The only thing she could liken it to was a sudden electrical charge enveloping her, leaving a tingling sensation on her skin. Before she even turned to see him, she knew he was there. Cooper. He quickly closed the distance between them, leaning in to kiss her softly on the lips before grabbing an empty chair and pulling it up to the table, right next to hers.

"You taste like my beer," he said. "That's delicious."

"Well, it tastes really good," she teased.

"Oh yeah, hotshot?" He leaned in, his eyes smoldering. "Have a marketing tip or two for me? Should I run an ad campaign urging women and men to share a bottle of the stuff as a way to spice up their love life?"

"I don't know. Give me five minutes to think about it!" She blushed crimson.

"Take as long as you need. I can wait," he smirked, grabbing the bottle from her hand and drinking down what was left.

"Okay you two. Enough with the veiled banter. I'm still here, remember me?" CeCe exclaimed.

"Well, ladies, the next round is on me. Let's toast to Ruby's success today." He pushed back his chair and walked up to the bar.

"He is so into you, I don't even know what to say," CeCe remarked, pretending to fan herself with a napkin.

"Do you think so?" Ruby let down her guard to the other woman. "I get so flustered around him…"

"You don't seem flustered. Excited yes. Flustered, no."

"I can't explain it to you, but there is just something about him that gets me going from zero to sixty in no time."

"Other than the fact that he's freaking hot? C'mon, it's obvious. And he's feeling it too. I can tell."

"How?"

"He seems different than he was last summer with Patti… you could tell that he wasn't really looking for any sort of attachment with her. But that boy has only got eyes for you now, it's obvious. He's got some serious game, let me tell you!"

Ruby watched Cooper at the bar, making small talk with some of the other men. His moved gracefully, patting one of the guys he'd been speaking to on the back before he picked up all three bottles of beer left by the bartender and returned to the table. She watched his hands, remembering the path they'd taken all over her body the previous night, how she had felt every fiber of her being under his touch. She wriggled in her seat.

"Breathe, girlfriend, breathe," she heard CeCe say, snapping her back from her wandering thoughts.

Then he was there, in front of her, and all at once Ruby began to regret that she'd been so emphatic about having dinner tonight in a public place. She no longer felt hungry for anything other than his mouth on hers, his hands on her body and the feel of his soft, cool sheets against her naked, overheated skin.

Chapter Eight

Marvin Gaye's soulful voice lifted into the air from the juke box and wrapped around the small bar in a lover's embrace.

"Oh geez. This is my cue to exit," CeCe said, pushing her chair back from the table. "You two apparently have a lot to talk about anyway, and I want to get in on that foosball tournament." She nodded her head toward the far corner of the room and the crowd that had gathered around the ongoing game.

"Are you going to the bonfire later?" Cooper asked.

"Wow. I forgot all about it, but yeah. First one of the season. See you there?"

"Probably," Cooper answered, turning to Ruby. "Ever been to a bonfire before?"

"Nope. What is it?"

"I'll let him fill you in. Have some fun, you two," CeCe said as she made her way to the other side of the bar.

Cooper smiled and then said, "We get together a couple of times a summer to have a bonfire on the beach. It's fun.

We hang out all night and generally stay to watch the sunrise. Are you game?"

"Um, I'm not sure I'd be welcome after I just cost the staff some of their hard- earned future income with my sales idea."

"You won't know unless you go. And besides, I'll be there…no one's going to mess with you, believe me."

She smiled and sarcastically said, "My protector, huh?"

"If that's what you want to call it, I'm down."

"What about dinner? You promised, and I'm starving!" she exclaimed.

"I thought of that. I packed up a little picnic for the beach, just in case you said yes." His eyes searched hers. "I hope that wasn't too presumptuous of me."

"I think that if you have some food, I'll follow you almost anywhere!" she replied.

"Anywhere?" he asked huskily.

"Well, the beach sounds like a fine place to start," she said in a rush, nervous energy rising to the surface.

He took her hand and led her outside to his truck. She could see a small cooler alongside a keg stamped 'Satin's Satin' in the flat bed, along with some blankets and firewood stacked neatly in a milk crate.

"Wow. You're prepared!" she remarked.

"I'm a pretty good boy scout," he smiled, opening the passenger door for her.

"I bet you've helped a number of old ladies cross the street," she teased.

"That I have. But for tonight, you're the damsel in distress. And I've got the cure for what ails you."

Ruby was glad that it was dark in the parking lot, because she felt a familiar blush rise, her face and chest grew warm and red. "Do you now?" she asked when he sat down in the driver's seat.

"Yup. Bread and cheese. Some olives. Melon and prosciutto…and some other delicious surprises."

Ruby drew in a breath at the innuendo. "Oh," she said. "Like what?"

"Well, now," he replied. "If I told you, it would ruin all my hard work, wouldn't it? And besides, anticipation only makes the experience sweeter."

She was melting into a puddle of pure desire in her seat. She knew that it would be impossible to resist this man. After he got into the truck and began to drive, she watched as he lightly held onto the steering wheel with one hand, offering his free one for her to hold. Ruby slipped her own small hand into his bigger one, feeling his warmth as he softly ran his thumb along the inside of her palm. Her entire body felt as though it was centered there, a mass of blatant longing concentrated in the center of the little circles he was tracing, causing her breathing to become erratic and her heart to race. When they pulled into the beach parking lot, she jumped out, needing the cool air to help bring her back to her rational self.

"Are you okay?" he asked with concern. She was leaning back against the door of his truck.

The last thing she wanted was to let on what she was feeling. "Oh yes, just faint from hunger," she kidded to cover the truth.

"Well, if that's it, I've got the cure for you," he said, leaning in and kissing her cheek.

"If that's not a loaded statement, I don't know what is," she replied.

"You wound me!" he said in mock horror. "I promised

you dinner in a public place, and by all things I hold holy, I vow to deliver!"

"Have you been watching some bizarre knight-in-shining-armor movie or something since last night? You sound like you're practicing bad dialogue from 'Robin Hood'!" she giggled.

"Nope. Just trying to keep a promise. Now if you'll help me carry some of this down to the beach, we can eat." He handed her two plaid wool blankets and lifted the smaller cooler easily out of the truck.

"What about that stuff?" she asked, pointing to what was left behind.

"That's for the bonfire. Wait and see."

"Sounds mysterious."

"Not really. Can't make a fire without some dry wood, right?" He pointed to himself. "Boy Scout, remember?"

"And the keg?"

"Well, that's my secret weapon. I'm supplying the libation tonight. If I can get these guys drinking my beer, maybe I can get them to suggest it to the patrons at the Hut."

"Taking a page out of my book, huh?"

"You were definitely my inspiration for this one. But I've got a few ideas of my own, you know."

"I'm sure you do," she replied, gingerly making her way down the steep dune toward the beach.

"Hold on. First, take off your shoes."

She leaned over and slipped off her sneakers, and he did the same.

"Just leave them up here at the top by the fence. They'll be here when we get back, don't worry. And there's no need to try and navigate this in the total dark," he said pointing the flashlight on his phone down to where her feet were sinking into the cool sand. "That's better."

"Wow. You really do think of everything," she said, clutching the blankets tighter, concentrating on each step.

"Well, it's not my first rodeo, you know."

And just like that, his words reverberated in her head, clearing her brain and reminding her that for him, she was another in a long line of summer flings. Just how many women had made this walk with him? Did he do this exact thing with Patti last summer? She cooled off considerably as they walked down closer to the shoreline. It was a new moon and the darkness highlighted the stars as they began to peek out against the horizon.

"It's high tide now," he remarked matter-of-factly, watching as the waves crashed onto the shore. We're good to find a spot anywhere here behind the waterline. He motioned to a place set back a short distance from the ocean.

Ruby shook out a blanket and placed it down on the sand, sitting as he opened the cooler. She watched as he pulled out two plates and two glasses along with a bottle of red wine. He then carefully lifted a series of containers out of the ice chest and scattered them between where the two of them sat. Hunger for the food in front of her overwhelmed her, allowing her to forget her doubts for a moment while she sampled some of the delicious treats he'd prepared. He opened a small Tupperware and offered her what was inside. It smelled earthy and delicious.

"What is that?" she asked.

"It's smoky eggplant. Try it."

He picked up the baguette he'd brought along and tore off one end, passing it to her.

"I know where you got this!" she exclaimed. "Phillipe is a family friend."

"Well, he makes the best bread for miles around." He took her hand in his and dipped it gently into the container, then lifted it to her mouth. She took a bite and relaxed some more.

"Wow," she said with her mouth full. "That's really good."

He smiled, looked relieved, and began to lift off lids from the other containers of food he'd prepared. There was homemade hummus, tzatziki and a tomato basil salad, along with a score of other small bites.

"I love this. It's tapas!" she exclaimed, continuing to eat as he poured the wine.

"What do you think about the idea of a tap room in town, where I can serve my beer, maybe some local wines and this kind of food?"

"It's great. In the summertime. But what happens to your costs when winter hits and no one is here?"

"Yeah, that's the hitch. But Terry seems to manage…"

"True, but you know what they say. Location is king, and she's got this," Ruby said, widening her arms to encompass the beach. A spot in the center of town might not draw a large crowd night after night."

"You have a good point." He looked down, crestfallen.

"Don't give up so easily," she said. "There are other ways to achieve what you're trying to do without a brick and mortar storefront, you know. Have you been to Boston? Seen the food trucks there?"

"Yeah, but you can't serve alcohol on the beach. Terry's the exception, she's grandfathered in."

"Right. But you can get a liquor license for beer and wine to sell out of a food truck. If you're parked right outside of the beach proper, well… not your problem if some of the patrons choose to walk down with their lunch or dinner to take a look at the ocean."

"I'm not so sure that's legal."

"Well, you can be my first pro bono case, just as soon as I actually start learning the law then!"

"Deal!" he smiled, popping an olive into his mouth.

Ruby lifted her glass to him and drank a large swallow. She loved their easy conversation and his company. She was feeling loose and languid from the wine and nearly missed her mouth with another bite of hummus. As she reached for a napkin, he stopped her, leaning in and swiping his tongue over the tiny bit of dip that had missed its mark. She shivered.

"Are you cold?" he asked, moving closer and pulling her onto his lap.

"A little," she said, trying to mask the truth. His nearness made her entire body shake.

He reached for the second blanket and wrapped it around them both.

"I like being here with you Ruby." He leaned in and kissed her, gently at first, but then with an apparent shift in urgency, rocking his body against hers.

She pulled back, a vision of Patti's face flashing before her eyes. "Wait," she said, trying to clear her mind. For as much as she willed herself to let go and not worry about what would happen to them when September rolled around, she didn't want to be discarded by him in three-month's time. She decided to keep up her prior argument. "I just can't get attached to you, Cooper. Summer's short. I'm here for a reason, I've got to keep my eye on my goal." She shifted herself off of him and back onto the blanket.

"Seriously? After what happened between us last night?"

She quickly added, "Let me finish. Don't confuse the issue. The sex was amazing, yes, but…I've been through a lot and I've finally decided what I need to do for me, and that's law school. I'm not going to deviate from that. Not for you, not for anyone." While she heard her own words, and knew that they rang hollow. She couldn't help but feel overwhelmingly sad. She wanted him. That was the truth. Not being able to continue to sit that close to him, Ruby threw off the blanket and walked down to the ocean, tears welling in her eyes, hoping to gain control of her raging emotions. The immediate attraction she felt for him left her utterly confused. Cooper was the complication she didn't need, but, a small part of her mind questioned if he was the anchor she'd been searching for all along? *No!* a little voice in her head screamed back at her. She stood still, arms wrapped around her body until she sensed him standing behind her, and when she turned, there he was. He reached out for her.

"I didn't mean to upset you Ruby. I was just being honest. I know we've just met, but I feel something for you that hasn't happened to me before. Last night was… special." His blue eyes locked with hers and he said, "you've got to believe me."

"You're right about one thing, Cooper. We've just met. We don't even know each other. We've got to slow down."

"If that's what you need, I can do that. I just can't give up on the idea that this thing between us is real." He took a step closer. "Give me a shot, Ruby. Please."

The sound of the waves pounding on the shore combined with the effects of the red wine should have been calming. Instead, she felt her heart racing. She knew that he was telling her the truth, and being honest with herself, she'd had to admit that she felt the same way. He was different than most of the Wall Street types she'd dated in the past. He was genuine in a way that made her weak in the knees. If she could let go just a little bit, relax and let nature take its course, then maybe this was a relationship worth pursuing.

"Okay Cooper," she whispered softly, her words lifting on the night air. "Let's get to know each other a little better before we have a repeat of last night's ending… as nice as that was, that's just not me."

He leaned in close and touched his forehead to hers. "I can respect that. I'll let you take the lead on this Ruby. You let me know where and when you're ready to spend the night with me again." He paused. "If ever."

"Okay," she replied so quietly that she was not sure if she'd even spoken the word out loud.

They stood there at the water's edge silently, the icy cold ocean tickling her feet until she heard the sound of cars pulling into the parking lot above them.

"People are starting to show up for bonfire," he whispered in her ear. "We don't have to stay."

She searched his face. His earnest, caring expression telling her all she needed to know.

"I want to stay. If I'm going to try and fit in, I've got to do the hard work."

"Well, I've brought enough beer to help ease your way," he joked. "What do you know about building a fire?"

"I don't have to know anything. I thought I came here with a bonafide Boy Scout!" she smiled.

He kissed her cheek. "That you did, Mademoiselle. Forever at your service!"

She smiled and they both turned to meet the crowd

beginning to descend down the steep dune. Summer was about to begin and Ruby was prepared to meet it head on.

An hour later the once empty beach was packed with people. Cooper had taken charge of starting the actual fire, a mixture of driftwood collected from the surrounding area and supplemented with the logs he'd brought down from his truck. Someone had set-up an old-school boom box – there was no internet service for wireless speakers on the beach – and a variety of dance music began to play from a far-off radio station. Cooper and Steamroller lugged the heavy keg full of

Satin's Satin down to where they were setting up for the night's activities, and Ruby watched with fascination as Cooper effortlessly hoisted the full metal container up onto the now empty milk crate. He then pulled a spout-like device out of his back pocket and quickly attached it to the silver keg with spare, graceful movements. He really was nothing like any other man she knew. In Manhattan, no one would think of fixing something in their apartment by themselves, they'd call in a handyman or the building's superintendent. She had once dated a guy who made multi-million-dollar deals for a stockbrokerage firm by day, but when confronted with a mouse in his living space stood on a chair holding his cell phone until help arrived. *Cooper seemed so much more,* she thought, struggling for a moment for what that elusive difference was. And then it hit her. *Masculine. He just seemed so masculine.*

He finished his task and walked back over to the blanket where she sat.

"Can I get you a beer?" he asked.

"If it's all the same to you, I think I'll stick with the red wine."

"Of course. We're going to light the fire soon. Why don't you come over with me? It's a real rush once you get that blaze going."

"Depends what kind of blaze," she thought to herself before remembering their prior conversation. She was the one who was pumping the brakes on their relationship. She shouldn't be sending any mixed signals. "Um, I think I'll hang back. You go ahead. I'm just going to stargaze for a bit."

"Ok. I'll be back once I get that fire going." He turned to return to his task.

Ruby poured herself some more wine, took a long sip and then sank back into the blanket to look at the dark sky. She didn't know much about the constellations – she most certainly couldn't see much of them in a very light polluted Manhattan – but she had a real appreciation for just how small a speck she was in the universe when she took in the magnitude of what was spread out above her. She could only identify the big dipper and the north star, but it didn't matter. As she watched more stars emerge above her as they came out into the sky against the reassuring pulse of the ocean meeting the shore, Ruby began to relax. She sat that way until Cooper returned from successfully starting the bonfire.

"I'm off duty. My work here is done!" he exclaimed, chugging down the remains of whatever was left in the red plastic cup in his hand. He lay down close to Ruby on the blanket. "What are you looking for?" he questioned, motioning to the sky.

She turned and lifted herself up on an elbow. "I don't know enough to know…" was all she said in return.

He reached up and ran his fingers through her hair. "I

meant the stars. Were you looking for something in particular?"

She smiled. "Oh. Um, how can you tell if you're looking at a star or a far-away planet? I've never seen the sky look like this. Can we see past our galaxy?"

"Well, I don't think we can see past our galaxy without the proper equipment, but planets are the stationary. Stars twinkle."

"So that's where the nursery rhyme comes from. Twinkle, twinkle…" she lay back down.

"Yup."

They lay there, side by side without speaking until Ruby saw something streak across the sky. "Did you see that flash of light? What was that?" she asked excitedly.

"A shooting star. Close your eyes and make a wish," he said, turning his face toward hers.

She did what he said, but even with her eyes closed, his face was the only thing she could see.

Chapter Nine

A few hours later, the party was in full swing. Cooper had enticed Ruby to join the others with a promise of a dance, and she acquiesced. He pulled her into the center of the crowd, and as the music changed to a slower tune, he took her into his arms and swung her around and around.

"I'm getting dizzy!" she exclaimed.

"Well then you'll just have to hang on tight," he replied, pulling her in closer. She could feel the warmth of his chest and the strong muscles of his thighs as they continued to move to the soulful beat swirling around them.

Out of the corner of her eye, she saw Patti filling her glass from the keg. The other woman seemed animated in the conversation she was having with a man Ruby hadn't met yet, and it made her feel relaxed. She would love to have the rest of the evening go by without any sort of weird confrontation. All of a sudden, she noticed a bunch of people beginning to remove their clothing.

"Skinny dip!" she heard one of them yell.

Next thing she knew, there was a rush toward the surf.

Naked bodies were everywhere, and people were flinging themselves into the frigid water. There was a lot of whooping and hollering by the participants, and Ruby found herself glued to the sand, watching the revelers in action.

"Isn't that dangerous?" she asked Cooper. "Aren't they risking hypothermia?"

"They're pretty fueled by booze, I don't know if they're feeling the water temperature at all. If they don't get out soon, I'll go down there..."

"You shouldn't have to do that! They're all adults. They should know better!"

"Wow, Ruby! So judgmental! They're just having some fun, is all."

She took a step away from him, aware that she'd said something she shouldn't have. "I just meant..."

Cooper said, "The first rule about trying to fit in is to watch and learn. This is just what we do, and we've been doing it forever. I know some of these people since elementary school. They've been jumping into the ocean since they were able to walk. They know their limits, but just in case, we look out for each other. If I think someone's in too long, I'll point it out, that's all."

"You aren't planning on going in, are you?" she asked wide-eyed.

"Nope. Too cold for me. But I never would try to stop someone from having a swim, if that's what they're into."

"You're right. Sorry. I shouldn't have said anything."

"No need to apologize," he smiled and added, "I'm pretty sure that there are people in the water right now regretting their decision to take a swim tonight," he chuckled. "That water is freezing!"

Sure enough, most of the party-goers stopped splashing

around in the surf and began to run back up the beach from the ocean, huddling in towels around the bonfire.

"Is that why you light…"

"Aha," Cooper interrupted her. "Now you're starting to catch on!"

"Oh. My city side is showing, huh?" she smiled.

"Just a bit. No problem. I find it endearing!" He reached for her. "Take a walk with me?" he asked, pulling a blanket up off the sand.

She took his offered hand and they began to move away from the crowd, the fire and the happy sounds of the party. As they walked down the beach in silence he put his arm around her shoulders, drawing her close until they got to a spot of total isolation. They sat down between two dunes, beach grass sprouting out in patches, the cool sand soft beneath her.

"I just wanted to be alone with you for a little bit, I hope that's okay," he said.

"Of course," she murmured. "It was getting a little bit crazy back there."

"Tell me more about what happened to your family, Ruby. How did things go so wrong?"

She sat still for a moment, trying to gather her thoughts. She really did want to share what she knew with him, but once he asked, she realized all that she didn't know.

"I'm embarrassed to admit how little I really understand. One day my life was pretty much as it had always been. I was away at school when it happened, I was a senior in college then – and the next thing I knew there were reporters camped outside the house I'd been renting off-campus with my friends." She shook her head at the memory. "The first time I opened the door and they jumped out at me… it was terrifying. And afterward…I was a prisoner inside for so long. When they couldn't get to me, they began to ask my housemates questions, or anyone else that tried to get to close the front door for that matter. My dad didn't really give me any warning, he had just said that his business was in trouble and that I shouldn't come home from Boston for a while."

"He just said he had trouble, without giving you any details?"

"Basically. And my mom totally shut down. I don't think she came out of her bedroom for days. It was so awful."

"So, what did you do?"

"I tried to avoid watching the news, but the reporters were relentless. I had a month to go before finals and graduation, but it became clear very quickly that I wasn't going to be able to stay and finish, I mean, it got crazy, and my friends were being harassed too. It was the final stretch at college, the part when you're supposed to feel on top of the world. You're done. You're about to get your degree. It's meant to be a happy go-lucky time…"

"Wait. You didn't graduate?"

"I got my diploma but I didn't get to walk with my classmates, no. I had all my work pretty much done and my professors took pity on me. I finished up by submitting my papers online. When it got to be too much for me to take any longer, I snuck out in the dark, at night, through the back door. One of my friends helped me navigate through the backyards of our neighbors and we came out on a different street where she had parked her car. She drove me home to Manhattan."

"Ruby. I'm so sorry."

"Yeah, it sucked. I'm still not over it even though it happened a year ago."

"What about law school?"

"Well, Harvard had accepted me, but I ended up taking a year deferment. The admission committee made it clear that it would be better for all concerned if I put some time and space between us. I was still welcome to attend, but not right away. I had to accept that, you know, and besides, if I had gone straight to law school, the reporters would have followed me there. You can't imagine how persistent they are."

"What did you do for a year?"

"I would sit with my dad when he'd come home from meeting with his lawyer every day. We wouldn't talk about what had happened at all, I'd just be there with him as he stared out the living room window at the park. I held my mom's hand when she couldn't bear the shame of not being able to keep up her lifestyle anymore. She didn't leave the apartment for almost six months, she couldn't deal with having an accidental run-in with any of her friends. Well, former friends. The whole group of them dropped her like she had some sort of plague. And then when it became clear that a plea deal was going to be offered in exchange for reparation money, I helped them pack up what was left of their belongings – and believe me, that wasn't much. Between what the government seized and what they were able to sell, there were only a dozen or so boxes. Then I moved them to Queens."

"That must have been hard, Ruby."

"I guess that was when I realized just how much it sucks to be an only child. It's just me and my folks, and they're pretty broken, you know?"

He shook his head for a minute before saying, "I can't even imagine how awful that was for you. Although I do understand the only child thing. It was just me and my mom for so long. But she's remarried now. And really happy."

"That's so good, Cooper. It gives me hope. The crazy thing about my family's situation is that I still don't really have all the details. My dad never wanted me to know, and I'm not sure what my mom understands. They both just shut down emotionally."

"Did your dad steal investment money from his clients? Did he move money around illegally?" He gently reached over pushed a stray lock of her hair behind her ear.

She shook her head, feeling the warmth of his fingers against her skin. "There was a point where I did want the truth. It's tough to see Federal marshals bang on the front door of your childhood home and start to pack up the computers and stuff…"

"Are you kidding?"

"No. Really early one morning there was a terrible banging on the door. A whole crew of men in windbreakers with the FBI logo came crashing through the house, throwing papers and laptops into boxes, telling us to sit on the couch and not touch a thing. It was pretty terrifying."

"Just like that?"

"Oh yeah. And an hour later, when they were done, they slapped handcuffs on my dad and took him away with them. My mother was in her bedroom. I remember the strangest things about it. It was at the beginning of November, the first really cold, blustery day of autumn, and it was raining, the kind of morning where you want to burrow back down under the blanket and stay asleep a while longer. My parent's room was dark because no one had turned any of the lamps on, and my mom just sat there on her unmade bed, crying."

"Were you scared?"

"I guess I was. But mostly I was confused, and I still am. But now I'm ready to find out what really happened."

"What if you find out that your dad did something really terrible?"

Ruby looked directly into Cooper's eyes. "I think that's a forgone conclusion, don't you? I still want to know."

"Why? What difference does it make now? You have your own life to live…"

"True. But I need to know. He wasn't in business alone. My dad had partners. They didn't have the same thing happen to them, they are still living the way they always did, the life my parents used to have. Why? How is that possible?" She hugged her arms around her own body. "My dad's a good person, I know he is. This whole thing is so fucked up."

Cooper shifted on the sand putting one arm around her shoulder and pulling her down to lay next to him on the sand. He placed a soft kiss on the top of her head. "Something tells me you'll figure it out. I just hope that when you do it doesn't change the way you feel about your father. It sucks not having your dad in your life, believe me."

She put her hand under his sweatshirt and over his heart, feeling the strong beat beneath his shirt. It was comforting and all of a sudden, she felt overwhelmingly exhausted. It was almost as if the retelling of the story was a confession of sorts. Now Cooper knew the truth, or as much of it as she did. Ruby closed her eyes and was soothed by the sound of the ocean hitting the beach and the warmth of his body next to hers. She couldn't get the jumbled thoughts about her past out of her head, but tired as she was, she drifted off to sleep.

Ruby opened her eyes to the shifting color on the horizon. There were still stars visible low in the sky, but now there was a hint of wheat colored light poking through the darkness. Her back was to Cooper's front and the blanket covered them both, fully clothed on the beach. She stretched out her legs and he stirred, pulling her closer to him. She could feel the hard core of him through the fabric of his jeans.

"Good morning," he whispered in her ear. "I'm glad we woke up before the sun did. The whole point of bonfire is to watch the dawn." He kissed the back of her neck and she felt a shiver run up her spine.

"Cooper…" she began, shaking her head.

"Don't say it, Ruby. I know. I can't help it. I'm attracted to you, but…" he sat up pushing the blanket away. "I can wait until you're ready. It's okay."

She sat up as well and stared wordlessly at the ocean as the sky began to brighten, bit by bit and watched Cooper stand, brushing the sand off his clothes before reaching out his hand toward her. "Ready to head back?"

"Yes," she replied as she grabbed onto him and was lifted up and into a quick embrace. She didn't stop him from kissing her, a warm and gentle reminder that she was equally torn between wanting to strip off her clothes and tumble back onto the dune with him or run away, as far as she could in an effort to protect her heart from the inevitable end of this type of summer romance. His lips were soft and his body told her all she needed to know. He would offer her warmth and comfort; the promise of a few months of intense passion, but she knew it would wane once Labor Day was gone. She wanted desperately to try and fall into that sort of easy, non-binding relationship. Could she? As he deepened the kiss and began to explore the inner recesses of her mouth, his tongue briefly touching hers, she moaned softly, knowing that all it would take was a signal from her for Cooper to lay her back down on the fine sand beneath them. She could tell that he was waiting for her to do just that. She pulled away.

"We should go. We've both got to be at work in a few hours."

He stepped back and lifted his hand, running it through his own hair, clearly trying to slow his own breathing. He grabbed the now discarded blanket up off the ground and said, "Okay, Ruby. Let's go."

They walked silently back to where the embers of the bonfire still glowed, red and yellow against the charred black wood that remained in a small pile on the beach. The stalwart souls that had stayed through the night were beginning to stir, calling out to one another, cleaning up stray red cups and now empty bags of chips and pretzels, folding blankets and towels and making their way back up the dune to the parking lot. Cooper joined in, throwing sand over the fire, insuring that it was fully extinguished before lifting the now empty keg and hoisting it up onto his shoulder. Ruby wordlessly picked up the basket that had held their dinner and dropped the empty bottle of red wine in a large, weathered metal garbage can before trekking back to Cooper's truck. It seemed to her like some strangely choreographed dance, each person taking a part, the large expanse of beach their stage. Once at the top, the sun now a bit higher in the sky casting a sheen of light across the waves, the surf seemed to be applauding their actions, grateful for the care they took to leave the place as they found it, unchanged by their visit. She recognized the healthy respect this group had for the beauty and splendor of their surroundings, something she'd taken for granted as a summer visitor. She was sure that as a child, she'd been guilty of leaving a soda can or two behind when the day was done, not really aware that it had been her responsibility to ensure that no trace of her remained. She felt both embarrassed and chagrined by this new awareness and vowed to change. She smiled, feeling energized and extremely awake. Her mind raced now. Maybe that was the first step toward fitting in, to accept and shift her focus, to watch and learn from this group of people, to understand what they valued and make that a part of her own life's philosophy. If she could let go of some of her own rigid rules, maybe she could try and live in the moment more. If she threw away some of the structure that drove her, perhaps she could slow down and take the time to enjoy the summer with Cooper, whatever that meant, no strings attached. If she could block the image of Patti in his bed, maybe…

"Hey, Ruby," she heard him say. "Are you going to get in the truck, or stand there all day?"

She reached for the handle, the teasing tone of his voice helping make her decision. She was going to climb in and take the ride.

After a quick shower and a change of clothes, Ruby was ready for work. The soft open of the restaurant was upon them, and she could feel the subtle difference in the atmosphere once she got to the Hut. The entire place was sparkling clean; the multitude of bottles behind the bar were full and shiny; lemons, limes and olives sat in their assigned slots, waiting to be mixed into drinks. The kitchen staff was busy chopping vegetables and garnishes, placing them in plastic containers to be used as mis en place, stacking their efforts in the large walk-in refrigerator. More importantly to Ruby, everyone was wearing a shirt emblazoned with the Hut's logo. And despite the all-nighter on the beach just hours before, the staff was humming with the energy of anticipation. The concession stand stood at the ready, so Ruby was drafted into helping the wait staff roll silverware inside of napkins. It was repetitive, simple work and she enjoyed the chance to lend a hand and take in the sound of the chatter around her.

"Did you enjoy the bonfire last night?" CeCe asked her.

Ruby looked up to see who else was listening before carefully replying. "It was fun. I did have a good time."

Patti snorted, "Yeah. Down the beach somewhere with Cooper. I bet it was special." Patti's sarcasm was apparent to everyone around them.

Ruby felt her blood start to boil as she slowly rolled the knife and fork she'd been holding into a napkin, put it on the pile of silverware that sat in the middle of the table and looked directly at Patti. "What the hell difference does it make to you where I was. Do us both a favor and stay out of my personal life."

All other conversations fell away as the women around the table set their focus on Patti's response.

"Feeling real full of yourself this morning, huh?" She turned to the other workers. "See, girls. That's what a night rolling around in the sand with Cooper will do for you…"

Ruby could feel anger rise and overwhelm her. She looked down at the knives on the table and for the briefest moment thought about taking one and putting it close to Patti's throat. She breathed in deeply to center herself. "We weren't doing anything more than having a private conversation, if you must know. Not that it's any of your business."

"Oh, it's my business alright. You come up here, take a job from a local and then try to run the place. Buy a tee shirt my ass…you bet it's my business!"

"Who do you think you are, Patti?" CeCe interjected. "The sheriff? Leave her alone."

Patti's eyes narrowed as she replied to CeCe. "You shouldn't talk. You're not really one of us either!"

CeCe moved over and stood in front of Patti, pulling herself up to her full height and not backing down. "Really? Like we didn't go to school together from kindergarten on? You gonna make this about skin color now? Huh? Tell me," she threatened.

The other women stood in shocked silence, not knowing what to do or say. Ruby reached out and put her hand on her friend's arm. "Don't worry about it, CeCe. She's angry at me, not you."

CeCe pulled her arm away. "No. I'm tired of the same bullshit." She looked around the group. "I belong here. Which one of you is going to tell Patti to shut up?"

The group remained silent, eyes cast to the ground. Ruby stepped forward. "I am," she said turning to Patti. In her mind, she knew what she needed to do. Bully the bully.

"Apologize to CeCe. Now."

Patti didn't move to speak.

"You really want to throw years of friendship with CeCe away because you're pissed that Cooper and I are seeing each other? Are you that foolish?" Ruby asked.

"Cooper's only interested in you for one thing, you know? Don't start thinking that he wants anything more than a piece of your ass for the summer. By the time September rolls around, you'll be nothing more than a memory."

"And who said that I'm looking for anything else, Patti? But really, you know nothing. Besides, I'm not talking to you about Cooper. I'm talking to you about CeCe."

No one in the assembled group moved a muscle. Finally,

Patti glanced over at CeCe who was standing, arms crossed next to Ruby. She blinked first.

"I shouldn't have said that, Ce. You know that I have a temper. Sorry."

CeCe acknowledged the apology with a nod of her head before picking up another napkin and rolling a knife and fork within it.

Ruby could feel the other women let out a collected sigh of relief as the tension began to dissipate. She was proud of herself for taking a stand. She just had the uneasy feeling that the feud between Patti and herself wasn't over yet. Not by a longshot.

Chapter Ten

By seven o'clock that night the first dinner shift was in full swing. While there was a steady stream of customers, not every table was filled, giving the staff ample time to work out the kinks that were inevitable at the beginning of the season. Aside from the two sweatshirts Ruby sold to a couple who had not dressed warmly enough for the cool evening air, both Louise and Patti each sold a tee shirt. The bar was where the main activity seemed to be centered. People sat around on the high stools, ordering clams on the half shell and shucked oysters, drinking beer and cocktails. From her high perch in the concession stand, Ruby couldn't see the bar, but every so often she would recognize Cooper's voice as he loudly shouted out a raw seafood order to one of the waitresses. The night moved along and closing time came around quickly and without incident.

As she closed the grate over the counter of the stand, Ruby rubbed the back of her neck. She must have been more nervous than she'd realized about this first real night of work and was grateful that Patti had sold a shirt. Maybe the doubting woman would see the value in Ruby's plan when she realized some profit from it.

"Hey, Ruby, over here. If you're done for the night I could use some help shutting down my station," CeCe yelled across the now empty restaurant.

Ruby walked over and started to help her friend put away ketchup bottles and salt and pepper shakers. "How'd you do tonight?" she asked as she wiped down a particularly sticky container of homemade barbeque sauce.

"Just okay. I mean, I only had my tables turnover once, but I'm not complaining. I prefer to ease into this, you know? Once season starts on Memorial Day this place will be hopping. I need to build up to the frenzy! What about you?"

"I sold some merchandise, but it was pretty slow where I sat," Ruby said. "But I'm just glad to have finally gotten started. The anticipation was killing me!"

"I bet it was," CeCe smiled. "Hanging out with Cooper tonight?" she asked with a smile, changing the subject.

"I really don't know. We haven't had a chance to speak all day."

"Oh, okay," CeCe said with some hesitation. "I'm just heading back to the Barn. I'm tired, and tomorrow's another day."

"I'll probably see you there," Ruby replied, looking around for Cooper. He was pouring another round of martinis for two older women at the bar, adding plump olives to each drink with a flourish. Even though the kitchen was closed, he'd work until the last patron left for the night. She started to walk over toward him when Terry appeared out of nowhere.

"Where do you think you're going?"

"Um, I, I was…" she began to stammer. She took a deep breath. "I was just going to ask Cooper…"

"Let me stop you right there. I don't care what either of you do on your own time but here, at work, you'll keep your distance from each other."

"What? I don't…"

"Cooper is here to sell alcohol. See those women at the bar?" she asked, turning Ruby's body in the direction she'd been talking about.

"Of course I see them," Ruby replied.

"Well, Cooper's the reason they're still drinking. And if they're still drinking, I'm making money. They can sit at that bar all night if they want to, and Cooper can continue to be charming and sell them my booze. That's the end game here. Got it?"

Ruby looked at her boss with incredulity. She couldn't even bring forth the words to say something. It was a ridiculous and outdated attitude, but all at once she understood why Terry had relented so easily on her idea of the tee shirts for the wait staff. It was a sleeker, sexier look, and the mere hint of something with any impropriety sold food and drinks. Mostly drinks.

"Got it," she said sheepishly.

"Good. Now turn your little self around and go to bed. Alone. Cooper's working. He's got no time for you tonight." With that Terry left her standing alone in the middle of the now empty restaurant.

Just then Cooper lifted his head, saw her and winked. One of the two women at the bar must have thought that he was flirting with her, because she threw her head back in laughter and then reached across the bar and took his hand. Ruby fished her phone out of her back pocket and quickly composed a text.

I'm going to bed. I hope you can do the same sooner rather than later tonight. See you tomorrow.

She replaced her phone and walked toward the parking lot when she felt a familiar vibration. She lifted the screen and read his response: *Miss you. Sweet dreams.* Smiling, Ruby sat down, turned on the ignition and drove to the Barn with every intention of closing her eyes quickly with the hope that she could summon up a dream that included Cooper within it.

By the time Memorial Day rolled around, Ruby had a much better understanding of just how busy the restaurant could be on a sunny beach day. On the Thursday morning of the long-anticipated holiday weekend, a line of cars stretched out along Route 6, the main road that ran through Bluff's Creek. Suddenly, the sleepy little town was fully awake. Every shop was open and bursting with merchandise, the sidewalks filled to the brim with tourists anxious to have their summer vacations begin. The weather had fully cooperated as well, with cloudless blue skies and warm breezes floating in off the ocean. The Hut's beach bar opened at ten in the morning, and lunch service started at eleven-thirty. Most of the staff worked a split shift, coming in at ten to set up for the day, handle the lunch crowd and then have a break at three. They'd all share the family-style dinner served to them at four-thirty and then they'd work straight through until nine o'clock when the kitchen shut down. The bar, however, remained open until at least midnight, and would continue to serve drinks until the last patrons stumbled out into the parking lot to their cars. During the holiday weekend, Terry demanded that all of the employees be at work, but after that, she allowed them each two days off during the week on a rotating basis. While the hours were grueling, no one seemed to mind. This was it, the payoff, the reason why they were all there: the season had begun.

Ruby's schedule was a little bit different. The concession stand operated at both the lunch and dinner shift, but she wasn't required to be there for the opening of the bar at ten. She could wait for everyone else to leave for work before showering, and she could grab a quiet cup of coffee at her favorite spot at the top of the beach before her long day of work would begin. She developed a routine. Each night she'd tally up the sales from the day before and the next morning she'd do an inventory of which designs were selling the best, along with which employee had sold the most. She kept detailed records on the legal pad in her car, with new ideas for unique merchandise to sell jotted in neat script along the margins. The weeks began to whiz by, one day blending into the next, with her falling into her bed each night thoroughly exhausted.

By mid-June, she was ready to talk to Terry about making some slight changes to help move sales along even further. Ruby had finally figured out that if she could increase Terry's profit margin, she could also be her most favorite employee. And Ruby had kept her promise, sharing her commission with the member of the staff that sold the most each week. So far, Patti had been the clear winner, smoothing the relationship between them by just the slightest margin. At least there was a break from the constant ribbing she'd been having to endure about her attraction to Cooper. For now.

As it was, Ruby had hardly seen Cooper at all during the last few weeks. Their days off hadn't jived and when he wasn't working at the Hut he'd been busy with his beer business, taking trips down to Boston to speak to a bartender in a small restaurant he knew by the wharf there, trying his best to widen his product distribution. As much as she'd hated to admit it, she'd missed him. She had wanted to steer clear of any entanglement, but now she knew that she wasn't able to stay away from him for much longer. Her body and mind were in a constant state of battle, and try as she might to have it any other way, her body was winning out.

On this Monday morning, Ruby had climbed up onto the hood of the Kia with her coffee to gaze out at the ocean, and now as she leaned back against the windshield and stared out at the calm water, she clearly remembered the heat of the bonfire and how he promised to let her take the lead in their relationship. Cooper had been true to his word; while she could feel his eyes on her while they were at work, he hadn't pushed her at all. She realized that he was hanging back, letting her come to him, to work out in her own mind just how she wanted to proceed. It had been easy in the frenzy of the Hut's season opening, they had both been so busy settling into a rhythm that she hadn't a spare moment to think about a summer romance. But now, with the sun warming her face, her mind drifted back to the night they'd spent together at his house, the way his fingers worked their magic against her overheated skin, his lips urgent against her own. She couldn't deny the truth of her feelings. She wanted him with every fiber of her being. The question of whether she could handle a relationship that came with its own built-in expiration date remained. The difference to her now was that she was willing to throw caution to the wind and go for it anyway. She sat up straight and stretched for a moment before deciding what to do next. Ruby knew that it would be up to her to let Cooper know if she wanted what he did, that she was willing to take the risk of losing herself to him.

She could hear the sound of increased activity in the parking in the lot. She jumped down from the hood of her car and watched the scene unfold before her – anxious parents applying sunscreen all over the squirming bodies of their young children; two boys tossing a football between the building traffic on the heated blacktop; a couple, each with one hand on a cooler and lounge chairs strapped to their backs, making their way down the sandy dune and onto the beach. Everyone was there for a day of relaxation and fun, meaning that she needed to take her cue from them and head into work. Once back in the car, she turned on the air conditioner. The day was warming up quickly, promising to be a scorcher by noon. There would be plenty to do at the Hut, especially for those tending the bar. Ruby rifled through some of the papers she had in a large manila folder on the front seat, looking for the printed schedule that Terry had handed out at the beginning of the week. She glanced at the names, searching for Cooper's to try and figure out if they had any time off together in the upcoming days. She ran her finger down the column, finding them both. He was off on Thursday, as was she. A thrill of excitement shot through her body as she sent him a text: *Wanna go to the beach with me on Thursday?* She threw the phone down on the passenger seat next to hers and shifted the car into reverse, waiting to hear the ping of a response. By the time she'd reached the lot's exit, she had his reply: *Hell yes.* Ruby could feel the smile stretch across her face. She turned her car onto the now crowded roadway and head into work.

Thursday morning dawned bright and clear. Ruby woke up with a nervous anticipation that fueled her as she carefully prepared for her date. She put on her favorite bathing suit, a red bikini that tied on each side of the skimpy bottom. There were pearl shaped, multi-hued beads lining the halter top, leaving a trail of color down her back, sounding somewhat musical as they bounced off each other with each step she took. Her skin was still pale, so she took care to apply sunscreen before slipping on a matching red cover-up. Grabbing a towel, she threw it into her beach bag and slipped into her flip-flops before she headed outside to meet Cooper in the parking lot. He was waiting there for her, standing outside of his truck, securing his surf board in the flatbed when she got outside.

Ruby stood still for a moment, watching his strong arms tighten the straps that held the board in place, his hands smoothing an apparent tangle in the nylon as he went along. The motion was all too familiar and she could feel herself sway a bit at the memory. She drew in a breath and walked toward him.

"Good morning," Ruby called out. She watched as he looked up, saw her and smiled.

"Now it is," he replied, reaching out as she got closer and pulling her in for a brief hug. "Ready to go?"

"I am," she replied, stepping into the truck and noticing the two to-go cups of coffee in the holders.

"I didn't want to waste time, so I picked up some coffee on the way. I wasn't sure how you drink it, so I brought a small container of milk with me. It's in the cooler… I mean, last time we hung out, we never made it to getting coffee…"

"That's true," she responded, feeling the familiar blush rise to her face. "Thank you."

"You're welcome." He reached over, took her hand and brought it to his lips where he deposited a light kiss. "I'm so glad we're doing this today."

"Me too," she said, allowing him to then place their still

joined hands down on his leg. She could feel the heat of his skin and reminded herself to breathe.

"Any preference of which beach we should go to?"

"Um, not really. Do you want to surf?"

"I'm not sure. I brought my board along just in case. I've been hearing about how great the chop is supposed to be today. There's a storm brewing down the coast. The churned-up water makes for some great surfing, that's for sure."

Ruby nodded her head. "Any beach then. Wherever you might catch the best waves works for me."

"Fantastic," he replied, steering with one hand toward the beach of his choice.

They pulled up onto a beach filled with surfers. Cooper had supplied everything they could need for the day: beach chairs, an umbrella, extra towels and a cooler full of sandwiches, beer, water bottles and cut-up fruit. It took them a few minutes to negotiate the steep dune down to the sand, but they found a spot near the water's edge and set themselves up for a day of relaxation. Once they were sitting, chairs close to one another in the shade of the umbrella, Ruby realized that Cooper had left his board in the truck.

"Do you need help bringing your surfboard down?" she asked innocently.

He laughed. "No, but thanks. I can handle it myself. I'm just now sure if I want to leave you to go surf. It feels like a long time since we've been alone together."

"That's because it has been…"

"But we're here now. That's all I care about." He reached over and took her hand in his before settling back to watch the waves.

She hesitated for a minute then finally said, "Can I talk to you about something?"

A dark look of concern crossed Cooper's face. "What is it? You can tell me anything.""It's just… well…I really like you Cooper. I guess I was just holding back after I spent the night at your house because I know that the summer is short and when it ends, we're over. It's been a rough year and I think I was just protecting myself, but I realize now that if I stay in my own little world, I'll end up there alone. I don't want…"

He lifted her hand to his mouth and kissed the inside of her palm, effectively stopping the jumble of words from continuing to spill from her throat. She could feel her skin sizzle beneath his touch.

"Ruby," he said in a hushed tone. "Why would you assume that this is a summer fling? What if I told you that I don't see it that way at all."

"We don't even know each other, Cooper. You can't predict the future, believe me. After what happened to my family, I wouldn't even begin to try."

"That may be true, but I'm all for us getting much better acquainted," he said, his deep blue eyes boring into her own.

Ruby felt her stomach flip. She was all in for knowing him more intimately. She hadn't stopped thinking of their first date, how it felt to have him kiss her from head to toe, how she felt when he touched her, their naked bodies intertwined. "Me too," was her whispered response.

Just then a group of surfers walked behind them on the beach, calling out to Cooper.

"Hey man, why is your board still sitting in the back of your truck? It's a perfect day for a ride!" Steamroller's voice rang out as he led a crew of others into the water.

Ruby broke into laughter as the supercharged air

between them dissipated. "Yeah Cooper. Go take your ride!" she teased.

He looked down at his feet, now covered in sand. "Will you still be here when I get back? You're not going to run off on me again, are you?"

She drew in a deep, steadying breath and then said, "I didn't really run. I just needed some space, and a chance to decide for myself."

A look of relief crossed Cooper's face. "I'm glad you did." He leaned in and lifted her up out of her seat, pulling her into a loose embrace. "Come for a ride with me…" It was a both seductive and suggestive statement, and Ruby planted herself firmly on the sand to avoid reacting to his most obvious meaning."No, thanks. Not right now. I'll watch from here though. I never did get a handle on managing staying upright on a board."

"I'd love to teach you sometime," he said, adding, "and there's no time like the present."

"Um, that might be true. But it's my day off. I think I'd rather just watch you…"

"Oh," he said with a sly smile, moving in even closer. "You'd like to watch. Ok…I like that idea."

"Leave it to you to turn something innocent into an entirely different sort of interpretation," she kidded.

"Who me?" he asked with mock indignation, leaning oh so close and whispering in her ear. "I would never try to compromise you. I'm too much of a boy scout!" His lips found hers and he kissed her, exploring the inside of her mouth with the tip of his tongue, before pulling away, leaving her breathless. He turned to go. "Stay put," he demanded. "I'll come back for you."

She couldn't have moved if she wanted to. In what seemed like a minute, he'd gotten his board out of the truck, back on the beach and was in the water, gracefully navigating the churning swells with ease. He paddled out with a group of surfers, beyond the smaller chop and out into more open ocean, waiting patiently for the perfect wall of water to build behind him. At just the right moment, he would ride along and then stand upright on his board in the bright sunlight, his leg muscles rippling with strength and determination. It was a mesmerizing sight.

Ruby could hear the group in the ocean calling out, coaxing each other to ride out one more wave, looking out for every person's safety as the water seemed to get rougher as the afternoon went on. Finally, they began to come back onto the sand, exhausted and exhilarated. She watched as Cooper scanned the beach, searching for the spot where he'd left her. When their eyes met, he smiled and she could feel her heart begin to beat double time.

"That was great!" he said, collapsing into his chair. "But not a good teaching day. That surf is rough. The storm must be moving in closer."

Ruby looked up at the sky, but it was cloudless. "It sure doesn't look like rain."

"The weather can turn on a dime out here. I've seen it happen countless times."

"Well let's hope not. I'm having the best day off ever," she said, stretching her legs out in front of her.

"If we have to, I'm sure we can move this inside. We can come up with something to do if that's the case," he said, winking at her.

Oh my, she thought to herself, wondering if she could will the rainclouds to appear, because with that one wink, she was lost.

"Are you hungry?" he asked, shifting in his chair and changing the subject.

"Maybe. What's in the cooler?" she responded.

He lifted up the lid and pulled out two thick sandwiches. "Brie, turkey and cranberry chutney on multi-grain," he smiled, handing one of the tightly wrapped packages to her.

"You're kidding. I used to insist on having peanut butter and jelly to the beach. I was a sticky mess by the end of lunch," she said.

"Well, maybe that's because you were a kid then. This is more my style," he teased, tearing back the foil and taking a bite.

Ruby peeled back the silver wrapping and lifted the sandwich to her mouth to try it for herself. When she had finished chewing she exclaimed, "This is so good. But please tell me that you didn't actually roast a whole turkey just to make us lunch. That would be excessive!"

He smiled. "No, I didn't. I thought about it, but went to the deli instead. I'm glad you like it!"

"I do!" she said, taking another bite.

He then grabbed two bottles of Satin's Satin out of the cooler and opened them, passing one to her. "Cheers!"

They ate while watching the waves crash onto the beach and following the path of the dark rainclouds as they gathered on the horizon. When they were finished with every last crumb of food, Cooper remarked, "I've seen that kind of low hanging sky before. The rain will be on us in no time. We should pack up and get going before we're soaked."

Ruby collected her towel and helped him with the cooler and chairs while he balanced his surfboard on the way up the dune. They made it into the truck as the first drops fell, and in just a minute later, the full fury of the storm hit, loud thunder and flashes of lightening crashing around them. "Wow," she said as water covered the windshield, making it impossible to see even with the wipers working at full speed.

"It won't rain this hard for long. Let's just sit here and wait it out a bit." He shut off the engine and sat back, one arm casually draped around Ruby's seat.

"Are we safe in here? From the lightening?"

"Of course. As long as the tires are making contact with the ground, we're good." Just then a large thunderclap resounded overhead. Ruby tensed and Cooper pulled her closer to him. "Don't worry, Ruby. Nothing's going to happen to us. It's okay." And then he leaned in and softly kissed her lips.

She felt her heart beat faster and she turned her body toward him, placing one hand on his chest and leaning into the embrace. Through the thin fabric of her bathing suit cover-up she could feel the building heat of his body, his desire apparent. The rain pounded down on the metal roof of the truck with a deafening sound, but it was a small distraction next to the feeling of her blood coursing through her veins with what seemed like incredible speed. He leaned into her, covering her with his broad chest across the front seat. "I want to take you home with me…" he whispered into her ear. "This isn't exactly the most comfortable place to do this…"

She nodded her head against his in agreement, trying to catch her breath as he sat up and turned the engine back on. It was still raining, but the intensity had lessened by the slightest bit and the thunder began to sound further away. Cooper was able to navigate the truck through the growing puddles in the now empty parking lot and slowly drive them away from the beach. It was rough going, but he finally made a wide turn around what looked like a newly formed lake at the foot of his driveway, and negotiated his way up to park close to the garage. "Wait here," he said, jumping out of the driver's seat and into the storm.

Ruby watched as he ran around the front hood to her door, opening it in a swift motion and grabbing her hand. Together they made their way through the still driving rain and into his house, both soaked to the skin, small pools of water gathering at their feet in the entry hall.

"Do you want to get out of those wet things?" he asked, eyes burning with suggestion.

She simply nodded and took his hand, walking past the display of Patti's photos and into his bedroom. She couldn't think of anything she wanted to do more than being naked with him on this very dreary rainy afternoon.

Chapter Eleven

At the exact moment that they fell into Cooper's bed, his phone rang. He ignored it, running his hands over her breasts, reaching down with his mouth to cover one nipple, gently teasing it with his tongue. Then it rang again. With a grunt, he turned over and lifted it up to see who was calling. It was Terry.

"Get over here, Cooper. We've got an emergency. I need everyone here to help put down sandbags. We're flooding!"

"Be right there." He threw down the phone and jumped out of bed, scrambling to find his pants. "Do you have any clothing with you? I mean other than your bathing suit?"

"No, why?"

"It's the Hut. We've got to get over there."

Ruby pushed herself off the mattress and reached for her wet bathing suit, struggling to get it back on. "What's wrong?"

"The storm. Water is rising and swamping the place. We need to help Terry stop it or we're all out of work this summer!"

Ruby dressed silently as Cooper gathered some supplies from his garage. He came back inside, dripping rain water all over the bedroom floor. Reaching into his closet, he pulled out one of his tee shirts and a pair of old sweat pants which she was able to roll up at both the bottom and the top to compensate for the bagginess of the fit, but at least providing cover for her body. Then he gave her a yellow rain slicker, that while way too large would at least protect her from the wetness of the storm. They hardly spoke as he concentrated on the slick road before them on the way to the restaurant, the pouring rain their constant companion. Once they arrived, he jumped out and grabbed a shovel from the back of his truck, handing it to her as they ran to join the others on the beach.

"Start loading sand into these bags," he shouted. "I'm going to see how bad it is inside." He turned to leave her there with both Louise and Patti.

"Here," Patti yelled over the wind on the wide shoreline, holding open a white burlap bag. "I'll hold it open. You fill it."

Ruby just nodded and began to work. Once the first bag was near bursting, Louise jumped in with an empty one. Both other women kept alternating for over an hour until they had a small pile ready to be transported up to the restaurant. After a while, Ruby's shoulders and neck ached, and large callouses started to form beneath her fingers at the top of her palms, but she kept at it. Steamroller and a few other men kept returning to where the women were working to bring the bags up to be stacked, but Cooper had not returned, and Ruby was beginning to worry about where he might be. The sky was even darker now that it was the end of the day, and there were no lights anywhere to be seen. She realized that the power must have gone out, increasing her fear even more.

A shadowy figure approached them, the wind blowing the hood back from a raincoat to reveal a soaking wet CeCe, her hair plastered to her scalp.

"You can stop now," she shouted. "The water stopped rising." Both Patti and Louise collapsed onto the soaked sand.

"Have you seen Cooper?" Ruby asked.

"He's inside with Terry. We were able to keep the ocean out of the kitchen for now, and lucky, high tide has passed. It looks like the power is out on this side of town, though. No dinner service tonight, that's for sure."

"I don't think that's a good thing," Patti remarked. "There must be a huge mess up there. Terry will have us all cleaning the place up until she can open again."

"Ugh," Louise chimed in. "I'm exhausted just thinking about it."

"It's not as bad as the time we got hit by Hurricane Arthur. Remember that?"

"How could I forget?" Patti said emphatically. "It killed the July 4th rush. What a bust."

"There were dead fish that washed up into the bar that time, it was so gross," Louise added, wrinkling her nose.

"Well," CeCe said. "The July 4th crowd is still two weeks away. We have time to get the place back together by then. I can't afford not to make mad cash over the holiday. I need the money."

"We all do," Patti said in an uncharacteristic moment of sisterhood, brushing herself off and stretching her arms over her head. "Let's go see what Terry needs us from us now."

The women slowly trudged up the dune, and Ruby

deposited the shovel back into the bed of Cooper's truck before following the others. When she got to the concession stand, she stopped to survey the damage. Her displays were all soaked; they'd need to be redone. Luckily, the merchandise was covered by the plastic tarps she secured when she'd closed up the night before. It had become a part of her routine – she didn't like to leave anything to chance because she couldn't afford to lose even a mere tee shirt. She knew that anything missing would be taken out of her paycheck. She was running a mental check-list of what needed to be done when Cooper rounded the corner.

"You're okay," he said, relief in his voice, pulling her into his embrace. "When you didn't come inside with the others, I didn't know what happened to you."

She winced a little bit when he hugged her shoulders. "I'm fine. Sore, but fine. What about you? Where were you?"

"In the kitchen. It was an all hands-on deck situation, keeping the water from the equipment. If it doused the pilot light that keeps the ovens going, it would have been major trouble. That's what happened last time. Nightmare. We were closed for over a week until the gas company came and gave the all clear for us to turn it back on."

"How did you stop the water?" she asked.

"Well, those sandbags you helped fill did most of the work. We kept stacking them up until we had a pretty sturdy wall of defense. And nature was on our side. The water stopped rising as quickly as it began, I guess. I mean, what the hell? Wasn't it sunny this morning?"

"It was," she replied softly. "We were on the beach…"

"Was that today? It sure doesn't feel like it." He leaned back against the concession stand, pulling her closer. "I was so worried about you. I'm glad you're okay."

"I'm tougher than I appear," she teased. "And besides. We're all in this together now. I'm glad I could help."

His deep blue eyes searched her face, as if to reaffirm that she was not hurt.

"And I was enjoying our day off, especially the part where you were in my bed."

"Me too. But I think that we won't be headed back there any time soon. There's work to do."

"I know. Just one thing before we get to it," he said, leaning in closer, pressing his lips to hers in a soft kiss. "Promise me that we will return there when this is finished. I can't think of another place I'd rather be."

She felt a warm rush of emotion pass between them and melded her body to his as she pressed herself against him. "Me too," she murmured, taking the moment to savor the connection between them.

He slowly pulled himself back and winked at her. "Get to work then. The sooner we're done, the sooner we can go back to what we were doing before this all happened."

Ruby smiled, turned and began to disassemble her display, all the while remembering the comfort of his bed, the warmth of his skin next to hers and the assurance that they'd return there when her work was done.

As it turned out, there was more damage to the kitchen than Cooper originally thought. Even after Ruby had freshly folded all of the shirts, restocked the shelves and freshened up small items on the counter of the concession stand, he and some of the other men were nowhere near finished mopping up the water and emptying out the heavy, wet sandbags back onto the beach. She had joined CeCe, Patti and the other waitresses as they righted the tossed tables and chairs, wiping down every surface and restoring the restaurant to order before Terry dismissed them for the night. Ruby looked around and spotted Cooper working with Big Red, emptying out the walk-in freezer and dumping the now rapidly defrosting food into large bins. She walked over to where he was standing.

"Do you need help?"

He smiled and shook his head. "No, but thanks. We've got to get this stuff over to the island's food bank while it's still fresh. Terry's going to donate it since they have power and we don't."

"Will I see you later?"

He hesitated for a moment and then said, "I don't know how long this will take. Do you want to wait at my house? The door is unlocked."

She could see Patti and the others starting to make their way to Louise's car. "No. I think I'll head back to the Barn. But I'd love a raincheck."

The both of them started laughing at her words.

"No more rain, ok?" he chuckled. "I think we've had enough for a while."

She blushed. "Yeah. Poor word selection, but you know what I mean."

"Yup. I do." He pulled her in for a quick kiss. "Tomorrow?"

"I hope so…" she answered as she left to catch up with her ride and to her own warm and dry bed.

The women were too tired to speak on the way back to the Barn. The storm had helped to smooth over some of the rough edges between Patti and Ruby, easing the tension that usually came between them. As exhausted as she was, Ruby needed a shower. She grabbed her things and walked into the bathroom, finding that CeCe had beaten her there, already in one of the stalls. She let the water get as hot as she could as she removed her borrowed clothing and then stepped into the spray, letting it cascade down on her weary muscles. She was tired, but she also had a feeling of satisfaction that she hadn't had in a very long time. She felt as though she was finally part of a team, closer than ever to being accepted as a member of this tightly knit community.

"Hey," CeCe shouted over the sound of the shower. "Where were you when you got the call from Terry?"

"I was with Cooper," Ruby replied. "We were…" she stopped speaking momentarily, remembering exactly what it was they were doing when the phone rang. "We had stopped at his house after the beach. It was raining so hard. We just wanted to get out of the storm."

"Uh huh," CeCe teased back. "Just wanted to get out of the storm. I bet!"

"Whatever," Ruby replied, shutting off the water in her stall and wrapping her towel tightly around her body.

CeCe did the same and walked over to the mirror, grabbing a comb to run through her hair. "No judgement. In fact, I'm envious. I wish there was someone here that I felt attracted to, someone to spend a rainy afternoon with."

"I didn't know you were looking," Ruby said with surprise.

"I'm always looking. Just not finding," CeCe replied.

"That's so funny. I wasn't looking at all. I don't even know how this all happened with Cooper, I really don't."

"But it did. And now what?"

"Nothing. It's like you told me before. It's just for the summer. I'm not expecting this thing between us to go past Labor Day. I'm just going to enjoy it for what it is."

CeCe's eyes widened in surprise. "And when did this

happen? While you two were just looking to get out of the rain earlier today?"

"Very funny. No. I've been thinking about it. It's been a tough year and I deserve a little diversion, don't you agree?"

"We're calling Cooper a 'diversion' now?"

Ruby picked up her toiletries. "Yes. No. Maybe… I'm too tired to think about this now. Can we discuss this tomorrow?"

"Oh, sure Miz Scarlett. Cause tomorrow, as you know, is another day!"

"Well we both know how that story ended. Rhett left her in the end."

"Cooper is not some fictional man. He's real. Rhett Butler wasn't."

"Something tells me that we'll have lots of time to review this over the winter in Boston. For now, I'm going to sleep."

As they returned to the hallway to walk to their room, Ruby couldn't help but chuckle as CeCe loudly hummed "Tara's Theme" from 'Gone with the Wind". Once inside, Ruby threw herself onto her bed, and quickly fell into a deep and dreamless sleep.

The weeks leading up to July 4th were so busy that Ruby barely had time to do more than work and sleep. The clean-up from the storm took longer than first anticipated, the damage more extensive than originally thought. Everyone was expected to keep up the frantic pace, and Terry cancelled all days off until the long weekend was over. Aside from restocking all the food that was needed for a normal lunch and dinner service, the kitchen staff now had to start planning for the larger holiday crowds. The waiters had to maintain the constant flow of food to the patrons of the restaurant, and the bartenders were mixing drinks double-time. They all navigated their way around repairmen and the inconvenience of the small reconstruction jobs that needed to be completed during their normal operating hours. Although the physical concession stand withstood the wind and rain unharmed, Ruby had to reorder a lot of merchandise as well as restock the shelves to prepare for a rush during the long weekend ahead. Terry had booked the first band of the season to perform on the Friday night of the holiday, and with all of the extra people expected to turn up for the sold-out show, Ruby hadn't had the chance to exchange more than a few words and a stolen kiss or two with Cooper for the last few weeks. She could not remember a time when she'd been more bone weary tired.

In the aftermath of the storm, the weather had been picture perfect, with sunny blue skies and warm temperatures predicted for the entire holiday weekend. Everyone was looking forward to getting on with it and then crashing after the crowds had packed up and left Bluff's Creek, leaving behind a quieter, slower moving week, their pockets lined with the cash they knew they could make over the four days and nights of intense work. Ruby was ready. She made sure that the concession stand was full of tee shirts, sweatshirts, keychains, shot glasses and the like; she had gotten really good at hard selling the semi-drunk clientele; the wait staff had become accustomed to wearing the logo shirts and selling them along with the other menu items. This weekend was Ruby's true test. She planned to make record profits for both Terry and herself.

On the Thursday night of the holiday, she could already tell that it was going to be a big money weekend. She had sold a record number of tee shirts, and it was a close contest between CeCe and Patti to see which one would be the staff's top earner. But nothing could have gotten her ready for the amount of sales that happened during the Friday night of the concert. She couldn't take in the money fast enough – there was an actual line of customers just waiting to snap up a Hut shirt, proving to those back at home that they'd been to the very popular beach bar destination. When the last concertgoer left and she tallied up the total for the two nights so far, it was a staggering eight thousand dollars. She stood back for a moment, stunned. She thought about going to find Terry and let her in on the good news, when she stopped and decided to wait until the weekend was over. Maybe the next night would bring her over the edge of ten thousand dollars. She'd have to wait and see.

Ruby was excited to open the stand the next day. She had on a fresh Hut tee shirt, one that she'd cut a deep V into down the front so that her tan lines were exposed a bit. She threw her now sun bleached blonde hair into a high pony tail and wore a pair of black skinny jeans. She was ready to make sales history. Business remained brisk and she was constantly busy, just as she'd thought she'd be -- until the end of the night. There had been a bachelor party at the bar, a group of guys who Cooper had been serving tequila shots to until he decided that they'd had enough, and called two cabs to come and collect them to bring the now very drunk men back to their rental house. As they staggered toward the exit, they stopped at the stand.

"Hey honey," one of the men said. "What'cha doing tonight? Wanna party with us?"

She smiled weakly, shaking her head no.

"C'mon preddy lady. Whad if I buy somthin? Would that change your mind?" he asked with a drunken leer, his watery eyes fixated on the deep cut down the front of her tee shirt and the soft cleavage that lie just beneath the fabric.

"No sir," she replied firmly. "You just get home safe, okay?"

One of his friends stepped up to the counter, so close that Ruby could smell the reek of alcohol on his breath. "My friend here wants you to come with us. After all, he's getting married soon. He needs one last fling…" The whole group of them laughed loudly.

"Yeah, honey. Do a guy a solid. Help him out…"

Ruby wasn't really afraid as much as she was annoyed. While the crowd in the bar had thinned out considerably, the whole staff was still there. She wasn't alone.

"Again, no…" she began. Just then the guest of honor lunged forward and reached up for her, grabbing her by the V of her shirt and pulling down, ripping it wide open exposing her lacy bra. Now off balance, Ruby tumbled over the counter, landing with a hard thud to her hip, onto the solidly packed sand floor in front of the stand. The impact made her woozy, and she closed her eyes as she saw the drunk groom-to-be lean down all too close to her face, attempting to give her a very wet and alcohol fueled kiss on the lips.

Chapter Twelve

The rest was a blur. She saw Cooper reach for the man who'd grabbed her, rage in his eyes. He wound up his arm, but before he could throw the first punch, both CeCe and Patti appeared behind him, each with a wooden baseball bat in their hands.

CeCe said, "Don't do it Cooper. He's not worth the trouble."Cooper looked at her, shook his head as if to disagree. Then Patti put her arm out and went to pull him away, but before she touched him, he stepped back, turning quickly to help Ruby to her feet, moving her behind him and shielding her with his body. Patti then stepped forward, holding the bat as if she were going to swing away.

"Hey asshole. When a lady says no, she means no. What part of that don't you understand?" she asked the man who had pulled Ruby to the ground, stepping in closer and menacing him with her bat.

The man shook his head. "I was just talking to the girl…"

A smoky-edged voice rung out from the back of the

crowd. "First of all, she's a woman, not a girl." All the assembled heads turned as Terry pushed her way through to come face to face with the culprit. "Secondly, she's a woman who works for me, and nobody puts a hand on one of my employees. Get out of here now, before I call the police and have the whole bunch of you arrested for assault. Go and never come back here. Do you understand what I'm telling you?"

Just then headlights appeared in the parking lot, and Terry turned her head to look in the direction of the newly arrived cars. "There are your cabs. MOVE." As she took a step closer, the men scurried away. "Good riddance," she remarked in disgust before turning to her employees. "Okay, there's nothing left to see here. It's been a long night, but let's get back to it. Except for you." She turned to face Ruby who had stepped out from behind Cooper once the others had gone. "Go home."

CeCe looked at Ruby and said, "Give me a few minutes. I was almost done cleaning up my station when I saw Cooper jump over the bar. I'll drive us back to the Barn in your car." Ruby looked up and nodded at her before CeCe went back into the restaurant with Patti and Terry. Only Cooper remained.

Ruby rubbed her hand over her hip, wincing in pain.

"How bad is it? Do you want me to drive you to the hospital in Hyannis?"

"No. No hospital. I just want to lie down. I'll be okay in the morning."

"Like hell you will. I'm taking you home with me. You need to take a hot bath. Then we'll need to apply an ice pack to that injury."

"No Cooper, really. I can go back to the Barn with CeCe."

His steely gaze met hers. “Not going to happen,” he said with an authoritative tone. Taking her arm, he led her through the parking lot to his truck, opening the door and helping her gingerly settle in before fastening the seat belt around her. “Give me your car keys.”

She knew it was useless to argue with him, so she reached into her pocket and pulled them out, slipping them into his open palm. “Wait and don’t move,” he commanded. “I’ll be right back.”

Ruby closed her eyes. Her right hip was throbbing and a shooting pain ran down her leg, causing her to feel breathless. In what felt like less than a full minute, Cooper was back.

“Don’t you need to put the bar back together?” she asked.

“Steamroller will do it for me. Besides, I’m following Terry’s orders. Take you home. CeCe will drive your car back to the Barn when she’s done here.” He reached over and laced her fingers with his own, squeezing them gently. She watched as he effortlessly steered one handed all the way back to his house. Once there, he jumped out and helped her out of the truck, directing her into his bedroom. He was all business. “Sit down,” he said, motioning to the bed. “I’ll start the bath.”

As she began to remove the sweatshirt she was wearing, her whole body started to shake.

“Why is it so cold in here?” she called out to Cooper.

He came out of the bathroom, concern sketched all over his face.

“It’s not. You’re in shock.” He helped her undress, bending to untie and remove her shoes, then helping pull her pants down carefully, hoping not to cause her any more distress.

Once stripped down to her bra and panties, he got her to her feet, getting a full view of the spreading, purple and blue bruise along her hip and leg. He let out a long whistle.

"That looks angry," he said. "Are you sure you don't want to have a professional take a look at it?"

"I just want to get into the tub and then go to sleep, Cooper. Really."

They walked into the bathroom and Ruby was overwhelmed by the scent of the lavender bath bubbles that he'd generously poured into the warm water, the same ones she noticed in the large glass bottle at the edge of the claw-footed tub when she was here last time. It was a lovely and thoughtful gesture. He pulled a large navy bath towel off the rack.

"Here. Wrap this around you. I'll give you some privacy while you get fully undressed."

"Privacy? That genie's out of the bottle. You've already seen me naked, remember?"

He smiled. "Believe me, I do. But…" His voice trailed off at the memory and he quickly changed the subject. "You'll sleep in my bed tonight. I can stay on the couch in the living room."

"Don't be ridiculous. I want you to sleep next to me."

"Ruby…" he shook his head.

"I hate to break it to you Cooper, but after this bath, I'm going to be asleep before you know it." She reached behind her back and unclasped her bra, letting it fall to her feet. She then put her arm out and had him steady her while she stepped out of her panties and carefully put one leg and then another into the tub. Sitting down and leaning back, she realized that he'd been right. The warm water was soothing and she could feel her stiffening muscles begin to relax.

"Do you see this?" he asked, motioning to a panel next to the spout. "It controls the jets. Do you want them on?"

She simply nodded yes and he reached over her to operate the controls. After he punched a series of buttons, the water started to pulsate, and she felt herself begin to feel an overall sense of calm.

"Hold on. One more thing," he said, ducking out of the bathroom. She heard a muffled sound of something clattering onto the kitchen counter. Before she knew it, Cooper was back with two Advil and a large glass of water. "This should help curb the inflammation. Or at least that's what it says on the bottle."

She took the pills, put them in her mouth and with a large sip of water, swallowed them down.

"I'll leave you to it. But don't even think about getting out of this tub without help. I mean it."

"Okay. Promise," she said, closing her eyes, trying to block out the events of the past few hours. It wasn't easy. All the time she'd lived in New York City, gone bar-hopping with friends, rode the subways late at night or been out until dawn, she'd never felt so afraid as when that man pulled her down from the concession stand. She saw the scene play over and over again in her mind. If it hadn't been for Cooper, Patti and CeCe, she didn't want to imagine what might have happened.

A little while later, Cooper knocked on the door. "Just checking in. Is the water still warm enough?"

"Yes, but I'm ready to get out. I'm so tired."

He walked into the bathroom and picked up the previously discarded bath towel. He then lifted her out of the tub, wrapped her snuggly in the soft terrycloth, walked into his bedroom and placed her carefully down on his bed. While she dried herself off, he rummaged around in his closet for a moment before finding a large tee shirt that he slipped over her head.

"You might not like it, but I think you need to put this ice pack on that bruise for twenty minutes or so. It will help with the swelling." He handed her a large package wrapped in a clean dish cloth.

Ruby lay back against the headboard and lifted the shirt up to expose her hip. She nodded and he gently placed the ice on her skin. "Oooh," she exclaimed. "That's freezing!"

"Ice generally is, sweetheart. Try coming up here in the winter sometime," he teased as he placed a blanket over her shoulders and leaned over her, depositing a kiss on her forehead. "You need to try and rest. I'll come back for the ice pack in a little while."

Ruby reached out her hand and grabbed onto his arm. "No. Please. I mean it. I want you to stay here with me."

He ran his hand through his hair, eyes on her the whole time. "It's not that I don't want to get into this bed with you, Ruby, because I do. I just don't want to take advantage of this situation. It would be wrong."

"How? I'm not talking about having sex. I just don't want to be alone. Please..."

"I told myself that I would not get back into bed with you until you begged me. Maybe this qualifies," he smirked.

She patted the empty mattress next to her and he scrambled over her carefully, laying down fully clothed.

"Was that so difficult?" she asked, blinking away the heavy-lidded feeling of sleep that was overtaking her now.

"No, never," he whispered in her ear.

"Can you hold the ice pack? It's getting very heavy…" she murmured just before the events of the night overwhelmed her and she lost the battle. She was asleep before she could finish her thought.

The next morning dawned brightly. When Ruby woke up, she was alone in Cooper's bed. The tee shirt had ridden up over her hip and was bunched around her midsection, leaving her lower body naked and exposed. When she opened her eyes, the first thing she saw was the enormous purple bruise, a reminder of all that had happened the previous evening. Despite having the urgent need to pee, she was afraid to move, feeling every inch of her injury just by straightening out her leg. But she had no choice. Slowly, she eased herself onto her good side and slid off of the bed to stand. A shot of pain ran up her leg as she put weight down on her foot, so she hopped her way into the bathroom to relieve herself, the sound causing Cooper to come running into the bedroom.

"What the hell are you doing?" he asked with concern.

"Isn't it obvious? I need to use the bathroom." She leaned heavily against his dresser.

"Don't be so stubborn. Ask for help!"

"I've been able to pee on my own for a number of years now, Cooper. I think I've got this handled."

"Well at least lean on me until you sit down in there. I promise to leave you alone until you're done."

"Um, if you insist. But we've got to move now!"

"Okay, okay. Bossy this morning, huh?" he teased, helping her over the marble threshold and depositing her onto the toilet.

She looked at him. "You promised you'd go. *Leave*."

"Anything you say. You're the boss." He turned to step out of the bathroom. "But call me when you're done. I'll help you up."

"Get out!" she implored, all but bursting. He smiled and as he closed the door, she peed for what seemed like ages, feeling a delightful relief. She was able to pull herself up by leaning on the smooth granite of the vanity. After she washed her hands and used Cooper's tooth brush, she tried her best to smooth her very knotted hair, but she didn't have anything with her on this unexpected sleepover, so it remained more than a bit wild. With a final glance in the mirror she tried to ignore the dark circles under her eyes. She called for Cooper.

"Ready for some breakfast?" he asked as he stepped back into the bathroom. "I didn't get to make you my pancakes last time. Now's your second chance."

"I am hungry," she said with surprise. "Lead the way!"

He put his arm around her waist and pulled her closer to him, slowly helping her navigate down the hallway to the kitchen. Once there, he gently lifted her up onto a stool. "Wow!" she said, looking at the bowl full of batter, plump blueberries peeking through. He'd already set out the necessary plates, napkins and utensils. A large glass of orange juice was placed in front of her.

"Start with that," he smiled, "Oh, and these as well." He handed her two more Advil. "The coffee is almost ready."

She picked up the glass he'd filled and took a small sip. Thinking about it, she realized that she hadn't eaten anything since the family meal at the restaurant the afternoon before. She was starving. Ruby watched as Cooper moved gracefully around his kitchen. It was clearly apparent that he'd designed the space knowing that he'd be the primary cook there. Everything he needed was within his easy reach and his movements were fluid. He dropped a large ladle-full of batter into a hot pan filled with melted butter, and she watched as it sizzled and formed a perfect circle. While the first batch of pancakes were cooking, he turned and poured some already warm maple syrup into a small pitcher and placed it in front of her. Then he filled her coffee mug, handing it to her across the counter.

"I could get used to this kind of service," she said teasingly.

He smiled. "That's actually something I want to talk to you about. You don't need to answer right away, but just promise to mull it over." He drew in a deep breath. "Move out of the Barn. Come live here with me this summer."

She sat back in her chair in shock. She hadn't expected him to say that and she almost couldn't process the thought. "That seems like a radical idea from the guy I had to convince to sleep with me last night, don't you think?"

"I did sleep with you," replied with a wide grin. "You were out for the count!"

She smiled back at him. "It's a really great offer, Cooper, but I'm good at the Barn."

"I know that. And while it might seem so, this isn't totally coming out of left field. I've been thinking about it ever since the bonfire. It's just that after last night…"

"That won't happen again, Cooper. Those guys were drunk, and Terry told them not to come back. It was just a random incident."

He flipped the pancakes over and quickly walked around the counter, turning her chair so that she faced him. "I want to make sure you're safe. I want you here with me." He kissed her face with a warm intensity, slowly pulling himself back, then running his hands lightly over her legs and said, "You're not getting away from me this time, Ruby. I mean it."

"Can we discuss this more later, after breakfast," she asked plainly, looking for a way to divert his attention from the topic. "It's all too much on an empty stomach." She didn't let on that his words caused a shiver to run up her spine. Live here, with Cooper? She couldn't. That would make it impossible for her to leave in the fall.

He placed a plate of fluffy pancakes in front of her, adding the syrup with a flourish. "Wouldn't you just love to have me make you breakfast every morning?" he asked with a wink.

"Um, not sure. I haven't tasted these yet!" she replied, cutting into the large stack in front of her. Chewing thoughtfully, she added, "You do make a good argument…"

Cooper smiled and it was all Ruby could do not to give in to his request, right there on the spot. "Eat," he said, "and then we'll talk."

A half hour later, there wasn't a pancake left in sight. Ruby sat back in her chair and put a hand over her stomach. "You are a man of your word. Those were delicious!"

"I am. So glad you liked your breakfast, Ruby." He reached over and took the napkin off of her lap, his fingers lingering briefly on her thigh. "Now, back to bed with you."

The warmth of his light touch was like a shock of electricity coursing through her body, from head to toe. She didn't argue when he lifted her off of her stool and carried her back into his bedroom, placing her carefully down onto the mattress and pulling the blanket up around her.

"You need to rest. Try to close your eyes for a bit." He turned to leave the room.

She sat up quickly, and tried to hide the wave of dizziness that threatened to engulf her from him. "Where are you going? Aren't you going to stay here with me?"

He smiled. "I'm going to clean up that wreck of a kitchen. I'll check in on you later."

"But I'm not tired. I can think of some other things we

could do instead," she murmured in what she hoped was her most seductive voice.

He shook his head. "Behave yourself, Ruby. It wouldn't take much to convince me to crawl in there next to you."

"So, why don't you?"

"Because, you're injured, and you need to sleep. It's the best thing for you now."

"But I'm not tired," she said, surprised by the yawn that escaped as she said the words.

"Ok, sure. Just rest." He closed the door.

For as much as she was disappointed by him leaving her alone, it didn't last long. Before she realized it, she was deeply asleep.

Chapter Thirteen

After another wonderful dinner, Ruby pushed herself back from the countertop and declared, "You missed your calling, Cooper. You should open a restaurant instead of a tap room!" She patted her very full stomach which was still covered by his tee shirt. She'd added her panties to her outfit, but didn't attempt to put her tight jeans back on over her injury.

"Which reminds me. You never saw my beer making lab the last time you were here. Interested?"

She smiled at the memory of their first night together. "Absolutely!"

He helped her stand up from the stool where she sat. The bruise was still spreading, but after a full day of ice packs and Advil, she was already beginning to heal, the pain lessening somewhat.

"Hold onto me," he said, leaning in to put his arm around her waist.

"Okay, if I really have to," she said teasingly, squeezing

in closer and resting most of her weight against his chest and legs. Together, they slowly walked out of the house and into the garage. Everything about it was surprising to Ruby. It wasn't a typical place to park a car anymore. It was spotlessly clean, with long counters of stainless steel spanning every wall. There was an enormous double sink sunk deeply into one end of a gleaming work table, and neat, precise shelving hanging above, ringing the entire space. Silver kegs were lined up underneath the countertops, and large clear plastic boxes sat stacked on the shelves, numbered and labeled. The space had a warm, yeasty smell to it, one mixed with some sort of lemony astringent cleanser. It was brightly lit by large, overhead fixtures fashioned out of old wine casks.

"Wow, Cooper. This is some operation you have out here. What's that?" She pointed to a strange looking piece of equipment on the far wall.

He walked over to the machine in question. "It's a bottle-filler. The problem is that as I increase production, I'll need something more efficient. It's too slow. And I'm thinking of adding cans to my bottle distribution. I've been looking into what goes into the canning process."

Just then Ruby shifted her weight and gasped at the sudden shot of pain she felt in her injured leg. He was back by her side in an instant. "I've got you, baby," he said, gently sitting her down on a chair he pulled out from behind what seemed to be his desk, a space carved out of one of the counters, papers and ledgers neatly piled on its surface.

"Are you okay? Do you need to go back inside and lie down?"

"No," she lied. "It was just a twinge. I'm fine now." The

pain had lessened, but she could still feel the aftershocks shooting up and down from her thigh to her ankle. "Tell me more about your business."

"So far, it's just been me, but I'm getting ready to expand. I need some help with sales." He turned to her with a sexy smile. "Looking for a part-time job in Boston when you start school? Big benefit package…"

"Really? You're offering health insurance?" she asked innocently.

"No," he smiled broadly. "Something much better..."

One look told her all she needed to know. She smirked and said, "very funny, wise guy."

"No, Ruby, really. Would I have asked you to move into my house if I didn't want something more substantial than just another summer fling?"

She felt an uncomfortable sense of panic begin to spread through her body. "I don't think I'm ready for that. I haven't even started law school yet. Who knows how much time I'll need to adjust to being a serious student again and besides, I know that the work load is overwhelming. What about the fact that you need to concentrate on getting this business off the ground. You can't be serious…"

"I've never been more serious about anything," he said with a quiet determination, eyes boring into hers.

She looked down to break the contact. "Now you're scaring me. We hardly know each other. And we met in the summertime, when everyone up here expects to have nothing more than an encounter, a tryst, a…"

"Don't throw your fancy vocabulary around, I get it. You're just not there yet." He moved in closer, leaned down to where she sat and tipped her chin up so that her eyes had nowhere to go other than to lock with his. "You will be, though. I'm sure of it." He kissed her then, gently at first but then with a growing intensity. When he pulled away, they were both breathless.

"Cooper, I don't know what to say…" she lifted her fingers to her lips, still feeling the warmth of his touch as it lingered there.

"You really don't need to give me an answer right now, but are you feeling any better?" The intent in his look was all too clear.

"I am," she countered, knowing exactly what he meant. "Much." She felt her stomach quickly flip, excitement beginning to build deep down inside of her.

"Good. Then let me give you a preview of what it would be like to live here with me." He scooped her up and carried her back into the house, pushing through the front door with his hip and slamming it closed behind them with a decided motion. He lowered his head to hers as they made their way down the now familiar hallway to his bedroom, showering small kisses all over her face, trailing them down her neck. Once in the darkened room, he gently placed her on the bed and quickly pulled his shirt off over his head, exposing his now tanned and well-toned chest. He then unbuckled his belt, and oh so slowly unbuttoned the fly front of his jeans, shaking them off, one leg at a time, exposing his desire clearly resting behind the thin fabric of his boxers.

Ruby sat back to enjoy the strip tease he was offering, anxious for his touch despite their prior conversation. She longed for him and reminded herself to stay in the present moment enough to enjoy what he was offering her, right now. She'd think about the future afterward. She felt the mattress yield under his weight as he made his way toward her, sitting her up and removing her shirt and panties. He threw the garments onto the floor, and kissed her forehead, making his way from there down to her lips, deepening the kiss before dipping down to lightly run his mouth over each breast, teasing her and sending shock waves from her toes to the tips of her fingers. She ran her hands over the broad expanse of his back, relishing the feel of his taut, overheated skin, almost able to feel the blood as it coursed through him in a rapid beat.

He quickly flipped her on top of him, careful to avoid the bruise that ran along her leg. "I don't want to hurt you," he whispered, his passion-filled eyes saying everything.

"You won't," she replied softly into his ear. "Never..."

A minute later they were joined, rhythmically moving in time, each climbing to a height that seemed nearly impossible to reach until the other caught up, swirled together into a vortex of feeling and pleasure. All of the cares and worries she had dissolved into pure sensation as the moon and the stars and the sky seemed to converge in a blinding, crashing pleasure that she'd never experienced with anyone else ever before. For Ruby, it was hard to deny that this was the place she was meant to be. As his breathing slowed and her own heart returned to its normal pace, she knew deep down that she wanted this blossoming relationship to work more than she'd wanted anything before.

In a fluid motion, he rolled off of her onto his side and then pulled her close, resting her back against his front, burrowing down into the warmth of their bodies under the blanket. "Stay with me Ruby," he whispered into her ear. "Stay..."

The enticing scent of him, the strength of his arms as they circled her in the comfortable nest of his bed and the soothing tone of his voice made it impossible for Ruby to vocalize her answer, because she knew if she were to respond right then, the only thing she would say was yes.

Instead, she leaned into him and allowed herself to be swept up into the most restful of sleep, knowing that if only for tonight, she would give herself permission to dream.

Morning crept into the room. The sunlight pushed against the window shades, reflecting off the walls enough to wake Ruby. She stretched out her leg, happy to find it considerably less sore than the day before. And for as much as she wanted to remain in this happy little cocoon at Cooper's house, she knew it was time to get back to reality. She had no idea how to answer his request that she move into his house with him. Could she make that kind of commitment, knowing that she was leaving in a mere seven weeks? What about school? It was crazy, she reflected, but now that he'd made his feelings known, she was conflicted. Most certainly, she'd love to stay with him, let him pick up the pieces of her shattered life. It would be the easy way… *Damn it!* She felt an unexpected rush of anger. *Why did he have to complicate this?*

As she lay back against the pillows, Cooper's arm still heavily resting across her as he slept, she began to work through the problem before her, in the only way she knew how, making a mental list to establish her case as to why she couldn't do as he asked. Firstly, school would require all of her time. She couldn't take her eye off of her goal because she knew she'd need to work hard constantly to stay ahead of her classmates. Harvard wouldn't accept an excuse for poor study habits; she'd be asked to leave if she couldn't keep up. Secondly, she wanted to excel. In order to get a good job, she'd need a recommendation. And of course, as always, there was the not so small matter of the cost. For Ruby, there were no second chances. She could not afford to waste the opportunity she'd been awarded to attend the most prestigious law school in the country. If she was meant to be with Cooper, he'd wait. That's all there was to it.

She turned her head to watch him sleep. He looked so peaceful and she knew that when he woke up she'd need to have a difficult conversation with him. She could only hope that he'd understand. Just then his eyelids fluttered open.

"How long have you been awake? Did your leg pain wake you?"

"No," she said quietly. "I actually feel a lot better. I had a great nurse after all."

He smiled, his hand trailing from her hip to her breast with a light, teasing touch.

"I guess I know all kinds of ways to make you feel good, then. Happy to be of service."

"Don't we both have to get to work today? I need to get back to the Barn and get dressed." She realized that staying in bed with him would make it impossible to tell him that she'd made her decision.

He continued to move his fingers gently over one nipple, then the next.

"No rush. We don't have to be anywhere right now. It's still early…"

Even though Ruby knew it was wrong to not address the elephant in the room, she couldn't help but be swept up in sensation as he moved over her and began to rain kisses down her stomach and past her navel, stopping only to kiss the soft inner skin on one thigh before finding her center and concentrating on her pleasure. At the very second when she was sure she could not stop the inevitable building climax from shattering her from head to toe, he moved slightly and entered her, heightening her senses and sharpening her awareness. She could feel him deep within her, as she marveled at the perfect way they melded together, both of them losing themselves to one another in that final moment of fiery passion that left them breathless and replete.

They lay there together silently, waiting for their pulses to slow when he said, "Would it be the worst idea to steal another day? Call in sick?"

Ruby laughed out loud. "Oh right. Let me picture it. Terry would be out of her mind if you didn't show up today, not to mention how pissed the rest of the staff would be if they had to cover for you again. Come to think of it, we both probably owe her a day now. No thanks. Off to work we go. Besides, if we don't get out of this bed now, I don't know if we ever will."

"You've uncovered my secret plan. That's exactly the point. You and me, here, just us. No intrusions. We do what we want, when we want to."

"For as lovely as that sounds, you know we can't." She leaned over and kissed him before continuing, "We've got to get up."

He put his arm over his eyes. "Ah, Ruby. You're halfway right, I need to get up. You need more rest."

"How about the promise of breakfast at the beach? We can go pick up coffee and croissants at Phillipe's and watch the ocean for a bit before work. Sound good to you?" *The beach is where I'll tell him…* she thought.

"Please take one more day off from work. Please."

"I can't afford it," she said softly.

"If that's the case," he said accepting defeat, "then I'll start the shower. That's just one more perk of having you here every morning."

"Sounds like a plan," she said, feeling the fresh dread of having to confess that she couldn't move in with him, then pushing the thought back down. *It could wait,* she silently told herself. *What was the harm in that?*

After a lovely and quick stop at the beach and the chance to allow the caffeine they consumed fully bring them awake and into their day, Cooper agreed to drop Ruby off at the Barn so that she could change into fresh clothing. She was relieved to find her car in the parking lot and went inside to look for CeCe. As she gingerly walked down the hallway toward her shared bedroom, the other woman was stepping out of the communal bathroom, her towel wrapped body absorbing the water dripping down from her freshly washed hair. Ruby could see the look of concern on her friend's face as CeCe watched her measured gait.

"Ruby!" CeCe exclaimed. "You're back! How's the hip?"

"Ugly and purple, but so much better than it was. I think I'll have a physical reminder of that night for a while, but I'll definitely recover."

"Cooper take good care of you?" the other woman asked with a wink.

"He did," Ruby smiled. "Lots of Advil, ice and rest. Just what the doctor would have ordered."

"Um hum," CeCe smirked.

"No, really. He took his nursing role quite seriously." She stopped speaking for a minute, deciding if she wanted to share her new found dilemma with her friend. Maybe CeCe would have some insight for her about Cooper's request. As they walked slowly down the hall together, Ruby asked, "Are you the last one here this morning? Have the others gone to work yet?"

"I'm not sure if Patti and Louise went to breakfast or

not. They were talking about grabbing some eggs in town before work today. I just wanted to stay in bed. Last night was crazy – my tables turned over like ten times during the dinner rush. I'm dog tired."

"Who worked at the concession stand?"

CeCe laughed out loud then said, "Terry. She sat there all night hawking your wares. It was hilarious."

Ruby's eyes widened and turned up in amusement. "Wow. I might have even paid to see that sight."

"And it would have been worth every penny. No one could believe it!" She shook her head at the memory, then turned to Ruby. "Do you feel well enough to go back to work today?"

"What's my option? I need the money."

"I understand. Believe me, I do." It took a while before they'd made it down the length of the hall and CeCe pushed their bedroom door open. Ruby walked over to one of the bunk beds and sat down on the lower berth.

"I'm exhausted already. I sure hope Terry doesn't mind if I bring a barstool over to the concession area. I won't be able to stand up all night on my leg. The pain in my hip travels down to my ankle. It's better, but I'm not close to 100% healed yet."

"Ha," CeCe replied. "Maybe she'll have some empathy having done your job for you last night. She looked pretty beat at the end of the evening."

"I wonder what her total receipts were. That number should be interesting."

"Right? That tough old broad is great at barking out orders. It was great to see her actually step up and do the work, though," CeCe smiled as she pulled her logoed tee shirt on over her still wet head.

Ruby drew in a deep breath as she gathered the strength

to change her own clothing. She stood up and went over to her cubby to get her clean things, stripping down and putting her worn items into her laundry bag. As she fastened a fresh bra across her back she decided to get CeCe's opinion on Cooper's request.

"Wanna hear something wild?" she asked gamely. "Cooper wants me to move in with him."

CeCe's eyes widened and her mouth formed a perfect circle. "Oh?" she asked before sitting down on the floor to slather moisturizer on her legs. "That's huge, Ruby. Huge. Are you going to do it?"

"I really want to, CeCe. But I don't think I can."

CeCe stopped what she was doing. "What? Why?"

"Because I'm leaving here in less than two months to start a whole new life in Boston. School's the real deal, you know? Lots of work, lots of studying. I can't be playing house here with some guy I've just met. I can't."

"Playing house? Is that what you think it means to Cooper? Because I've known that boy a real long time. He hasn't ever lived with a woman. Never. I don't even think Patti spent a full night in that house the whole of last summer."

"What?" Ruby asked, truly surprised.

"You heard me. She'd be over there, doing what I'm sure you can imagine for yourself, but she was back here at a certain point before sunrise. I should know. I was her roommate then, too."

"But he's got her photographs up on the wall near his bedroom. She must have meant something to him…"

"She was the woman he was sleeping with, that's all. They were friends long before that, and I think they still are. It was just a fling between them. Believe me, if Cooper had asked Patti to move in with him, she'd be there now," she replied matter-of-factly, returning to her moisturizing routine.

Ruby stood still for a moment, her clean tee shirt still hanging from one hand, trying to process what she'd just heard from CeCe. She moved to put it on over her head, then she stepped into the short navy blue lycra skirt she'd pulled out of her cubby. To hell with the entire dress code today. Her leg still hurt. Terry would need to deal with it. She watched as CeCe struggled into her black jeans, legs still slick from the product her friend had just finished applying to herself. Once done, CeCe stood and zipped up her fly, smoothing her tee shirt down and tying the excess fabric up in a knot to one side so that the fabric landed just at the waistband of her pants.

"So, you plan to say no?" CeCe asked bluntly.

"I don't see that I have a choice," Ruby answered.

"You always have a choice, honey. That's the definition of free will. You just don't want to live with him."

"That's not entirely true either…" she threw herself down onto the bed again, putting her head in her hands, tears welling up in her eyes. "You know what, CeCe? It was a real shitty year for me. Coming up here was a whim. I knew I needed a job, but what I really needed was to put some time and space between all that happened to my family and the new life I thought would start when I got to Harvard. I didn't expect to meet Cooper, or feel the way I do about him. I like him. I do. More than I care to admit to myself."

"Then what's the harm in taking a chance? Move in and see where it leads."

"CeCe," Ruby whispered. "That's just it. I don't think that once I do that I'll be able to leave."

The other woman came over and sat down next to Ruby. "And what's so horrible about that?"

"It would mean giving up on me and the future I have planned out for myself. I could lose myself into Cooper's world, but really? No. I can't. I just can't do that."

"Suit yourself, Ruby. Just let him down easy, huh?"

Ruby felt the tears start to fall down her cheeks onto her lap. She nodded. "I'll try," was all she said.

Chapter Fourteen

Ruby didn't expect to have the reaction she did when she reentered the Hut with CeCe. The whole scene from the last night she'd worked came crashing down around her and for a moment she felt dizzy. She instinctively rubbed the bruise on her hip. She saw Cooper lift his head in surprise at seeing her arrive and he quickly walked toward her from where he'd been working at the bar. She swayed for a moment before reaching up and grabbing the counter of the concession stand. CeCe put a steadying hand on her arm and said, "Are you okay?"

As she fought off a wave of fresh pain and nausea, she replied, "Yeah. Give me a minute. I'll be fine." Just then Cooper was by her side.

"I told you to stay home today, damn it! I should have been more forceful. You could be safely tucked into my bed right now," he hissed. "You shouldn't be here. It's too soon."

"Cooper, please!" she said sharply. "I need to do this, to get back to work. I will be okay, I just got a bit...overwhelmed. It's already passing."

He raked his hand through his hair in an exasperated manner. "I just wish you'd let me take care of you the way I'd like to. You're impossible!"

"And you're being ridiculous. I'm fine. See?" She carefully stepped up into the stand and started to straighten up the merchandise. In one evening Terry had managed to leave the entire shop in disarray and with a glance Ruby could tell that she had her work cut out for her. Even with her back turned, she could feel Cooper's presence, his eyes boring into the spot between her shoulder blades. "I know you're still there, Cooper. Please. Go back to whatever you were doing at the bar. I'll check in with you after I sort out this mess."

"Ruby…"

She pivoted around on her good leg to face him. "Please, Cooper. I'm good, I promise. Go."

Ruby watched as he fought back the words he'd meant to say, instead just shaking his head and turning on his heel, retreating to his work. She let out a sigh and leaned heavily against the wall. It wasn't even lunch time and she was already exhausted. Sweat beaded on her forehead and formed in the valley between her breasts. Cooper had been right, she most probably shouldn't be here, but she had no choice. She began to refold the shirts and resort them by size when Cooper returned, a barstool in his right hand.

"What's that for?" she asked.

"For you." He climbed into the stand, placed the chair down, took her by the shoulders and gently sat her on it. The space seemed all too small with him in it next to her. Ruby could feel his anger radiating off of his chest and onto her body.

If he'd brought her two dozen roses it would not have been a more thoughtful and appreciated gift. "I don't know if Terry will let me sit while I work," she stammered, his closeness making her nervous.

"Don't worry about Terry, let me handle her for you, at least. You can't stand up for the next twelve hours anyway. I'll be driving you to the hospital if you try. Sit," he commanded.

"Okay, okay already. I hear you." She felt nothing but relief when she took the weight off of her bruised leg.

"You can really be so frustrating," he said. "Don't let me see you standing again." He turned to go, then stopped. "And you can be sure that I'm watching you." He finally squeezed past her to go, their bodies touching as he made his way out of the stand. He turned back for a minute and reached out to lift her chin with his hand.

"I want you to take it easy. Please," he bent down slightly, his lips gently brushing hers. "Swear to me that you'll stay on this chair."

"I give up. Promise," she replied, pressing her lips to his, giving into the undeniable warmth of his kiss, allowing his tongue to tease her own, making her both breathless and lightheaded at the same time.

He pulled himself away and smiled. "I knew I would convince you to do the right thing. I'll be back later!"

She sat for a minute and her heart slowed a bit. As she went back to work, all she could focus on was the methodical folding of shirts and sweatshirts. She didn't dare try to review the last two night's sales numbers; she knew she didn't have the head for it. All she could think about was Cooper, the tangled sheets of his bed, and how she'd need to store up all these memories to keep her warm for the long winter that would inevitably come all too soon.

By mid-July the summer was definitely in full swing. The sun was out most days and there was a delightful breeze blowing off of the ocean through the restaurant. Luckily, there'd been no more rain other than a brief passing shower here and there since the big storm the month before. Business was brisk at the Hut, from the minute the beach bar opened each morning through a busy lunch service and well past the last dinner order was served. The staff was doing what they did best and as a result, they were lining their pockets with dollar bills like squirrels storing nuts away for the cold lean months to come. Even though Ruby's hip was almost all healed now, she kept the barstool in the concession stand and grabbed a moment or two of rest whenever she could. Standing for hours in the confines of the small space had taken a toll on her body, her lower back hurt at the end of her shift as well as the soles of her feet, and no matter which shoes she wore, they throbbed in pain after a long night of sales. She'd been so busy, in fact, that she hadn't been to Cooper's house in the two weeks since he'd asked her to move in with him. Ruby was somewhat relieved that he hadn't made an issue out of her lack of an answer to his request; she just didn't want to face the inevitable. She had fallen into the zone, as CeCe put it: work, sleep, work, day off, work again, just like everyone else at the Hut. Acceptance by the rest of the staff, though slow, was closer than ever. She'd gained the respect of everyone she worked with and even Patti had to admit that the extra money from the sales of merchandise was a great perk. Ruby felt a true sense of accomplishment, having succeeded where most people would have expected her to fail.

In the late afternoon on a beautifully cloudless and sunny Tuesday, she allowed herself the luxury of filling her plate from the array of food set out for the staff before heading down to the beach for a few moments of quiet before the restaurant began to fill with the dinner crowd. She picked out a sunny spot and kicked off her sneakers. She wanted to soothe her aching feet in the cool, soft sand, and was even considering dipping them into the ocean and just letting them soak there for a bit. It was Cooper's day off and he had driven down to Boston to try and sell Satin's Satin to some more pub owners. He'd been slowly adding more bars to his customer list and it looked like his home-cooked brew might actually have a chance at a wider distribution than he had originally imagined. Once she finished her salmon and salad, Ruby set her now empty plate down next to her and stared at the horizon. The sun was bright in the sky and she could feel its rays bathe her face, warming her whole body with a balm-like effect. She really loved it here in Bluff's Creek. She always had, from her earliest days as a child. Now it meant even more: it represented a freedom she'd craved, a place where she had staked out a claim to live her life on her own terms.

Then another thought crept into her mind. *Cooper.* The memory of his face, his eyes boring into her own while he covered her with her body, the two of them joined in the most intimate of embrace flooded her vision. She did miss being in his bed, feeling the spark of his naked skin ignite against her own, but she couldn't risk having him repeat his request to move in with him. The pace of their summer work schedule had kept them apart, but she knew that they had a shared day off at the end of the week. The inevitable was upon her. She would have to tell him no.

Just then, she saw a shadow creeping up behind her. She turned to find Steamroller, wet suit on and surfboard in hand. He gracefully sat down next to her on the sand.

"Hey there Bumblebee, what's happening?"

She smiled at the old nickname. For as many times as she'd corrected him this summer, he persisted. "Just taking a break before it heats up again." She cocked her head toward the Hut. "You know how it is."

"Oh yeah. I must have shucked at least two thousand oysters since Saturday."

She looked down at his hands. Despite the heavy Mylar and steel reinforced gloves he wore behind the raw seafood bar in the restaurant, they were heavily nicked with small cuts. She reached out and touched one of the older scars. "Do these hurt?"

"I guess I'm used to it. I barely feel anything. I just slap on a bandage and keep shucking. I hold the speed record, you know." He smiled broadly.

"I've heard," she emphatically responded before turning her attention to the ocean. "Are you heading in?"

"Yeah. I thought I'd ride for a bit before my shift starts, you know, clear my head. Wanna join?"

"I haven't surfed since my lessons with you when I was a kid. And besides, I don't even own a wet suit. That water never warms up, does it?"

"It's tolerable. I mean, it's never gonna be like the chop in Maui, you know? This is the east coast, after all."

"Exactly. I'll pass."

He stood up and zipped the front of his neoprene suit closed and said, "Okay, but if you ever change your mind…" He took two steps toward the water before turning back. "Oh, and Bumblebee? Any truth to what Jenny told me about your dad?"

Ruby's head shot straight up as she felt a ripple of fear shoot up her spine.

"What are you talking about?"

"You know, that he stole all his client's money out of

some fund and tried to blame it on the market going south. Something about putting accounts off something and hiding the money for himself… not offline, um, what's it called again?" He rubbed his hand against his forehead and then added, "off shore. That's it. Off shore."

"What?" Ruby asked, feeling her heart almost beat out of her chest. "He would never have done that. He was trying to protect his clients' money, to minimize the effects of the Ponzi scheme that he didn't see coming. He was a victim too. We lost everything." Her head was swimming, but she thought to ask out loud, presumably to the man in front of her, but actually to the universe, "if he put money off shore, where is it now?"

Steamroller picked up his surfboard. "It's all above my security clearance Bumblebee," he said in a teasing tone. "Ask my sister if you really want to know. Jenny told me that's what happened and that you're hiding out here. No worries, though. Now that we've gotten to know you, we all like you just the same." With that he waved and head into the approaching tide, all but disappearing into the fresh churn of expansive ocean.

All of a sudden, Ruby could not sit still. She jumped up and grabbed her empty plate, tossing it in the nearest garbage can. She then pulled her cell phone out of her back pocket, not at all surprised by the lack of signal on the beach. She hurried up the dune to the one spot in the parking lot where she knew she could reliably make a call and dialed her father's number as fast as her fingers could move over the keyboard. Once connected, the call went immediately to voicemail. She made a second attempt with no luck. Drawing in a deep breath, she tried her mother's phone, but had the same result. It was absolutely maddening. She looked down at the screen. It was already close to five fifteen. Jenny should be at the restaurant by now, setting her station up for the dinner rush. With a determined motion, Ruby shoved her phone down into the back pocket of her black jeans and set out to find Jenny, who, according to Steamroller, was a treasure trove of information.

Fifteen minutes later and now in a full sweat, Ruby was still unsuccessfully looking for Steamroller's sister. Instead, she found CeCe. "Hey, have you seen Jenny anywhere?"

"No," her friend replied. "But check the master schedule. I think she's off tonight."

"Okay, thanks," Ruby said, pushing past her friend.

"Hey where's the fire?" CeCe called out as Ruby kept walking straight through the double swinging doors that led into the Hut's nerve center -- the kitchen. She had barely been back here since that very first week when she broke Terry's dishes trying to prove that she was something she was not. She hardly noticed the enormous vat of milky New England Clam Chowder bubbling away on one burner of the massive stove, heading straight to the back wall where each week's schedule was posted. She searched for Jenny's name and slid her finger across the page until she found today's date. Just as CeCe thought. Jenny wasn't due to work today. "Damn it!" she muttered under her breath.

"Hey there, you. Little one. All okay?" Big Red's voice boomed loud and clear across the space. Ever since the incident on July 4th, the entire kitchen staff had become incredibly protective of her.

She took a deep breath to calm herself and said, "Yes. I'm fine. I was just checking to see when my next day off is…"

"Ah yes," Big Red replied. "We could all use some time off to admire the fine sunset I suppose. But that day is not today, is it now?"

"No..."

"Well then little darling. You had better make like a ghost and disappear before the big boss lady finds you in the wrong place at the wrong time!"

His words snapped Ruby out of her panic for a moment. Big Red was right. If Terry found her in the kitchen, she'd fire Ruby without a second's hesitation. She'd been warned once, she knew that Terry didn't offer any second chances.

"Thanks, Big Red," she smiled weakly at the big man. She needed the truth, and to get it, she'd need a plan. Ruby shuffled off to the concession stand to give herself the time to work out the details of what it was that she was going to do next.

It was nearly midnight before Ruby was done tallying sales figures and submitting her report to Terry. Her phone had remained silent in her pocket. Neither of her parents had returned her calls, and now her anger was replaced by a nagging sense of worry. She'd been speaking to them both sporadically over the summer, but she'd always been able to reach one of them when she dialed their phones. It hadn't been the highlight of her week, speaking to her mom and dad. They always sounded so defeated, so tired. She actually felt guilty that she was up in Bluff's Creek without them, despite the changed circumstance of her being there. Her surroundings were still magnificent, the beach, the sky, the ocean air; they faced the same closed four walls of their tiny apartment in Queens. It had been a particularly hot and humid summer in the city. She knew just how miserable they both must have been, but she had been able to compartmentalize. She needed to work, as did they. Her job was just in a better location.

A nagging thought began to form at the back of her mind. Her day off was Thursday. If she woke up really early, she could drive down to New York, visit with her folks and drive back in the late afternoon. Maybe she could get her father to finally open up and tell her the details about what had truly happened. But even if she couldn't, she could at least see for herself that they were okay. She was calculating the cost of the tank of gas it would take to make the trip as she pulled the heavy metal grate down over the concession stand, locking up for the night. Everyone else had already left for the Dive, but she was bone tired and looking forward to slipping between the cool sheets of her narrow bed instead. As she made her way across the parking lot, a pair of headlights appeared. She immediately recognized Cooper's truck heading her way. She stopped and leaned against her car as he pulled around, a wide smile on his face.

"I was hoping to find you here!" he said gleefully. "I had such a great day. I signed on with two more bars in Boston. I was hoping to get you to come celebrate with me…"

"Well that makes one of us. My night took a turn…" she replied.

"What happened?" he asked, shutting off the engine and coming over to stand next to her.

She wrapped her arms around her body and leaned back onto her car door. "Steamroller told me that somehow Jenny had uncovered the not so small fact that my dad dumped money into an off shore account, money he'd stolen from his clients." She shook her head. "All this time, the one thing I held onto was that my dad was innocent. I really believed him when he told me that he was just caught up in the vortex of this thing. I can't believe how gullible I was."

"Don't do this, Ruby. First of all, how credible is the source of this information? How would Jenny know more than you?"

"She doubted me from the first day I met her. Who knows? Maybe she did the digging I should have done."

"Or she's guessing. You need to speak to your father and ask him yourself." He moved in closer to her, his warmth enveloping her in a cloud of reassurance. "That's the only way to get the truth."

"I know," she said quietly. "I've tried that before, he's never been forthcoming with information. It's like he's not willing to talk about it."

"No? Or maybe he's just trying to protect you. If you don't know, then you can't be held responsible for anything he's done. You can't hide what you have no knowledge of."

"I called him and my mom earlier, but neither picked up their phone. You know, it's interesting. I think I should be concerned that I can't reach them, but I'm not. They like to ignore the outside world now, I know that. Besides, they might have both been working earlier when I tried."

"So, dial them now," Cooper urged. "Put this whole thing to rest."

Ruby glanced at her phone, pressing the middle button which illuminated the screen. It was almost one in the morning. "It's too late now. If I call, they'll be panicked. And if they don't answer now, I will be..."

"What's the plan? You need some answers, if for no other reason than to shut Jenny's gossip machine down."

"I'm off on Thursday. I think I'll head to New York to see them in person."

"Let me drive you," he said, shifting to put an arm around her shoulder, pulling her in close to him.

"Not a good idea, Cooper. As much as I appreciate the gesture, I don't think it's a great time to meet my folks."

"I don't need to meet them. I'll just tool around until you're ready to head back. You shouldn't drive alone, especially when you're this upset. Let me do this with you."

She started to cry. "If this is true, then everything I've believed about my father all my life is a lie. I've always thought him to be this honest and true maverick. He seemed to have it all together, you know? He was my hero…"

Cooper didn't hesitate. He gathered her up in his arms and held her close to him as racking sobs shook her body against his own.

"I'm soaking your shirt," she said after a few minutes. "I'm sorry."

"No apology necessary. What will it take for you to understand how I feel about you? I want to be there for you. I want to help." He lifted his hand to her face to wipe away her tears.

The soft touch of his finger against her cheek broke the dam of emotion that had been raging in her all night, and she couldn't help herself. "Take me home with you Cooper. Please."

"You don't need to do this, Ruby. I know you've been struggling with how you feel about me, about what I asked you. I don't want to push you into doing something that makes you uncomfortable. I want you to come back to me when you're ready. Not like this…"

She drew in a deep breath, feeling like she couldn't win for trying. All she wanted right now was to cling to him, to feel the strength of him filling her, to lose herself in the sensation of his naked skin against her own.

"How about we put the issue between us on hold and you just help me get through tonight? I need you Cooper."

Even though it was dark in the parking lot, she could tell that he was searching her face, trying to determine what to do next. He was clearly torn between doubt and desire. She needed to act on what she wanted, so she leaned up and kissed him, trying to sway his decision. As soon as he responded, she knew what would happen next.

"Get in the truck, Ruby, before I change my mind."

A shot of anticipation ran up her spine. She didn't hesitate.

Chapter Fifteen

It wasn't long before they turned onto Cooper's driveway. Ruby drew in a deep breath and waited for him to come around, open the door to his truck and take her inside of his house. He was there in a flash, pulling her close, kissing her as they walked together through the front door, down the hallway past Patti's photographs and into his bedroom. It was exactly as she remembered it all those nights alone in her single bunk bed at the Barn, when she conjured up the image of a very naked Cooper motioning her to join him there; the soft down-filled comforter, the oversized pillows, the indulgent high thread count sheets, and him, all of him, wanting her. She drew in a deep breath.

"Are you okay?" he murmured, ever so slowly running his hand down her back in a blissful caress.

She nodded her head and he took that as a signal. He didn't hesitate. Grabbing the hem of her tee shirt, he lifted it over her head with one hand while the other hand unhooked the clasp of her bra. He bent down to kiss her right breast, his tongue making lazy circles on her skin as he worked his way to her left side, mimicking the same action there. Then he kneeled in front of her and oh so slowly unzipped her pants, pulling them down until they rested at her ankles. He looked up at her. "Just tell me again. Tell me that this is what you want…"

She could barely breathe, let alone speak. She heard a deep humming sound and realized that it was coming from her throat, signaling him to continue. Having been given the go-ahead, Cooper pulled down her thin cotton panties and drove his tongue into her soft flesh. It was all Ruby could do to remain upright as the pleasure continued to build from a place deep down inside of herself. She moaned.

"Tell me that you want to be here with me Ruby," he whispered against her most sensitive skin.

"I do," she said softly, shivers of intense sensation beginning to build at the base of her spine. Her head fell back as she grabbed on to his shoulders, no longer able to hold herself up.

"Good." He smiled at her. "Now don't think. Just feel." With those words, he grabbed both cheeks of her rear end and massaged them with nimble fingers until she felt the room around her fall away. As she climbed up to the edge of a cliff of pure sensation, he shifted her onto the bed, threw his own clothing off and onto the floor and joined her there, both of them joined in an age-old rhythm, climaxing together in breathless passion.

A few minutes later, when she felt her heart begin to return to its normal pace, Ruby lifted her head off of his chest and shifted her body to lay back against the pillow.

"Cooper, that was…"

"Don't say it, Ruby. It was most certainly a moment."

"But…"

"I told you. Don't let your thoughts run away. You tend

to over analyze everything. Sometimes you just need to connect with someone, right? I want to be that someone for you Ruby, I really do. You're not comfortable with the thought of moving in here, I get that. But if you think I'm going to disappear after Labor Day, you're dead wrong."

In that moment, Ruby realized just how well he knew her. *Was he so deeply connected to her that he could read her thoughts?* She hesitated a minute, then quickly blurted, "I've been trying to come up with a way to tell you. I'm so overwhelmed. I'm worried that I won't be able to compete at school, you know. It's Harvard. And now this thing with my dad is crashing down on me…"

"Whoa, Ruby, slow down." He flipped over onto his stomach and rested his head on his folded arms, propping himself up to look into her eyes. "Do you think that Harvard would have admitted you if you weren't able to cut it there?"

"Well, my last name opened a lot of doors in the past, I mean before this whole scandal with my dad. And they did ask me to defer a year, which I did. So yeah. I'm a bit concerned."

"I'm not. Look at what you did at the Hut with the concession stand. You changed the whole business model by yourself. You're smart, Ruby, really smart. You'll do just fine."

"And what about this whole thing with my dad? Jenny was able to get a piece of information that I should have known. I understand that people are curious. Damn, I am too. I can only hope that I get the truth, and that when I do I can handle it."

"I'll be there, right beside you," he murmured. "Just let me in."

"That's hard for me, Cooper," she said as newly formed

tears sprung behind her eyes. "I have some serious trust issues, as you can see."

"That may be true, but I always find that if you go with your gut, you're most often on the right path. What does your heart tell you, Ruby?"

His words gave her pause. She wasn't ready to tell him that yet. Instead, she pushed him onto his back and rolled herself on top of him.

"Really?" he smirked.

"What's the matter? Not up to the task?"

"Are you kidding? I love a challenge!" He wrapped his arms around her and rained kisses down her neck, effectively ending the conversation and giving her a much-needed reprieve. As his lips softly brushed against her cheek, he breathed into her ear, "Give me a chance to show you just how great we can be as a team, you and me. You won't be sorry."

She allowed herself to sink more fully into the embrace that she so craved, blocking out all traces of the trouble that lay outside of his bedroom door. *Just for tonight,* she told herself. *I can pretend just for tonight that I am as carefree as I want to be.* Instead of speaking, she let her body answer for her, opening herself to him fully and losing herself to the night.

They were both awake before dawn. As dim light began to creep ever so weakly around the window shade of Cooper's bedroom, she stretched before getting out of his bed and rummaging around for her clothing.

"I'll need a ride back to the Barn. I've got to change before work, and if I'm heading down to New York on Thursday, I've got to get in early today to order some more inventory for the weekend."

"How about this for an idea," Cooper began. "You don't officially move in here, but you leave a few things for mornings like these. A toothbrush, some underwear, a pair of jeans and a clean tee shirt for starters."

"Holy crap, Cooper, you are relentless! And what's wrong with me using your toothbrush?"

"Nothing, really. But you having one here keeping mine company would give me hope!"

Ruby laughed out loud. "Okay, okay. You win. I'll go buy an extra toothbrush and leave it here," she said, rummaging around on the floor and finally finding her bra tangled in a heap under the bed. "But for right now, I need some coffee. Let's get going."

"I like to hear you laugh," he said, picking his car key and wallet up off of his night table. "It's a beautiful sound. You should do it more often."

"Yeah, I know," she said wistfully. "I wish I could."

They walked out of the house together and climbed into his truck. He went to start the engine then stopped, turning to her. "I do want to do the drive with you on Thursday. I can get Steamroller to switch days off with me and I can go… if you'll let me."

Ruby thought about it for a moment, all the while looking at the concern for her reflected in his beautiful dark blue eyes. "Okay," she heard herself say.

"Wow, that's great," he said, the surprise showing on his face. He leaned over and squeezed her knee before turning the ignition key. "I promise to stay out of your way with your folks. I can make myself busy, no worries."

"We'll have to leave really early in the morning if we're going to do this trip in one day. I hope you're good with that."

"Earlier than this?" he asked. The sun was just beginning to make its way over the horizon with a hot and hazy lethargy. Despite the hour, it was already warmer than was comfortable. They'd been pretty lucky with the weather so far this summer, despite the storm the month before. And the sunny skies had brought record numbers of tourists to the Cape, making everyone at the Hut very happy. They were all on their way to earning more than enough money to help finance their winter adventures.

"At least this early," she replied, a wet, humid breeze coming at her through the open windows of the truck. "Ideally we arrive at my folk's apartment before either of them needs to leave for work. It's a five-hour drive, so figure we need to hit the road around four…"

"Ugh. Brutal."

"You don't need to…"

"Oh, I'm coming with you. I think it might be best if you spend Wednesday night at my place, though. That way we can save some time, if I don't need to swing by the Barn to pick you up."

"You just don't give up!" she exclaimed. Then, in a conciliatory tone said, "But in the spirit of partnership in this particular endeavor, I'll come to your house after work, shiny new toothbrush in hand."

He let out a breath. "Wow. That was a whole lot easier than I thought it would be!"

"Don't get ahead of yourself, Cooper. It's a practical suggestion."

"Ok. If that's how you want to look at it, I'm good with that. For me, however, it's a night with you in my bed that I can look forward to."

A small shiver ran through her body. "We'll need to sleep. No funny business."

"Funny business? I can't promise…"

Just then he turned into the parking lot of the Barn. "I'm going to head to the beach to find Steamroller. It's low tide. Something tells me that he's out surfing."

"Let me know if he's cool with you switching days."

"Oh, Ruby, no worries. I'll be very persuasive."

She had no doubt about that, considering how far he'd gotten her to compromise, new toothbrush notwithstanding.

They were halfway to New York City on Thursday morning before Ruby felt fully awake. Cooper was driving her car, both of them agreeing that it would be easier to park her smaller vehicle there. They had fallen into bed the night before, their lovemaking more relaxed than it had been; maybe it was the now familiar shape of each other's body, the way they perfectly molded together; maybe it was the languidness of their bones after a long day standing at work, no matter. Ruby's last thought before sleep was of just how good he could make her feel as she wrapped herself tightly around him and woke the same way. She could no longer deny that she had deep feelings for Cooper, she just needed some space and time to process exactly how she could make things work between them.

She looked up at the road signs on the highway and saw that they were already in Hartford Connecticut, halfway there. She straightened in her seat and turned to Cooper.

"Would you like me to drive? It might be easier, I know the way once you cross the Throgs Neck bridge."

"No, that's okay. You can direct me, though."

Ruby continued. "I've been running through a few different scenarios in my mind. I don't think my dad will be willing to tell me the truth, even if I confront him with what Jenny told me."

"He probably just wants to protect you. Or maybe he's told himself so many times that he did nothing wrong that he believes it. Then again, for what it's worth, what if he's innocent?"

"Innocent, huh?" She shook her head. "I'd really love to go with that, you know?"

He reached over and grabbed her hand in his, resting them both on her lap. "Of course you do. That's understandable. He's your dad."

"Yeah," she said softly, squeezing his hand tightly in her own. "He sure is…"

Two and a half hours later they were circling the streets that surrounded her parents' apartment building, looking for a place to park. After the third unsuccessful attempt, Cooper said, "This is nuts! Who can do this every day?"

"Most New Yorkers!" Ruby answered enthusiastically. "Although, I must admit, I haven't missed this ritual since I've been on the Cape."

"Wow. I'll tell you what I think. I'll drop you off and I will eventually find somewhere to leave the car. I'll text you my location. You can let me know what you want to do after you speak to your father."

"Thanks, Cooper. Sounds good." She could feel the apprehension build as they pulled in front of the building and she got out of the car. "Thanks for driving, by the way. I can drive us back."

He winked at her. "Let's see how you feel after this conversation." He nodded his head toward the entrance.

"Okay," she said, leaning back in and across the front seat to give him a kiss. "Wish me luck," she whispered before turning to go inside.

The drab lobby of the building was dimly lit, but Ruby barely noticed as she made her way into the tiny elevator. It was nothing more than an ancient steel box, non-descript and basic; it couldn't be further from the lushly carpeted, wood paneled, modern device she was accustomed to in their Park Avenue condo. She stepped inside and pushed the button for her parent's floor. As the lift creaked under the effort of rising up through the shaft, Ruby ran through her questions again in her mind. All too soon the doors opened into a hallway that smelled vaguely of old onions and cabbage. She stepped out and briskly walked to the last apartment on the left. She remembered what her mother had said when her parents had moved here. "At the very least, darling, we have a corner unit. Lots of windows." Ruby had chaffed at her mother's use of the word 'unit'. *Geez. It wasn't a luxury building or an exclusive real estate deal. It was a rental apartment*, she had thought. *Nothing more*. Once outside their door, Ruby lifted her arm and knocked loudly. She heard stirrings inside, and then the sound of approaching footsteps.

"Who's there?" her mother's voice called out.

"It's me, mom," Ruby replied.

"Darling…" her mom's surprised voice matched her face as the hollow metal door swung open to reveal her mother standing there in her frilly nightgown, an open bathrobe trailing its belt behind her. "Is everything alright? What are you doing here? Did you lose your job in the Cape?" Her mother's face looked old and edged with concern.

"No, mom. I'm fine. It's my day off. I need to speak to dad."

"He drove a late shift last night, he's sleeping."

Ruby let out a sigh. "What time do you think he'll get up? I don't have much time. I've got to be back tonight."

Her mother adjusted her robe, tying the errant belt tightly around her waist. "Do you want some breakfast?" she asked.

"No," she replied, all the while trying to remember if her mother had ever asked her that question before. Throughout the years she lived at home, there was always someone else in her parent's employ to provide meals for her. First her nanny, then the cook. Her mother never stepped a foot inside of the kitchen, at least not that Ruby could recall, unless it was to refill the Cartier ice bucket they kept on the bar.

"Well, I just made coffee. Maybe just a cup?"

"You made coffee?"

Her mother stopped mid-step and turned back. "Yes. I did. Lots has changed here, you know."

"Right, mom. I know. Sorry."

"No need to apologize, dear." She continued into the small galley kitchen with Ruby following behind her, where she spotted the Keurig machine on the counter. That made a lot more sense. Her mother's version of making coffee was still merely touching a button. Her mother picked up her already brewed mug, sipped briefly and asked, "So what do you need from dad?"

There was a small café style table in the corner with two chairs. Ruby sank down into one of them and motioned for her mother to join her.

"Phillipe says hi, by the way," she said.

"Phillipe? From the bakery in Bluff's Cove? How wonderful!" her mother smiled. "Please do send him my very best regards."

Ruby stared at her mother for a moment. Even in these

shabby surroundings she still sounded like the Park Avenue socialite she'd been her entire life. "Right," she began, getting back on topic. "Listen, Mom. My presence on the Cape has stirred up some of the old gossip about what happened to dad. When I heard some of the stories, it made me realize that I never really knew the whole truth. I think I deserve some answers."

"Ruby!" her mother exclaimed, loudly banging her mug down on the table, coffee sloshing over the side. "We're done with all of that now. Leave it alone."

"No mom," she replied calmly. "I can't leave it alone. I need to know."

"You already do!" her mother said, jumping up and grabbing the sponge out of the sink to clean up the expanding mess.

"No, mom, I don't. I only know what dad told me. I most certainly don't know the details."

"Well, maybe I can help. What is it you want to hear? How dad was accused of some very terrible things that he didn't do? Or that we're ruined financially and none of our old friends will have anything to do with us? Perhaps you want to know just how much our old neighbor, Mrs. McNair spent yesterday in the shop where I work. *Thirty-five thousand dollars. On three dresses and a handbag!*"

"C'mon, mom. You used to do the same thing."

"I might of. But I wasn't a saleswoman at the time. It was humiliating!"

Ruby hesitated a brief moment. Her mother's whole world was upside down and forever changed. She needed to tread lightly with her. "I'm sure it was, mom, and I'm sorry you had to go through that."

They sat in silence for a few minutes as her mother

sipped at the remaining coffee in her mug. "Dad won't tell you anything," she finally said.

"Why is that? Is there nothing more to tell, or will he take what he knows to the grave?"

"I'm not sure if he does know anything else, but I've asked a million times. He won't talk about it anymore." She then reached out and put her hand on Ruby's arm which was resting on the small table. "We all need to move on."

"Then why am I hearing rumors about off shore accounts and hidden money? Most gossip has a small kernel of truth to it, you know it does."

"Probably because most people love to speculate, and they most certainly enjoy seeing someone at the top fall off their high perch. People are often mean and thoughtless. Or at least that's what I've come to understand."

Ruby looked up at her mother. The harsh, florescent lighting in the kitchen accented the weariness in her face. It wasn't just a sleepless night's exhaustion, either. It was the weight of her life bearing down on her each and every day that had entirely transformed her mother's appearance, from vibrant to drab, in what seemed like the briefest of moments. Before she could answer, they both turned to face a sound in the doorway. Her father had woken up.

"I thought I heard your voice, Ruby! What a great surprise to see you!" He stepped into the small space to give her a hug.

"Hi, dad," she said standing.

"What brings you to New York?" he asked.

"Well, I tried calling, but neither of you ever answers your phone. I just wanted to..."

"Come inside to the living room," her mother interrupted. "It's more comfortable to sit on the couch. Sam, do you want coffee?"

Her father smiled. "That would be great sweetheart. Thanks." He turned to exit the kitchen and Ruby went to follow, but her mother grabbed onto the hem of her shirt as she turned to go.

"Leave him alone, Ruby. He's been through enough," she said in a low, stern voice.

"I can't, mom. I need to know." She pulled away and stepped into the living room, her mother trailing behind her and they both sat in the low loveseat next to the couch, facing her father.

"Listen, dad. I heard some crazy stuff up at the Cape about what happened to you and I realize that there's so much I don't know."

"It's not worth talking about, Ruby." He turned his head away from her and toward the window.

"It is to me, dad. What's the truth about you hiding money in some off-shore account?"

His head snapped back. "Look around baby girl. Does it look like I stored a ton of cash somewhere?"

Ruby felt embarrassed for both herself for asking, and for her father, for having to reply. "I'm sorry. I just can't get away from it. This damned thing followed me up to the Cape, and you can be sure it's going to rear its ugly head at Harvard."

"You can't repeat what you don't know," he so softly that she wasn't sure she'd heard him correctly.

"What?" she asked sharply.

"There's nothing to know, that's all," he said. "And I'm done discussing it. Look, I'm not in jail. I've got a job and so does your mom. We're getting by. I suggest you do the same."

"That's not really an answer, dad."

"It's the best I can do."

Just then there was a knock on the door.

"Who could that be?" her mother asked them both, rushing over to find out.

As she opened the door, Ruby saw the familiar shape of Cooper in the hallway.

"Hi," he said. "You must be Mrs. Tellison. Is Ruby still here?"

"Cooper?" she called out. "What are you doing?"

"I'm sorry, Ruby. Can I come in?"

"Of course," Ruby's mother said, stepping out of the way and ushering Cooper inside.

Ruby had made her way over to him in time to hear him whisper, "I'm about to bust and I didn't want to pee in the park. Where's the bathroom?"

Chapter Sixteen

Ruby stepped back, allowing him some space to enter the apartment. "Of course, Cooper. Come in. Down the hall, first door on the left.

He smiled widely and made his way past her and head quickly toward the bathroom. Ruby's mother turned to her, the front door still gaping open.

"Who's your friend?"

"He works at the Hut, and he has his own artisanal beer business as well." She blushed, not sure why she felt she had to qualify that Cooper was more than a bartender to her parents.

"That's nice, dear. And when you say 'friend'... what does that mean exactly?"

She could feel both sets of her parents' eyes fixed on her face. She also knew that Cooper would be back in a moment. The pressure was almost too much to bear.

"We've been, um... dating. He offered to make the drive here with me, that's all." She could hear the water running in the sink down the hall. "Please, please, just leave it at that." Ruby knew how intrusive her mother could be at times and right now all she could do was pray that this wasn't going to be one of those moments. She heard Cooper open the bathroom door and make his way down the hall back to the living room.

"Thanks. I wouldn't have come up if I could have helped it. I'll wait downstairs for you Ruby."

"No, Cooper, It's nice to meet you. And besides, you're here now. Don't be ridiculous," her mother said. "Can I offer you a cup of coffee?"

"That would be great, ma'am."

"Come with me," she said, giving him her best Park Avenue smile, crooking her finger and leading him away.

Ruby turned back to her father for what she knew was her one last attempt at an answer.

"He seems like a nice young man," her dad said, as though their prior conversation had never taken place and her surprise visit was an ordinary enough experience.

She realized that she had limited time before Cooper and her mom returned to the room. "Dad. Please. Some answers."

He sighed and shook his head. "None of the past matters now honey. What's done is done, I can't change it. I've paid a hefty price for my mistakes. Don't make my trouble your own."

"Now you're just talking nonsense, dad."

"No. I'm not. You're about to start law school, to become an officer of the court. If you truly don't know anything, no one can ever question your ethics or your motivation. I've thought long and hard about this, Ruby. I'm your father. My job is to protect you, always."

"Protect me?" she hissed. "How have you protected me?

Everything I had is gone. You and mom are barely surviving. You can't protect yourself, let alone help me!"

He sat up sharply on the couch. "Ruby! That's not true! I may not have money to give you any longer, but your mother and I… we're always here for you."

She saw the raw desperation in his eyes and it completely disarmed her. She had seen her father vulnerable before, but not like this. He wasn't going to tell her anything, that was certain. She went and kneeled at the sofa where he sat and took his hands. Sitting there, still in his bathrobe and pajamas, he looked old to her for the very first time. "I know you are," she whispered, squeezing him tightly. "I just wish I understood, that's all. It's tough when complete strangers claim to know more about what happened to your family than you do."

"I'm sure it is," he responded. "You need to trust me on this. Let people talk, it doesn't matter. Keep your eye on the prize, sweetheart. You have three tough years ahead of you. Get that degree and you'll be fine."

Ruby realized that it was futile to argue with him any longer. "Okay, daddy," she said. "Okay."

Just then Cooper and her mother returned to the room amid peals of laughter.

"What's so funny?" she asked.

"Oh, dear, Cooper was just telling me about his first attempt at making his special beer. He had a boil-over. Thankfully it was a small batch and he was able to get out of the way. He had to hop on one foot out of the garage to prevent himself from getting burned. One of the neighbor's kids saw him and started to imitate him from across the street! Can you imagine? This poor boy is trying to get away from a potential disaster and the kid starts jumping around on his own front lawn? What a sight that must have been!"

"You never mentioned that, Cooper," she said smugly.

"I guess I was just trying to impress you with my beer making prowess. I sort of left off that detail." He blushed brightly.

"Do you have time to stay for lunch? Mom and I'll just get dressed and go across the street to the diner. C'mon. That's a New York tradition you just can't get up on the Cape."

She didn't see a way around it, but asked Cooper anyway. "Is it okay with you?"

"Of course. Sounds like fun."

Taking a deep breath, she said, Okay. Let's do it."

An hour later Cooper was trying mightily to pull the remains of his chocolate egg cream up through his straw. "What an awesome drink. Maybe I should brew a chocolate beer!"

"That has possibilities," she offered. "I'd try anything that has chocolate in it!"

Ruby's father motioned the waitress to bring the check and Cooper reached for his own wallet.

"No, you don't. You're my guest today."

"Mr. Tellison. Thank you, but…"

"Not another word." The older man put a ten-dollar tip down on the table and they all stood to leave.

"Thank you for lunch," Cooper said.

"It was our pleasure to meet you. Ruby doesn't bring a lot of friends around to the house anymore. We enjoyed the time with both of you."

"Okay, dad. Enough with the guilt. I've been working."

"I know. But this was still a great surprise."

They all walked outside and Cooper led them to where

he'd parked the car. Ruby hung back a bit and held onto her father's arm. "Listen. If you change your mind – not today or tomorrow, but whenever – I'd like to know the real story of what happened."

"Maybe someday, Ruby. Just don't count on it."

She nodded, realizing that it didn't matter as much to her anymore. Her parents were broken people, but they loved her, and her father just wanted to keep her safe, even if that meant leaving her in the dark.

"And Ruby," he added. "Your mom doesn't know anything either. It's just better that way.

"If you say so dad." She drew him into a hug just as they got to her car. "I'll text you once we're back on the Cape."

"You do that, Ruby. And your young man – is he making you happy?"

She hesitated at her father's bold question, but once she thought about it for a moment, she said, "More than I thought."

"Well, it was really great of him to come here with you today. He must have some pretty strong feelings for you, don't you think?"

She didn't get the chance to answer before he added, "I love you, Ruby. My only wish is that you find a place in the world that makes you happy."

"I know, dad." Ruby could feel tears begin to well up and she didn't want her father to see her cry. She glanced over to find Cooper huddled in deep conversation with her mother. In a short time, they'd become fast friends. "I'll be sure to send you a six pack of Satin's Satin, Mrs. Tellison. But only if you promise to give me your honest opinion."

"Would I lie to you Cooper?" she said with an air of

innocence that stopped Ruby in her tracks as she made her way over and opened the door to her car.

"There's no way for him to know that, now is there mom?" she asked, now suppressing a smile.

"That's okay. I'm looking forward to hearing what your mom has to say, no matter what," Cooper replied politely.

"Oh boy," Ruby remarked. "Hate to break up this love fest, but we've got to get on the road."

"Of course, dear," her mother replied before she stood on her tip toes to give Cooper a kiss on the cheek. "Come visit again," she said cheerfully.

Cooper turned to her father, shook his hand and said, "Thanks for lunch. It was great to meet you." He walked over to the driver's side and got into the car next to Ruby. She watched both of her parents wave on the sidewalk as Cooper pulled the car into traffic, leading them back to the highway that would take them to the Cape.

"What was that back there?" she asked.

"What do you mean?"

"I'm sure you had to pee, Cooper, but I thought you were going to wait for me by the car."

He flashed her a brilliant smile. "It was an emergency," he said.

"Okay. Sure. Whatever you say."

"I think it worked out okay, don't you?"

"Well, my mom's a fan, that's for certain."

"I was trying to distract her enough for you to have some alone time with your dad. Did it work? Did you find out what you wanted to know?"

"He wouldn't tell me anything." She shook her head. "There's definitely more to the story though. I just couldn't get it out of him."

Cooper reached across the gap between their seats and took her hand in his. "I'm sorry Ruby."

"Don't be. I'm going to work on being okay with it. I have to respect his wishes. I can't change the outcome anyway. He thinks he's protecting me by keeping me out of the loop."

"Maybe he is. And you left him with his dignity intact. That's the important thing. I'm sure he's been through enough."

They sat silently for a long while, watching the regal Manhattan skyline recede as they crossed back over the Throgs Neck Bridge and into the Bronx.

"Your mom is great, by the way," he said a little time later. "I had fun with her."

"You mean you had her eating out of your palm!" she teased.

"Yeah, that's me. Great with the older women, not so good with the younger set."

"Oh, I think you do just fine." She smiled and squeezed his hand. "Do you want me to drive for a while?"

"No. But talk to me."

"Okay," she said. "What should we talk about?"

"You mentioned that you're worried about school. Tell me why."

She was surprised at his question and took a long moment before answering him. "I guess it's all so overwhelming. I'm a really good student, Cooper, I know what it takes to study the work and be prepared for class. I'm a pretty good test taker, too. I think what concerns me most is the cost, and what happens once I graduate. What if I hate the law? What if I don't want to be some corporate attorney living out my life in that highly pressured atmosphere." She paused. "Do you remember one of our earliest conversations, when we talked about this and you asked me when I would have time for me?"

"Of course."

"I've thought about that ever since. You were right. What if I spend the best years of my life doing something that I'm not passionate about? What then?"

"Whoa, Ruby. Back it up. You won't know that until you try, right?"

"But once I start school, the clock is ticking. Each semester I'll sink more and more into debt. Maybe I shouldn't even go."

He turned away from the road to look at her wide-eyed for a moment and sighed. Shaking his head and returning his attention to the building traffic in front of them he said softly, "You have to."

"What? Why?"

"Don't compound your father's mistake. You obviously wanted to go to Harvard Law. If you didn't, you wouldn't have applied in the first place. And, even more importantly, they accepted you. Do you have any idea of the odds against you on that, even with perfect grades and board scores? I read somewhere that only about fifteen percent of all applicants get in."

"It doesn't matter."

"Yes, Ruby," he said firmly. "It does." He turned the car toward the next exit, pulling into the first gas station he found.

"Do we need gas? We should have been able to make it on one tank…"

"No. I just need a break. Let's go in and get a coffee."

They both walked into the small convenience store behind the pumps, drawn to the smell of caffeine and donuts.

"What would you like?" he asked, eyeing the array of colorful pastries.

"Small black coffee. Thanks."

"Nothing else?"

She shook her head, watching as he added cream to his cup before securing the lid tightly on top with careful assurance.

"What would you do if you didn't go to school in the fall?" he asked.

"I.. I'm not sure."

"What's your plan? You must have one, I mean, you say you've been thinking about this."

She looked down at the small white cup in her hand. "I don't have one. For the very first time in my life, I just don't know."

"Well then, until you do, stay the course. I think you'll be sorry if you don't."

"Why are you so insistent that I go? First you want me to move in and then you want me to leave. Which is it?"

"Wow," he said, paying for their coffees and pushing through the glass door back to the car. "You must be kidding."

She reached out and put a hand on his arm. "I'm serious."

"So, that's what you think? That I want you to stick around the Cape and play house with me? How awful would that be for you? You'd resent me in twenty seconds, and you know it! Besides, how do you know what my winter plans are anyway?"

"I don't, I guess. Why don't you tell me?

He ran his hand through his hair, a gesture that she recognized as a sign that he was feeling stressed. "Cooper. Just tell me."

"I was waiting for the right time to talk about this with you. Let's get on the road. We can discuss it tonight once we're back on the Cape. Right now, I just want to drive."

"I see. All of what you said about this being more than a summer fling was a lie. I'm nothing after Labor Day, huh?" she challenged.

"Ruby!" he said sharply. "Don't!"

"Don't what exactly? I need to leave for school when I said I would so that you can move on, right? Have you picked her out yet?"

"Picked who out yet?"

"Your next conquest. Do you have someone lined up to warm you this winter while I'm in Boston?" She regretted her rash words as soon as she spoke them.

"I'm going to ignore that and let you cool off, let myself cool off, because right now, Ruby?" He spoke in an even, measured tone. "Right now, you're acting like a child and making me insanely angry!"

They both climbed back into the car in silence, and remained sitting, a mere two feet from one another, eyes forward to the road ahead without a word passing between them until they were on the driveway at Cooper's house, her coffee still in the cup, undrunk and as cold as the air between them.

"I'll let you drive yourself back to the Barn. I think you know the way."

She felt tears begin to prick the back of her eyes. "I'm sorry Cooper. I shouldn't have said that about you having another woman waiting in the wings. I didn't mean it and it was wrong of me. I just don't want you telling me what to do."

He sighed. "I'm sorry, too, Ruby. I'm not trying to tell you how to live your life. I just want you to keep your eye on the prize, whatever that means to you. I really believed that you wanted to go to law school, but hey – who am I to tell you to go if you have doubt."

She wiped a stray tear off of one cheek. "Are you going to tell me where you're going this winter?"

"This isn't the right time. We've had a long day, and we're both tired. Come inside and we'll talk about it in the morning."

"You realize that you're sending me very mixed signals, here. I don't want to argue anymore, but I don't think sex will solve anything."

He smiled for the first time since leaving her parents behind on the sidewalk. "As much as I hate to admit this, I agree. It's a bad idea. Let's just shower and go to sleep."

All of a sudden, her limbs felt heavy and exhaustion threatened to make it impossible for her to drive herself anywhere. She slowly stepped out of the car.

"You can shower first," he offered as he opened the front door.

She walked down the hallway to his bedroom and ever-so slowly stripped off her clothes, folding them and leaving them on his dresser. She then went into the bathroom, turned on the shower and waited for the water to get as hot as possible before stepping in, hoping that the sound of the spray would drown out what she was sure to be a torrent of her own tears.

Chapter Seventeen

Ruby wrapped a large bath towel around herself and went back into Cooper's bedroom. She was exhausted from the entire day and crying in the shower just made things worse. She looked around and realized that she only had the clothes she'd worn that day, she had nothing else.

"Cooper," she called. "I need to borrow something to sleep in."

"Top drawer on the left of my dresser. Help yourself."

"You can shower now," she yelled back, but there was no answer. She shrugged and walked over to get a clean tee shirt. She slid the drawer open, and in front of the neat pile of folded laundry was a piece of paper with the logo of an airline across the top. Knowing she shouldn't look, but unable to resist, she quietly lifted the folded document out and held it up to the light. It was a ticket to Amsterdam, one way, no return, on a flight that left right after Labor Day. *Was he going to tell me about this?* she thought, heart pounding rapidly in her chest. She quickly replaced it, grabbed a shirt, slipped it on and slid into the bed.

Ruby stared up at the ceiling. She realized that she should have never looked at his personal papers, but now that she had, it wasn't like she could forget what she'd seen. He most certainly had not mentioned going to Amsterdam, or anywhere else for that matter. Was he planning on taking an extended vacation after the Hut closed? Why wouldn't he have told her? And who the hell was he going with – as far as he knew up until today, she had every intention of starting school in the fall. *Besides*, she reminded herself, *he hadn't asked her to go with him. Oooh!* She turned her pillow over, trying to get comfortable on the bottom side's cooler surface. It was so infuriating that he would keep something like this a secret and not share it with her. Ruby could hear Cooper's steps in the hallway coming toward the bedroom. She closed her eyes. *Should I say something?* she thought to herself. *Or should I wait until he tells me... if he tells me!* She heard his deliberately quiet steps as he made his way to the shower, turning the water on and closing the door behind him. It wasn't long before she felt him get into bed, still a little bit damp, smelling of the delicious rosemary scented soap she'd used herself, just a short while before. After a quick moment, he was gently breathing, and she knew that he'd fallen asleep. Ruby considered sneaking back to the dresser to get another look at that ticket, but she knew that the information she'd seen earlier would still be the same.

Just then Cooper moved closer, pulling her to him, molding his body around her without even waking up. She wasn't getting any answers tonight. She breathed in deeply, trying to stop feeling so anxious, to convince herself that he'd tell her about his planned trip when he was ready, that she was making something out of what she was sure would turn out to be nothing. She felt her eyelids grow heavy as the warmth of his skin and the comfort of his bed overwhelmed her, and she slept.

The next morning, he was already out of bed when she woke up. Ruby could smell fresh coffee being brewed in the kitchen. She pushed off the blankets, put on her clothes from the day before and went looking for Cooper. His back was to her as she found him at the sink, carefully slicing a banana into a bowl of oatmeal. She took a minute to watch the sleek muscles of his back contract with his small movements. It was such a domestic and tranquil scene, it almost caused her to forget his airline ticket that she'd found the night before.

"Good morning," she said softly, not wanting to startle him while he was still using the knife.

He turned and smiled. "How are you today?"

"Um, better than I was last night, I guess," she lied.

"Would you like some oatmeal? I just made a batch."

"No thanks. Just some coffee." She moved around him to pour her own, knowing where to find the mugs and utensils, reaching into the refrigerator for the container of milk. She finished preparing her drink and walked back over to sit on a stool at the counter. Watching the steam rise from her cup, she said, "I'd love to talk about what you brought up yesterday, you know, about your winter plans."

He swallowed the cereal in his mouth. "How about we have that discussion tonight after work? I think it might be a long one, and we don't have the time now."

"Do you want to give me a hint?" she asked.

"No. It's not that big a deal, Ruby. I just don't want to get into it now." He turned and put his empty bowl in the sink. "I can be ready to drive you to the Barn in ten minutes. Sound good?"

"Of course," she said, sipping slowly at her coffee, itching to demand information about his mystery trip right now.

Cooper left the kitchen and went into his bedroom, leaving Ruby with her thoughts. She had all day to figure out just how to get him to tell her about that airline ticket, and she meant to have him spill out all the details tonight.

The Hut was slammed with customers, extending the closing time by an hour. Ruby barely had a moment to catch her breath, between the constant demand for paraphernalia at the stand and filling the orders as they came in from the wait staff. After the last patron was served, she still had to tally all the receipts from the day, which was complicated and just the kind of detail-oriented work that she had no patience for. All she wanted to do was get the truth out of Cooper. Plain and simple. She still had her head buried in her ledger book when CeCe stopped in front of her.

"Let's get a drink. I'm so ready to relax." She rolled her shoulders in an attempt to ease her weary muscles.

"Hold on. I'm not sure if I'm meeting Cooper tonight or not."

"Really? You two have been together every night this week. Spare a moment for this girl, okay? Besides. I met someone and I need to fill you in on all the crazy details!"

For as much as she was dying to get to the bottom of that mysterious airline ticket, CeCe was right. She'd been pretty much ignoring her friend for days now, and she realized that she shouldn't do that.

"You met someone? Holy crap, CeCe, that's awesome.

Okay then. The Dive." Ruby said, throwing her car keys to her friend. "Meet me in the parking lot. I'm just going to tell Cooper I'll hang with him later."

"Much later!" CeCe laughed. "I might have two drinks, you know! And we have a ton to catch up on!"

A few minutes later Ruby walked over to the Hut's main bar where Cooper was swiftly wiping down the counter. "I'm going over to the Dive with CeCe for a drink. She needs some girl time. Can I meet you at the house later?"

"Of course. It's going to take me some time here anyway. Crazy night."

"Tell me about it. Almost a new record for my sales."

He winked at her and Ruby could feel her resolve start to fade. She wanted to forget all about the confrontation she was pretty sure she would have with him over that ticket. She wanted to leave her car with CeCe and ride home with Cooper right now and get into his bed. But she knew that she couldn't. She had to spend some time with her friend.

"See you, sweetheart. I'll be sure to wait up." His tone was pure honey.

Ruby had to physically push herself away from the bar. "I won't be long," she said, turning to go.

"Ruby, wait," he said, quickly moving through the half-door that separated him from where she stood. He swept her up in an embrace and gave her a long, deep kiss, gently teasing her with the tip of his tongue. "Just a little incentive for getting you home to me sooner rather than later," he whispered before releasing her and setting her firmly on her feet, leaving her both panting and breathless.

"Cooper…"

"Go on now. Spend some time with CeCe."

Gathering her wits back around her, she drew in a deep

breath and nodded to him, then head out toward the parking lot to find her friend.

An hour and two beers later, Ruby was feeling much more relaxed.

"So, dish it out. Who's the guy?" she asked her friend.

"For as much as it's against everything I stand for, he's a customer."

"You better not let Terry find out," Ruby said. "She'll have your hide!" "I'm not letting that old bag spoil this for me. Besides, he spends his money in her fine establishment. That should keep her happy."

"Okay, so tell me how you met him," Ruby asked."He'd been coming into the restaurant and asking to sit at my station every weekend since July 4th. Then he bought two tee shirts and a sweatshirt one night. I thought he was just flirting, no big deal. But then he came back and gave me one of the shirts as a gift! Crazy, right?"

"No. You're awesome. He sees you for who you are…"

"So, wait. Let me tell you the rest."

"First tell me his name."

"Oh yeah. Carl. His name is Carl. And he's really cute."

"Where's he from?"

"He told me the name of the town, I just don't remember right now. Somewhere in Connecticut."

"Really? And he's here every weekend? Does he have a house up here?"

"Yes, his family does, over in Truro."

"Have you been there?"

"Not yet. But he's invited me over next week on my day off. He's coming up early just to spend the day with me!"

"Wow, CeCe. That sounds serious!"

"No, Ruby, no way." She took a long sip of beer and then paused, a look of concern crossing her face. "Wait. Do you really think so?"

"Well at the least, he sounds really interested in you. So, when do I get to meet him?"

"Whoa, baby! I barely know him. I don't think I should overwhelm him with my friends just yet."

"Somebody's got to decide if he's good enough for you. Might as well be me!" They both broke out into tipsy peals of laughter. CeCe struggled to regain her breath, gulping in air to try to compose herself.

"Yup. You're a good judge, alright. You can't even see that Cooper is madly in love with you."

Those words sobered Ruby immediately. She sat up straighter in her chair.

"In love? I don't know... In lust is more like it."

"You're out of your mind! The guy is head over heels. Why the hell else would he have driven all the way to New York City with you on his one day off? He doesn't need to impress you just to get you into his bed. I mean, you're already there. No way. He's in love. It's obvious to everyone but you."

Ruby felt like CeCe had thrown cold water all over her. She had avoided the simple truth of her own emotions, but if Cooper was feeling the same way...she couldn't even think about that.

"What did happen with your dad?" CeCe asked, bringing Ruby back to the present.

She then filled CeCe in on the afternoon spent with her parents and the lack of information she'd obtained.

"You know what I think?" CeCe asked reflectively. "Your dad isn't ready to tell you anything, so stop asking. I mean, what's the point?"

"If you were me, wouldn't the truth be important?"

"No, I don't think so. Your father is doing his best to steer clear of your life and to not jeopardize your schooling. Let him alone. Give him the chance to maintain the only thing he's got left, his love for his family. He's doing his best for you, Ruby."

"Maybe. I just can't stand the gossip."

"Here's what I've learned from living up here my entire life: they're going to talk about you anyway! Who the fuck really cares what other people think?"

Ruby thoughtfully bit down on a plastic straw. "Do you really mean that? You don't care about how others see you?"

"Listen, honey. Up here, most people see the color of my skin and not all that much more. No one knows the real me. You're the only one who seems to have an interest in what I do anyway. Well, you and maybe Carl."

"That's one way to look at it."

"What else matters?" CeCe reached across the small table and took Ruby's hand. "You're the first person who even asked what I do all winter. And I've known most of these fools all of my life! They can be small, petty people. So yeah. Who the fuck cares?"

Ruby slammed her now empty bottle down on the table in affirmation. "You said it! I'm adopting a new attitude. Fuck 'em!"

"At'tah girl. Now you're talking!" She took a final pull out of her drink. "One more?"

"Uh, no. I've got to drive us out of here. And besides, I have some unfinished business with Cooper."

"Back to him, huh? Can't keep your hands off of each other?"

"No. Well, yes, but no. We need to finish a chat we started yesterday."

"Do you now?"

Ruby lowered her eyes, growing serious. "I found something in his dresser last night that I probably shouldn't have seen. An airline ticket."

"Yeah, so?" CeCe asked.

"To Amsterdam. Right after Labor Day."

"Just for him?"

"Yup. And it was only one way."

CeCe leaned back in her chair, eyes wide now. "What the hell is that all about?"

"Well, I'm trying not to dwell on it without the facts, but, to be honest, I'm not succeeding."

"Are you upset that he's going, or is it that he didn't ask you to join him?"

"I couldn't go, CeCe. I'm starting school, or at least that's my plan. I do have my doubts about that as well."

"What?" her friend asked alarmingly. "You've got to be kidding. You're going! Not only are you going to be one powerhouse of an attorney one day, but I need you in Boston. Our campuses are so close to each other. I'll say it again – you're going!"

"I know, I know, and I most probably will. I'm freaking out over how much debt I'm going to be in when it's done. Let's save that whole topic for another day. For now, I'm just confused as to why Cooper hasn't said a word to me about his trip."

"You worry too much, Ruby, about pretty much everything," she said, leaning in with a smirk on her face. "Maybe he's waiting for the right moment, you know, when you're naked together in his bed," she said teasingly, clearly trying to lighten her friend's mood.

"I'll try to resist," Ruby answered with a smile. "But it's not easy! He's just so damned…" She paused, reflecting for a moment on how quickly she'd fallen for him and how unexpected this whole summer had been. Cooper, CeCe… these were people that she didn't know a few months ago, and now the season was almost over, school was to start in a short two weeks and she couldn't imagine her life without them. She reached across the table for her friend's hand. "C'mon. I'll take you home."

Ruby drove to the beach after dropping CeCe off at the Barn, got out of her car and sat on the warm hood looking up at the moonless, star-filled sky. She had to swear on everything she held holy that she'd go to school in the fall – CeCe wouldn't get out of the car without that promise from her. Deep down Ruby knew that she'd attend classes, how could she not? It was her plan all along, and she'd stick to it, debt-filled life be damned. She let the sultry ocean air surround her, the sound of the waves pounding against the sand lulled her and helped her think. Maybe she was destined to be an attorney so that she could help her father clear his name in the court, once and for all. Or maybe she was meant to help people who couldn't afford to pay for their own defense, to do pro-bono work for those less fortunate than herself. She may not have a bank account, but she was going to have one hell of an expensive education. Only time would tell where she'd use her degree.

As for Cooper, she had to face the truth. She'd fallen in love with him, but he was going to Europe and she was headed to Cambridge. She wasn't even sure if she'd be back at the Cape the following year – she knew that many law students vied for the few coveted clerkships offered by the big law firms in New York and Boston because they often led to high paying jobs after graduation. She'd have to consider doing whatever it took to get one of those, pounding the books and getting near perfect grades. She had her work cut out for her.

Despite the warmth of the air, Ruby wrapped her arms around herself, closed her eyes and just sat for a moment, trying to blot out all of her jumbled thoughts and focusing on taking in even breaths. It was a calming meditation, one that she so desperately needed. In the inky darkness behind her lids, she pushed down her anxiety over the plane ticket she'd found in Cooper's dresser. If he wanted to tell her, he would. She hoped that he did. But she had no real hold on him, other than the memory of the time they'd spent together this summer. If CeCe was right, and if he felt the same way about her as she did for him, maybe they could work it all out. She honestly didn't know. She opened her eyes in time to see a star shoot across the sky, and she knew that she should make a wish on it, but she didn't. Instead, she climbed down from the hood, got back into her car and drove over to Cooper's house, prepared to live out the next two weeks with no expectations, but rather, just to enjoy the pleasure that they offered one another for as long as she could.

Chapter Eighteen

Ruby opened the door to Cooper's house and found him sitting on the couch, shuffling through a stack of papers, a bottle of Satin's Satin on the end table near his elbow.

"Hi," she said. "Reading anything good?"

"It's the manual to the new canning machine I'm considering buying. I downloaded it off the internet, but I'm not having much luck figuring out the instructions. I'll probably understand it better when I see the thing in person."

"Oh?" she asked. "Did you get it? Is it here in the garage?"

He looked up at her and motioned for her to come sit down next to him. "That's part of what I want to talk to you about. C'mere."

Ruby sat down. "I'm all ears," she said.

"I'm going to Amsterdam. To buy this machine…" he began. "And it comes with lessons. I'll be there for a while."

Her eyes widened in a mix of relief and surprise. "What constitutes 'a while'?"

"At least eight months. I've been offered the opportunity to study with a real beer master."

Ruby felt all of her previous tension and worry about the plane ticket deflate as she considered his words. "When do you leave?"

"The second week in September. But, Ruby, I want you to come over for Christmas. You'll have a break from school. I'll send you a ticket. Think about it."

"Wow. That's quite an opportunity."

"Yeah. And I have you to thank. I started thinking about school, and how you were committed to going. I want to make a real effort to be successful with my business, and to do that, I need to learn more about the process of brewing."

"But, Cooper, Christmas? I can't promise you that."

His face fell. "Why not?"

"Because I don't know what my work load will be, and I don't know if I can make that trip."

"Oh," he said, finishing his beer with a long swallow then walking into the kitchen to throw the bottle into his recycling bin.

"It's not that I don't want to, Cooper." She shifted on the couch to face him as he stood behind her. "It's just that I don't have any idea what will happen by then."

"Or who else you may meet at school? Some trust fund baby getting his degree?" he asked sarcastically.

"Take that back! You can't be serious!"

"I've never been more serious!"

She was surprised by his anger, but felt her own blood begin to boil. "And, by the way, why did you wait so long to tell me this? School starts soon and now you're leaving? What the hell?"

"I just decided to do it, Ruby. I wasn't sure that I had the guts to go back into a classroom. It's not my favorite thing, as you know."

"Like it's mine? But you wouldn't hear my argument for not attending."

"You have to go," he said coming back to the couch, calmer now, and sitting down very close to her. "Just like I do. We both want the same thing, to better ourselves."

"But…"

"No. Listen, Ruby. If you can't come over at Christmas, I'll try to understand. Just keep an open mind. But if you think it's at all possible, tell me you will." He leaned in and grazed her softly on the mouth with his lips, deepening the kiss and melting her anger with away as she responded.

"You're not playing fair," she said breathlessly.

He pulled back for a moment and said, "Life's not fair, Ruby." With those words he shifted his body, laying them both down, covering her from head to chest with soft caresses, igniting something deep within her. She pulled at his shirt, lifting it over his head with one swift movement. She made to undo his belt when he stopped her.

"Promise me you'll try," he breathed into her ear.

"I can't…"

"Yes, you can," he whispered, running his hand under her thin tee shirt and tugging at the cup of her bra, springing her right breast free.

"I don't know…"

"There's nothing to know," he responded, undoing the clasp of the restricting garment at her back. "I'm going to miss you. I just want to hold onto the promise that we'll reconnect at Christmas. Just say yes…" he lowered his mouth to her breast, lightly kissing the sensitive skin and tugging gently on one nipple with his teeth.

Ruby felt herself giving in to the sweet sensation that was centered in her chest but rapidly spreading downwards. "I can't promise. Just know that I'd love to if I can, but I don't want to commit to it. I don't even know what my work load will be like yet. Cooper, please…"

"Please what, Ruby? Stop asking? Stop kissing you? Or is there something else you'd like?"

"Stop asking. At least for now," she choked the words out. "Let's revisit this conversation when I have more information. And besides," she said in a voice barely above a whisper. "I can't think about anything in this moment except getting all of these clothes off."

"Your wish is my command," he said roughly, sitting her up briefly to pull her shirt up over her head and tossing the bra to the floor. He lifted his own shirt off and lay her back down on the couch, showering kisses everywhere and ever so slowly working his hands to the waistband of her jeans, unfastening them and tugging them off of her one leg at a time. He then sat up and leisurely rolled down her panties until she was naked before him. "You are so beautiful," he said before her dipped down and concentrated his attention on the most over sensitized part of her body, using his tongue to bring her to the edge of pleasure before quickly removing his own jeans and slipping deeply inside of her.

He felt incredible and Ruby tilted her head back against the pillows and let the fullness of him guide to new heights, shattering her in pieces as they both climaxed together. "Ruby," he gruffly whispered in her ear. "I can't let you go. You need to come to Amsterdam…"

As her heart slowed to its normal pace, she shifted out from under him. "You are a broken record, Cooper! Don't ruin this moment, please. I told you that I'm not even sure that Harvard is a good fit for me – you know how I feel. I'm hoping that I survive there until winter break." She looked up into his blue eyes and felt her resolve begin to slip. "If I can make my way to you at Christmas, great. But if I can't…"

He leaned in and kissed her soundly on the mouth. "I'll take that, Ruby, really. Let's leave it at that."

She drew in a deep breath before saying, "Cooper. I just like to be able to keep my word once I give it. So, it's a provisional agreement. If I can, I will."

"You're starting to sound like a lawyer already!" he said with a wide smile, standing and extending an arm out to her. "Let's go to bed."

"For round two or to sleep?" she teased.

"Name your pleasure. I'm here to serve you," he replied.

She stood up and stepped into his embrace. "Well, I'm not tired. How about you?"

"Round two it is." He took her hand and together they went into his room. Sleep would come later, but for now, Ruby was determined to fill up on all of him, to store the memory of this night to sustain her through the long, cold winter ahead.

It seemed like before she could even catch her breath, it was the Thursday of Labor Day weekend. Although Ruby had never witnessed it before for herself, by the time the last patron was served on Monday night, the Hut would officially close for the season in a last-minute flurry of activity. According to CeCe, the major clean-up would begin this morning. All extraneous supplies were brought into the storage container where Ruby had originally found all of her inventory for the concession stand last spring. No new orders of food or drink would be delivered – they sold whatever they had on hand at this point, down to the last oyster. It was the restaurant equivalent of an acrobatic trick, the kind with no net beneath the performers, and it required all hands-on deck almost 24/7 until the final minute when the doors were locked and they all went on their way. From the time Ruby arrived at work that morning, she got caught up in a wild flurry of activity. She knew what merchandise would sell out and what had sat for most of the summer without interest from the customers, so she began to pack up the items she wouldn't need and place them high up on the shelves of the storage unit. It was tedious work, but it kept her mind off of the thought that she was leaving on Tuesday morning for Cambridge, and that Cooper was headed to Amsterdam shortly thereafter. The only saving grace was that CeCe would be nearby all winter at school in downtown Boston. She'd have a friend she could count on if school got too tough to handle. She was up on the highest rung of the ladder, reaching to pile the last box at the very top near the ceiling when she heard Cooper's voice.

"Ruby," he said in an even tone. "Don't move a muscle."

Fear shot up her spine. "Why not?" she asked.

"This ladder isn't sturdy enough for you to be up that high. It could topple over. I'm going to hold the base. You step down slowly, one foot at a time."

She was too surprised by the seriousness of his voice to do anything other than what he said. As she made her way back down to where he stood, he let go of his grip on the ladder and reached up to pull her into his arms.

"Is this really necessary?" she asked. "I was fine. And I was almost done. Now who's going to put the last of this junk away?" She pointed to the box she'd left on the top step.

"You don't have the occasion to climb up on ladders much, huh? You're never supposed to stand on that last step. You could have fallen off and broken your neck!"

"You worry too much. I was fine!" she said indignantly, secretly happy to be in his embrace. He set her on the ground and quickly climbed back to the top of the ladder, stopping near the top.

"This is how it's done," he shouted down to her, leaning his body weight against the aluminum frame and reaching up to wedge the last box in place. He was back down next to her in seconds.

"Thanks for the ladder lesson. I'm not sure when I'll use that information again, but you never know."

"I'd like to think that I've taught you a thing or two this summer," he winked, looking around to check to see that they were alone.

She could feel a crimson heat begin to bloom on her neck and face. "Cooper. Not here. Not now."

"You really know how to kill the mood, Ruby. And here I just saved you from impending disaster…"

"Ha!" she laughed before asking, "What were you doing in here anyway? The extra liquor doesn't go here, does it?"

"According to Terry, there should be no extra liquor. I'm supposed to sell it all before the weekend's over. But no, if there should be a spare drop it goes into a large lock box inside of her office." He paused. "I was actually looking for you."

"You found me," she smiled.

"Yeah. It's about the final bonfire."

"What about it?"

Will you be my date?"

"Why of course! You know I will."

"I had a feeling you'd say that. But isn't it nice to be asked?" he leaned in and kissed her softly on the lips.

She felt so comfortable being in his arms and didn't want to think about anything else, but they both did have to get back to work. "Should I come over tonight, after closing?"

"You never have to ask, Ruby. The answer is always yes."

She nuzzled her face against his chest. "Good to know," she replied.

After one very long kiss, he walked her back to the concession stand and they both got pulled into the frenzy of the day. He didn't even make it to the family meal later that afternoon, and Ruby sat with CeCe as Big Red plopped down an enormous bowl of the quick pasta dish he had whipped up for them that night.

"You know how you can tell it's the end of the season?" CeCe asked as she looked into the steaming serving dish of linguini.

"No, how?"

"The dreaded tinned anchovy." She had dished herself a serving and then picked out a remnant of the much-maligned fish and moved it to the side of her plate with the tines of her fork. "Terry lightens up on ordering fresh seafood the last weekend. The staff feels it first."

"Ugh. I might need to go to Benny's for a burger later. I hate anchovies. Too salty."

"Look at you! Speaking like a true local. One for the road tonight?"

"Absolutely." Ruby pushed herself away from the table, downing an entire glass of water before she left. "I'll regret drinking that if I get busy and don't have a break tonight. But what the hell!"

"Ha! I know exactly what you mean!" CeCe replied as she pushed her uneaten plate away and drank down the contents of her glass. "Time to get going," she added. They walked into the restaurant, parting at the entrance. CeCe went about setting up her station and Ruby stepped up into the concession stand. She was busy rearranging what was left of her inventory when Patti stopped by on her way into work.

"Hey," she called out, causing Ruby to whip around to the front of the counter to see who was speaking.

"Hi, Patti. What's up? I don't have many tee shirt sizes left. You should check with me before upselling the customers tonight."

"Yeah, okay. But that's not what I'm here for." The other woman shifted her weight from one leg to the next, signaling her unease.

"What do you need, then?"

"I just want to say… when I'm wrong, I admit it. Selling tee shirts this summer really put a lot of extra cash in my pocket. It was a good idea." She looked away, as if there was someone else she needed to speak with in the distance.

"Thanks, Patti. I appreciate you telling me that."

"Yeah, well… will you be at the bonfire on Monday night?"

"Wouldn't miss it!" Ruby said with a smile.

"I'll see you there." With that, she tucked her head and walked into the restaurant.

Ruby stood still for a minute, still processing what had just happened. The woman who had pretty much promised to be a thorn in her side all summer had just sought her out with genuinely nice gesture. Shaking her head, Ruby greeted the first customer of the night, unfolding the last of the extra small women's shirts for the young woman's approval. *Wow,* she thought as the picky shopper in front of her examined her options. *Look how far you've come. You made it!*

On the morning of the bonfire, Ruby was restless. She had packed up all of her things and moved out of the Barn the day before, spending another night with Cooper in his bed. He'd gone out early, and she was still lazing around, sitting on his couch before taking a much needed shower before her last shift at the Hut. The entire summer had gone by all too quickly, leaving her feeling both nervous and nostalgic. She sipped at the coffee that Cooper had brewed before leaving the house, but it tasted flat and flavorless. She knew she had to shake off this feeling of melancholy; she wanted to enjoy her last hours of freedom with the man she'd come to love.

Maybe that was it. She loved him, she knew it deep in her heart, but she hadn't told him yet. She was pretty sure that he felt the same way, but they'd never said the words. Ruby was deep in thought, still in the same spot where he'd left her when Cooper came back home.

"Hi, babe," he said. "I hope I didn't wake you when I left. But I brought breakfast!" He held up a white bakery bag with a buttery smear across one side. "Chocolate croissants from Phillipe's shop. You know you want one…"

He was so damned attractive. How was she going to leave him behind when she had to go to Boston tomorrow? She could feel the tears forming behind her eyes and she blinked them away. *No. I won't let it end with me crying,* she thought to herself. "I do!" she said with as much enthusiasm as she could muster. "Let me just wash up. Be there in a minute."

Ruby ran down the hallway and into the bathroom to splash some cold water on her face. She glanced at her image in the mirror. She may look the same, but she was definitely a different person today than she was when she got up to the Cape last spring. She drew in a deep breath and walked back to the kitchen, determined not to let Cooper see how shaky she felt. He had already plated the pastries and was drinking another cup of coffee. He held up the French press.

"Some more?"

"No thanks." She pulled apart the soft pastry and chocolate oozed out onto the ceramic dish. She took a small bite. It was delicious but she could barely eat much of it at all, and pushed it away.

"Ruby? Do you feel alright? That's a fresh chocolate croissant. It's your favorite, isn't it?"

"It is. I'm just not hungry right now." She reached for the waxy bakery bag and put the confection back inside, rolling down the top.

"What's going on?" he asked with concern.

"Nothing, Cooper really. I guess I'm just sad that the summer is over. I'm being childish, I know."

He walked over to where she sat and put his arms around her. "I get it. I feel it too."

That was it. Tears flooded her eyes, rolling down her cheeks and soaking his shirt. "I don't want to go. I want to stay here with you."

"You can come to Amsterdam at Christmas, Ruby. We can have a real vacation, and you can be my date for New Year's Eve."

"It's not enough, Cooper."

"If you truly hate school, Ruby, I mean, decide that it's not for you, come to Amsterdam and learn to brew better beer with me," he teased.

"Don't offer if you don't mean it."

"Are you serious? I so mean it. Ruby… don't you know that I'm crazy about you? He paused. "I'm head over heels in love with you."

There it was. The words she needed to hear, yet all she could do was throw herself against him and sob.

"I love you too, Cooper. So much." She had trouble getting the words out through the torrent of her tears.

He kissed her then, starting at the top of her head and working his way down to her mouth.

"How about this?" he asked wiping away some of her waterworks. You start school. If you hate it, I mean really hate it, then come to me. I'll be waiting."

She nodded her head in affirmation, and accepted the tissue he offered her from a box on the counter.

"Okay," she stammered and reached up to put her hand on his shoulder. "That helps."

"Does this help as well?" He asked, kissing the back of her neck.

She could not suppress a giggle. "It tickles!" she exclaimed.

"Wow, talk about ruining the mood!" he exclaimed.

"You didn't ruin my mood Cooper," she said, standing on her toes to kiss his lips. "Now, where were we?"

Chapter Nineteen

After the last customer was served and the final drink poured, the entire staff of the Hut gathered once again on the beach for a bonfire. They trickled down the dune as they finished their tasks at the restaurant, gleefully calling out to one another, jubilant and in the mood to let loose and celebrate. By the time Ruby and Cooper got there, the party was in full swing. Steamroller had built an enormous fire and a bunch of people were standing around it, beer one hand, a long stick pierced with marshmallows toasting in the other; some were already skinny-dipping in the warm ocean water, and others were just sitting in groups, discussing their upcoming winter plans. From the top of the parking lot, Ruby could tell that this was to be an all-night affair.

"Are you ready?" Cooper asked as he came around to her side of the truck and opened her door for her.

"Ready as I'll ever be!" she exclaimed, actually looking forward to joining her friends on the beach.

"How about going for a swim?"

"You mean naked?"

"That is the tradition."

"I'm not that ready, then," she laughed.

"Maybe next year," he added, pulling her out of the truck. "Actually, maybe not. I don't want you naked with anyone else but me."

"Ditto," was her reply.

They walked hand-in-hand down the soft dune to join the party, stars twinkling overhead in the moonless night. Before Ruby even realized it, a red cup of beer was put in her hand and she made her way around the beach, talking to everyone as she went. She lost sight of Cooper for a while, but felt his presence there with her. After a while, she sat down next to CeCe.

"Looks like another successful season," her friend said. "I've got more than enough cash to pay my tuition, room and board. Best of all -- we'll be in the same city, Ruby! It's not gonna matter how cold this winter will be – we've got each other!"

"I know, CeCe. It's the thing I'm counting on most!" she replied, meaning every word.

"It'll be okay, you know. The Cooper thing, I mean. He'll do his training, and you'll do yours. You'll find your way back to each other."

Ruby gulped in the salty sea air in an attempt to clear her head of doubt. "I hope so," she said quietly.

"I'm pretty confident," CeCe replied. "And what do you know? Here comes the boy now."

They both watched as a shoeless Cooper made his way to where they sat, finding a soft spot next to Ruby on the blanket she'd smoothed out on the sand. "How's it going, ladies?" he asked.

"Cooper, tell this woman that everything's going to be

fine, okay? I'm done trying to convince her for now. I'm off for another drink. Anyone else?"

Cooper lifted his full glass and Ruby shook her head no.

"Alright then, you two. I'll catch you later." She stood and walked down the beach, leaving them alone.

"So much has happened since that first bonfire, huh?" he asked.

"You can say that. I feel like I've become more of a local, that's for sure!"

"You have. Even Patti says so. She told me before just how much she appreciates the extra cash she made this summer. Everyone does. You really made an impact here."

"Maybe Terry will actually let me come back and work next summer."

"She better, or else she'll lose her best bartender in the bargain."

"You don't mean that!"

"I do. We're a package deal now," he smiled and leaned in to kiss her cheek.

"So how long do you plan on staying here tonight?" she asked.

"Tradition dictates that we watch the sunrise all together…"

"Do you think they'll miss us if we sneak off for a bit?"

"What did you have in mind?" he asked with a sly smile.

"Oh, I'm sure I can think of something fun." She traced her finger along the inseam of his shorts, stopping where the fabric met his skin and dipping her thumb up underneath the hem for a moment. "What do you say?"

"I say let's go." He quickly stood, pulling her up in a swift motion. "I'd rather watch the sunrise in my bed with you in it than just about anything else in this world, Ruby."

"Me too," was all she said, but we don't need to go all the way back home to do what I'm thinking of."

"Is that right?" he feigned surprise. "Where do you want to go?"

"Just down the beach a bit. Like we did the last time we came to a bonfire."

"You don't need to ask me twice," he said jumping up and pulling her off of her feet in one motion. He looked around and picked up the blanket they'd been sitting on. Satisfied that no one was watching them, he whispered in her ear, "C'mon."

They quickly put some distance between the party and themselves, and once they were alone, they spread the blanket on the sand and sat down facing each other.

"I'm going to miss seeing you every day, Cooper. More than you'll know."

"You'll be too busy learning the law to notice. You won't have a lot of spare time to think about anything else but school."

"Not true." She lay down on the blanket and looked up at the star-filled night.

He lay down next to her and they held hands for a long while, not speaking, watching the sky as it filled with constellations in spectacular fashion.

"Look!" she said as a star shot across the sky. "Make a wish."

"I already did," he answered. "And it was granted. I have you."

She snuggled closer to him, reveling in the warmth and comfort of his body, storing the memory of this moment in her mind to have in the long winter they'd spend apart.

Ruby most certainly did not know what lie ahead, what waited for her in Cambridge. She could only hope that when the seasons turned, she would find herself back here, with him. Only time would tell.

"I have an idea," he said.

"That sounds intriguing," she replied, rolling from her back to her side and propping herself up on her elbow.

"Pick a star."

"Huh?"

He pointed at the sky. "If we both choose the same star, then anywhere we are, we can look up at the same time and be together."

"Cooper… that's so…romantic!"

"I mean it, Ruby. Even if we haven't spoken that day, when you look up, you can just imagine this moment, when we picked the star out together."

"Okay," she replied, rolling back onto the blanket, searching the heavens. "How about that one?" She pointed at the bottom of the little dipper.

"You mean Polaris? The North star?"

"Figures. I picked a famous one. Should I try again, maybe for something a little less obvious?"

He thought for a minute. "No. It's actually perfect. The North star. I mean, you're my true north."

"Is that a thing?"

"Don't you have a romantic bone in your body?" he teased, turning toward her and lifting his head off the blanket to put a kiss on her cheek. "Of course, it is!"

"What does it mean?"

"You're my constant. The North star is always in the sky, you can always see it. And it was known to sailors everywhere as the guide to bring them home."

"That's really lovely, Cooper."

"Well, Ruby, the way I see it, you're my home. So, go to

Cambridge, and when you're done with school, come back to me. I'll be waiting."

Ruby looked up at the sky, tracing her way down the Little Dipper to Polaris. It twinkled, a bright shining beacon in the dark night. She closed her eyes and made a simple wish. When she opened them again, she looked at Cooper, and smiled.

Epilogue

The winter to follow was harsh, with extreme cold but little in the way of rain or snow, causing a drought-like condition as spring emerged. The promise of long, hot and hazy days ahead made conditions ripe as the blue speckled caterpillars slowly awoke from their slumber, and got to work, weaving cocoons in the still leaf-less trees. They had been brought to this part of the country from France over a century before, by a misguided entomologist who believed they'd make him rich with the silk he was sure they'd spin. Instead, once they became gypsy moths, their primitive instinct caused them to chew the foliage of the mighty oaks and graceful willows, humming away as they rapidly defoliated entire forests. They were a sign of things to come…

Next in The Seasons of Us Series

vinci-books.com/AlmostUs

The bar's on the line. So is her heart.

Back at Bluff's Cove, Ruby's reeling—Cooper's distant, his "friend" is moving in, and The Hut is on the brink of closure. With her heart on the line and the clock ticking, Ruby must fight for love, friendship, and the beach bar that feels like home.

Turn the page for a free preview…

Almost Us: Chapter One

"Ruby… Ruby… Hey, Ruby!"

The incessant knocking on her car window brought Ruby out of her trance. She turned to look at the source of the annoying sound only to find her friend CeCe standing on the sidewalk, luggage in hand.

"Wow, girl. You can zone out like no one I know. Pop the trunk, would ya?"

Ruby complied, reaching down to engage the lever before hopping out to help the other woman load her bags into the old Kia.

"It's a gift, I know," Ruby teased. "It comes from countless hours in the law library." She put her hands on her forehead. "Ninja focus."

"Ninja, nothing," CeCe replied. "You were off daydreaming again. Pay attention. We've got a lot of road to cover in a short amount of time."

"Do you mean mileage or information?"

"Oh, that's right, madam prosecutor. You're all no nonsense and strictly business now, huh? Well, I'm just anxious to hit the road. It was a long winter and an even longer academic year. I need to blow off some steam."

To say that it had been an incredibly hard nine months would be an understatement, Ruby thought. Between the overload of schoolwork as a first- year law student and the unbearable anxiety over losing touch with Cooper, she felt off-center and adrift.

"When do you plan on doing that exactly?" she asked. "Terry's expecting us at work tomorrow."

"I know, I know, we're cutting it close. But the Dive is already open, and the gang is there tonight."

"What did you do? Call ahead and have them ice down a couple of cans of Pabst for you?" Ruby turned the car onto the open highway in front of them and merged into the left lane.

"Ha! No. I just spoke to Patti earlier, and she filled me in. Everyone is back up at the Cape already. They're just waiting for us."

"Not everybody…"

"You still haven't heard from Cooper?" CeCe asked with concern in her voice.

"Nope. Not a word."

"Wow."

"You could say that. Or you could say what I'm thinking. He's just not ever coming home. Or if he is, he's just no longer interested in pursuing a relationship with me."

CeCe shook her head. "Impossible. He's crazy about you."

"Then how do you explain it? I couldn't get over to Amsterdam at

Christmas like he wanted me to. I had to stay at school and work on that case I told you about for my criminal law professor. I had no option. You don't get asked twice, and there was no way I could say no if I want a shot at a good clerkship next year. Things just deteriorated from that point, and now, radio silence. I haven't spoken to him in over a month."

"I know. But I still can't believe that was the problem. Are you sure he's okay?"

Ruby winced as she glanced over at the other woman. If it hadn't been for CeCe being so close to Cambridge at her campus in downtown Boston, she couldn't imagine how she'd have made it through the year at all. She was her sounding board, her emotional anchor, and her best friend. "We've been through this, CeCe."

"You can't believe what you see on social media, Ruby. You of all people should know that."

Ruby's family had been dragged through the press after her father had lost all their personal wealth in a Ponzi scheme two years ago. The reporters and gossip columnists had dogged them so steadily that the powers that be at Harvard had asked her to defer her admission to the top-notch program for a year after she graduated from college. She did and now, after months of nonstop study, she was headed back up to her summer job at the Cape's most famous beach bar, the Hut.

"On his very own Instagram and Facebook page? What do you think?"

"It's all very confusing. Who was that chick again?"

"He told me that she was his mentor. Some master brewer something-or- other. I don't know. All I'm sure of is that he's no longer talking to me."

"You might really be making too much of this so-called brew bitch. I saw those photos. They were innocent enough…"

"You mean the one where she's sitting on his lap with

her arms wrapped around his neck? You call that innocent?"

"There must be a reasonable explanation. Cooper is a one-woman type of man."

"Right. I'm just no longer that woman."

"I think you've got to wait until you are face-to-face before you write him off altogether."

"Let me ask you something, CeCe. If it was Carl, and you saw some really incriminating photos of him with another chick, what would you think?" Carl had been a patron at the Hut who had been smitten by CeCe the summer before when she waited on his table one night. He had barely left her side since.

"I'd ask him about it, that's for sure. You know? Have a conversation before I dismissed him from my life without another thought."

"It's maddening, CeCe. I examined all the facts. I've come to the most reasonable conclusion I can."

"Except you don't have 'all the facts' as you claim. You're speculating at best. You need to sit down with the boy in person and have it out."

"Well, that will be impossible. He's nowhere to be found."

"Really? Have you contacted Interpol?"

"Stop kidding around, CeCe. You know what I mean. And guess what?

I'm a mess over it."

CeCe reached across to put her hand on Ruby's arm. "Okay, I'm sorry. I just want you to take a breath. I'm sure someone up on the Cape knows where he is, and you'll have an answer soon enough."

"I'm really not sure that I want to know. I just don't want to deal with the fact that it's over between us."

"You can be such a drama queen. There's no proof that it's over between you. Maybe he was just so into finishing his program that he had no time to talk. Did you ever think about that? I mean, you were guilty of that same thing this spring as we got closer and closer to final exams. I barely spoke to you at all."

Ruby considered her friend's words as she drove. CeCe did have a point. Weighing the argument, however, didn't change her mind. She shook her head. "You know what the difference is here, CeCe? I wasn't sleeping with you!"

"True, but not conclusive. You were immersed in studying and look at the result. Top of your class. Very impressive. I spent every waking moment in the library preparing for my own exams. Same result. Cooper was probably doing that very thing. I'm sure he'll fill you in when he gets back to the States."

"Which, if my memory serves, should have been last week. So, why didn't he call?"

CeCe let out a deep sigh. "I don't know, but I'm sure he's got a reason.

Innocent until proven guilty, right?"

Ruby smiled weakly as she turned onto the Bourne Bridge that would put them on the Cape. "You're watching too much *Law and Order*. With the fast pace of the twenty-four-hour news cycle, no one is allowed to be presumed innocent anymore. There's always another opinion."

"That may be true, but I, for one, will be keeping an open mind. I think he's going to get back home and come looking for you."

"I love that you hold on to your 'happily ever after' attitude!"

"You can thank Carl for that. And one of us has to. That's what best friends are for."

"You really like this guy, huh?" Ruby said, all too happy to shift the attention off herself and onto her friend.

"I still pinch myself. He's been so great, so generous. He really wined and dined me all over Boston this year. The more I get to know him, the more I want to be with him. This is serious."

"That's amazing. What did you decide to do about his offer to have you live in his Cape house this summer?"

"Yeah. I wanted to talk to you about that. Would you be okay in the Barn without me? I mean, you're comfortable with the girls now, right?"

"Of course! I haven't really spoken to anyone this winter, but I'm fine. And Terry cracks that whip anyway. We're not there much, except to shower and sleep."

CeCe let out a laugh. "True. But living with Carl will mean so much more…"

"Too much information, CeCe. Don't overshare. I'll be jealous!"

Both women laughed out loud, and Ruby could feel the tension in her shoulders ease just a bit.

As they drove around the rotary and through the town of Orleans, CeCe asked, "Do you want to drop your stuff off, or do you want to go straight to the Dive?"

"I'm in no rush to get to the Barn. Patti is probably there torturing some new employee anyway. I'd rather go to the Dive and get a drink. I could use one."

"Okay. Carl's meeting us there. I hope you don't mind."

Ruby smiled. She knew that her friend was itching to see her current heartthrob, and she fully understood how that felt. She'd been the same way last summer when her relationship with Cooper was heating up. Their long separation had been difficult for her, and the realization that he no longer wanted to continue what they'd begun felt impossible. But she had to keep moving forward, or at least that's what she told herself. As they got closer to the Dive, she could sense CeCe's anticipation of seeing her boyfriend charging the air inside the little car.

"Do I look okay?" CeCe asked, pulling down the visor with the mirror on it to check her makeup.

"You look beautiful, as always," Ruby replied, pausing at the stop light on Route Six to glance over at the other woman. Her tight mahogany curls spilled onto her shoulders, the sunset outside the car window reflecting off the red and golden highlights of her hair, her tawny skin flushed with excitement. Sitting in the close confines of the Kia, Ruby felt drab and tired next to her friend. It had been such an emotional roller coaster of a year. Law school was hard, much harder than she could have imagined when she began. All her free time was spent with her books and her study group, so much so that she had absolutely no social life at all in Cambridge. The last people she wanted to see in her few moments of relaxation were her classmates, with their constant chatter about the law and their endless arguments about the minutia of each and every exam they took. No, she wanted Cooper, only Cooper, in her bed, in her world. But he had, by ignoring her as summer drew near once again, made his intentions known. She was in his rear view now. There was someone new.

"Come back to me," CeCe teased. "I get the sense you were somewhere else just now."

"Sorry. I'm here. Actually, we're here." Ruby pulled off the main road down a small dirt path to the Dive. It was an old bomb shelter, left over from the Cold War when the residents of the Cape felt that they were vulnerable to foreign invasion, as they were situated so close to the Atlantic Ocean. Its location was a closely guarded secret among the locals of Bluff's Cove. It was not a place for tourists. It was home.

As Ruby turned into the parking lot and shut off the engine of the car, CeCe turned to face her.

"I know you're feeling a bit blue, but c'mon, girl, put just a little lipstick on."

"Oh. Yeah, I guess I should do something so that I don't scare the natives, huh?" She smiled.

CeCe handed her a brush, and Ruby pulled the elastic band out of her blond hair, releasing it until it fell midway down her back. She worked through some of the tangles until it was smooth, put some sheer lip gloss on, and pinched her cheeks to raise the little bit of color she could manage. Even her green eyes, which usually sparked with life, seemed to take on a dull appearance. "Any better?"

"You'll do. That didn't take that much effort, did it?"

"No need for sarcasm. I'm just not feeling great about this. I mean, what do I tell everyone?"

"First of all, since when do you care what anyone else thinks? Besides, they probably won't ask. But the truth works, you know. You haven't spoken to Cooper since prepping for finals, and no, you don't have any idea when he'll be back."

"You mean 'if' he'll be back."

"I'm sure he will be, sweetie," CeCe said, speaking to Ruby as if she were a child. "He lives here. Owns that awesome house and everything that goes with it."

"If you say so." Ruby shrugged and opened her car door, taking note that the parking lot was full of familiar pickup trucks and cars. The gang was gathered, that was for certain. "Let's go."

Together they walked, arms linked, into the bar.

It was actually a joyful reunion. All the people who had been strangers to Ruby the summer before were now her friends. She and CeCe entered to a rousing cheer of hellos; there was a round of hugs and the constant chatter of a group happy to see one another after a long winter. Mostly everyone had traveled somewhere exotic and fun, endlessly chasing summer and the ocean waves that they craved as they surfed around the world. It all sounded so intriguing to Ruby, and she was thrilled for the distraction, even though the only person she was hoping to find there was noticeably absent. Cooper had apparently not made his way back to the Cape yet, as she'd hoped, or was at least choosing not to come over to the Dive if he had. It left Ruby with a sinking feeling in the pit of her stomach; she stood up from her chair at the long table they had strung together from a mismatched set of smaller ones, making her way over to the bar to get another drink.

"Hey, Bumblebee," Steamroller said as she approached, holding his own draft in one hand and putting his free arm around her shoulders. "I'm glad you came back to us." He called her by the nickname he'd given her when she was a teenager and he was her surfing instructor. Now he was simply a good friend.

"Of course! Where else would I go? It's summer, and that only means one thing! The Hut!"

"Spoken like a true local!" He looked directly into her eyes. "So, tell me.

How was your winter? Work your ass off at that fancy school of yours?"

"Ugh, yeah. Don't remind me. I'm still waiting for my final grades. It was hard, Steamroller, really tough. I feel like I haven't slept a full eight hours in who knows how long. I can't wait to get back to the simpler life, you know, selling cheap tee shirts at Terry's concession stand."

"I hear you. Summertime always just seems easier, doesn't it?"

"It sure does. Tell me about your winter."

"Oh, well, Jenny and I went back to Maui. She has a waitressing gig there at a beach bar, and I teach tourists how to surf."

"You spent the winter with your sister?"

"Yup. But she met a guy this time and decided to stay."

Ruby was almost embarrassed by the relief at hearing that Jenny wasn't back up on the Cape. She was the person who had harped on Ruby's family scandal the previous summer, raising all sorts of questions that Ruby still hadn't found the answers for.

"That's something, huh? Meeting a guy at a beach bar. I can't imagine how that ever happens," she replied with a sarcastic laugh.

Steamroller raised one eyebrow as he thoughtfully chewed on a plastic straw he'd plucked from a container on the bar. "Happens all the time, I'm told." He turned to lean his elbows on the worn wooden surface, tilting his head up to look directly into her eyes. "Speaking of which, what do you hear from Cooper?"

"Nothing. We haven't spoken in a while. Have you heard from him?"

"As a matter of fact, I have. He called me this morning."

Ruby felt a wave of panic rush from her toes up to her head. She knew that she should remain calm and unaffected, but it was a real struggle to stop her heart from racing. "Really?" she asked as steadily as she could, trying not to give in to the inner turmoil she felt. "Where is he?"

"On his way up here from Logan Airport by now, I

should think," Steamroller said, glancing down at the small illuminated space on the cover of his antiquated flip phone, checking the time. "He was due to land around five. He said if he wasn't too jet-lagged, he'd stop by tonight."

"Did he?" Ruby questioned. "Is that all he said?"

"Uh, yeah. And that he was glad to be coming back home. I think he's had enough of that European living for a while."

"Interesting," Ruby replied, finding her center and feeling calmer now. "I wonder if he's bringing that woman home with him."

"What woman?"

"The one he met there, the one who was splashed all over his social media pages?"

"Who?" Steamroller asked. "You're not talking about his instructor, Anya, are you?"

"Not sure of her name, but that curvy redhead? That's who I mean."

Steamroller smiled widely. "That's her. But they're not a thing. I asked him about her when we spoke. He made it clear that it's all professional between them.

"It sure looked like they were close. She was hanging all over him, sitting on his lap and…" Just then Ruby could feel a subtle shift in the air around the bar. Before she even heard everyone shout out their greetings, she knew that Cooper was there, the pulse of him moving through the crowd with the speed of an electrical current straight to the core of her being.

"Well, I guess you could ask him yourself."

Ruby heard a familiar voice as Cooper stepped up behind her. "Three Satan's Satins, please," he said, asking the bartender for his very own brew, the one he'd gone off to Amsterdam to perfect. Ruby stood stock-still for a moment before turning around to see him. He looked even better than she remembered. Once the icy cold bottles were put down on the bar, he handed one to her and one to Steamroller.

"Thanks, man," his friend said, grabbing Cooper in a bear hug. "Good to have you back home."

"It's good to be here." Cooper patted Steamroller's back before stepping out of the embrace. "How's things?"

"Oh, you know…good. Pretty much the same."

"Glad to hear it. Let's get some dinner in a couple of days, once I settle back in. I have an interesting business proposition for you."

"Cool, man." Steamroller winked at Ruby and said, "See you later."

Ruby watched as Steamroller walked back over to the assembled group and sat down at one of the tables before turning to Cooper. "Hi," she said shyly.

"Hi yourself," he said with a smile, and she felt herself begin to shake with nervous energy. "I'm glad you're here."

"Well, if you'd been in touch with me this last month, you'd have known

I was coming back up."

He grimaced. "Why don't you finish your beer and then head out of here with me, back to the house? I'm really exhausted, but I think we have some catching up to do."

"Your house? Cooper, I don't know. We haven't spoken in so long, and you're tired. It can wait."

"Really, Ruby? You may be able to hold off on the inevitable, but I'm not." He leaned in and softly kissed her behind her ear. "I've been looking forward to seeing you," was all he said before reaching for her hand. As much as she wanted to stay put, the warmth of his palm melted her resistance, and she let him lead her out into the parking lot, anxious to hear what he had to say.

Almost Us: Chapter Two

Ruby pulled herself back from Cooper's nearness. The overwhelmingly familiar musky scent of him was making her lose her resolve. She could not fall back under his spell; he'd ignored her texts and e-mails for a month. She mustn't let him charm her with his smile. What she truly wanted was an explanation.

"Where've you been, Cooper?"

"Furiously working, trying to master this new brew method. It's so exciting, Ruby. I'll fill you in on everything, I promise. But for right now, I'm beat. Can it wait until the morning?" He reached for her hand. "I really missed you."

She stared back at him, not moving, and crossed both of her arms across her chest, ignoring his gesture. "Sure, have it your way, Cooper. I'll see you at work tomorrow."

"What? Wait...aren't you coming home with me now?"

Ruby just shook her head. "You must be really jet-lagged, because you're just talking nonsense. You haven't been in touch with me for over a month and you think I'm going to fall into your bed? Have you lost your mind entirely?"

He ran his hand through his hair in a familiar gesture. "I was in the lab with no internet connection, day and night for the last six weeks, Ruby, so yes, I was out of touch. I had no way to get to one of the cafés with free Wi- Fi. The six-hour time difference didn't help the situation either." He shook his head in apparent disbelief before continuing, "When I got off the plane in Boston, my phone was dead, or I would have tried to send you a text to let you know that I was on my way to the Cape. But, sure, have it your way, darling. We can talk about it some other time." He turned to leave, but then looked back. "Or is it something else? Because I know just how busy you were with finals. You made it clear that you had no time for me. For shit's sake, you couldn't even leave your precious study group over the holidays to come spend a few days in Europe with me when you did have a break from classes."

"We've been over this, Cooper," Ruby replied. "I didn't really have a break then. I was doing research for one of my professors. He truly needed me to finish the case work for him."

"Yeah, Ruby, so you've told me. But news flash. I needed you more. I was miserably lonely there without you."

And then, without even missing a beat and before she could stop the rush of words, she said, "I don't know, Cooper. The pictures of you on Facebook painted a different picture entirely."

"Pictures? You mean the ones with my classmates in the pub on one of our rare nights out?"

"Yup. I especially enjoyed the one with your so-called mentor sitting on your lap. It sure looked like your student-teacher relationship had turned into something else. Anything you want to tell me about that?"

He narrowed his eyes and shook his head. "Green's not your color, Ruby.

I'll see you at work tomorrow."

All Ruby could do was watch as he got into his truck and drove away, leaving her standing alone in the parking lot. She shakily drew in a breath, feeling tears begin to well up in her eyes, then looked up at the multitude of stars in the dark sky. When she located the one star that she and Cooper had designated as their own last summer at the final bonfire of the season, the one they pledged to look at together from opposite sides of the Atlantic Ocean, the one star she would go out and search for when she was missing him most, she began to cry in earnest. Then she got back in her car and drove over to the Barn to get some sleep. She had a sinking feeling that tomorrow was going to be quite a day.

Ruby woke up with a start. She had barely made it into her old room the night before when a semi-tipsy Patti, Louise, and Ronnie arrived.

"Ruby! It's so nice to be roomies with you again!" Louise engulfed Ruby in a boozy embrace.

"Yeah, hot shot! Done any real lawyering yet?" Patti asked with an air of amused interest.

Ruby smiled tiredly, in no mood for an extended conversation with any of these women, especially when they'd been drinking. "No. Not yet. And it's great to see you as well, but I'm beat. I think I'm just going to go to sleep." She lifted herself onto her old top bunk without even pulling a sheet onto the beat-up mattress and turned away from them, facing the wall. "Goodnight, girls."

"Hey there, not so fast," Patti said, jumping up on the bottom bed and pressing her face close to the back of Ruby's head. "I saw you standing outside the Dive with Cooper. What gives? Is he up for grabs again, or are you two still an item?"

Ruby could feel the hot, alcohol-laced breath of the other woman on her neck. She knew that there would be no sleep until she dealt with her nosy roommates. She sat up sharply.

"Okay, here's the story. I finished my first year of law school and feel like

I haven't come up for air since I saw you all last. It was hard, really hard, and I'm so tired that my eyelashes hurt. I have no real idea if Cooper is back on the market or not because we haven't spoken in a month; that is, other than the conversation you witnessed in the parking lot, Patti. And now, if you'll let me, I just want to go to sleep. Is that okay with all of you?"

"Wow, Ruby. No need to get your panties in a twist! It was just a question. Sorry to have disturbed you," Patti said before stepping back down. She turned to the other women and in an exaggerated whisper said, "C'mon, girls. Let's leave Miss Fancy Pants alone to sleep." She lifted a bottle of cheap red wine off the desk that sat between the two bunkbeds. "Nightcap, anyone?"

The others followed Patti out of the room, leaving Ruby blissfully alone, where she slept in the same exact position the entire night, waking at sunrise to find herself still dressed in her clothing from the day before and stiff from head to toe. She quietly slid down to the floor from her elevated perch, grabbed a towel, clean underclothes, jeans, and a tee shirt along with her toiletry kit, and stealthily opened the bedroom door. She did not want to wake the other women and face the continuing interrogation that had begun the previous night. She walked down the hall into the communal bathroom, stripped off her dirty garments, and turned the hot water on in one of the shower stalls. She then stepped inside and let the steamy spray soothe her aching muscles. When she finished scrubbing her hair and rinsing the remains of her body wash away, she stepped back out and made quick work of drying herself and dressing before the others woke up. She wanted to grab a quiet cup of coffee before having to face what she knew would be a grueling day, stocking the concession stand and dealing with the multiple personalities that comprised the rest of the staff at the Hut.

They were truly an eclectic bunch, mostly local residents with a handful of foreign-born kitchen workers thrown into the mix. Ruby had been the outsider last summer, but she had made her way into the core of the group when she had offered to split her commission from the sales of tee shirts and other paraphernalia with the member of the wait staff who sold the most merchandise over the course of the season. It was a moment of pure inspiration because it had immediately bonded her with a majority of her fellow employees. It took longer for some of the others to accept her—Patti primarily—but eventually Ruby had worn her down as well. Over the winter months she'd kept in touch with her boss, Terry, and made sure that she'd be welcomed back to the famed beach bar and restaurant once again for another season. Now, in what felt to her like a blink of an eye, summer was about to begin anew.

Ruby drove her car into the parking lot at the local Cumberland Farm convenience store and shut the engine.

Grabbing her wallet, she stepped inside to make herself a large cup of hot coffee before heading off to her favorite spot to watch the waves for a bit before her work day began. She paid for the brew and took a long sip. Feeling a bit stronger with that first rush of caffeine coursing through her blood, she went back outside and pointed her Kia in the direction of the beach. When she arrived, she saw the familiar pickup trucks that belonged to the dedicated surfers who all worked at the Hut. She could spot them chasing the surf from her vantage point high above

on the dune. Even though she'd survived an entire winter away from this place, in that moment Ruby felt as if she'd never left.

She stepped out onto the blacktop and grabbed her coffee, sat herself down on the warm hood of her car, and leaned back against the windshield. The early morning sun had not yet begun to heat up the day, but she could feel the true promise of summer on her face as she closed her eyes for the moment to grab and store some serenity for when she knew she'd need it most.

An hour later, feeling a bit more refreshed, she threw her empty cup into the trash. There were a few small gypsy moths flitting about the garbage receptacle, and she absent mindedly watched them take flight and fly off together looking for something better to eat than the drained beer bottles and empty pretzel bags that lined the bottom of the big green can. Drawing in one last gulp of delicious ocean air, she returned to her car and drove over to the Hut.

As Ruby pulled into the parking lot of the infamous beach bar, she could see that not much had changed over the winter. The location was what made the place such a draw. It sat high up on a sandy dune, and over the years it had expanded, with several decks that jutted out overlooking the ocean. There was a large bar along the water's edge of the outdoor portion of the restaurant, another bar inside where the concert stage sat, as well as a beach-level bar at the end of a long row of wooden steps that opened each day at eleven in the morning. The menu of the restaurant was simple enough. Fresh seafood caught by local fishermen was served all day, along with the standard hamburger and nacho fare that most people enjoyed with a cold beer or frozen margarita. The owner, Terry, ran a tight ship. She expected a lot from her loyal employees, and, in turn, they were able to pocket an enormous amount of money for their short season's work.

Ruby had originally come up the previous summer with the hope of being hired as a waitress, but instead, Terry had hired her to run the concession stand that sat at the main entrance. It was Ruby's responsibility to stock the shelves and sell as many tee shirts and sweatshirts to the clientele as she could. The record-breaking tally from the year before would be hard to beat. She hoped she was up to the challenge.

As Ruby walked closer to the main building, she could see stacks of boxes sitting just outside the stand. Someone had helped her out by giving her a head start, saving her quite a few trips from the storage container at the far end of the parking lot. She had her work cut out for her, she could see that, so Ruby did the one thing she knew would take her mind off Cooper for the next few hours—she went looking for Terry to get the key for the lock on the metal grate that secured the stand. She walked past the main entrance and into the back of the empty bar, where she knew her boss's office was located, and found the other woman sitting at her desk behind a large, messy stack of papers.

"Hi, Terry," she said.

The distinctive hair of the woman she had first thought looked something like Cruella de Ville had an even wider streak of gray than she'd had the previous September, when Ruby'd seen her last, and there were large bags under her eyes as well. She slowly lifted her head at the sound of Ruby's voice.

"You here for the duration now?" she asked, her voice as raspy as ever, and in true Terry fashion, cutting right to the heart of the matter.

"Yes. School ended a few days ago. I need the key for the lock on the concession stand."

Terry lifted one of the large stacks of papers off her desk, only to knock an entire file onto the floor.

Ruby knelt to help gather the sheets when she spied the logo of a large law firm from Boston across the top of one.

"Everything okay?" she asked apprehensively.

Terry narrowed her eyes. "It's a work in progress. I'm handling this mess, believe me." She rummaged around until she came up with a key and passed it to Ruby. "Get to work. I want that stand in top shape for the soft open at the end of the week. You've got a lot to do. Go."

The older woman hadn't changed a bit. Still gruff and bossy. "Right. I'm gone." Ruby slipped the key onto the ring with her own and went back outside to organize herself for the day. When she unlocked the stand, she immediately realized that nothing had been touched inside since she walked away from it last September. There were dried leaves piled high in one corner that needed to be swept out and more than one cobweb up on the highest shelves. She went to the storage unit and grabbed the bucket and sponge that she had stored there the summer before and busied herself scrubbing down the entire stand, from top to bottom. She hadn't even had a moment to look at her watch, but from the height of the sun in the now cloudless sky, she could tell it was nearly noon. She was drenched in a combination of sweat, dust, and dirty water when she realized that she hadn't eaten a thing yet today. She took the bucket of murky suds, walked across the parking lot, and drained it behind the Dumpster at the far end and put her cleaning supplies back into storage. She then headed into the bathroom to assess how much personal washing up she needed to do before tracking down CeCe and getting some lunch.

The women's restroom was empty, so she took her time rinsing the streaks of dirt from her face. The ponytail she'd hastily pulled together earlier that day had come undone, so she pulled out the elastic tie and let her blond hair fall in loose waves around her shoulders. She had taken off her long-sleeved button-down shirt when she started to work in earnest, knowing how dirty she'd get. Her white tank top was truly grimy now, so she removed it, put the other garment back on, and rolled up the sleeves against the growing warmth of the day. Her jeans were still wet in patches from washing down the stand, but she knew that they would dry quickly when she set up her display of merchandise after she ate something. Just then her cell phone buzzed against her leg from the pocket of her pants. She reached inside and answered the call.

"Hey, CeCe. You're a mind reader. I was just about to come find you. Are you here at the Hut?"

"On my way. Do you need some food? I can stop for sandwiches. I'm leaving Carl's house now."

"Sounds good to me. Did you have a good night?"

"Oh, you know how nice an overdue reunion can be. It's hot!"

Ruby winced. "Yup. I bet. Um, could you get me an iced coffee too?"

CeCe answered, "Be there in ten minutes. Meet you at the picnic table out back."

"I'll be waiting." Ruby shut off her phone and went to sit under the shade of the large trees that lined the back of the parking lot where the designated employee break area was located. It was nothing more than a few old rickety tables, but it was outside of the venue and sheltered from a bit of the seasonal craziness when summer was in full swing. It offered some peace and quiet in what could often be a never-ending grind when the bar and restaurant were packed beyond capacity. From this vantage point, Ruby could watch the bustle of activity as deliverymen showed up in a constant stream, dropping off provisions for the cooks to prepare in anticipation of the soft open.

There was a beautiful, cool breeze rustling through the trees, and Ruby closed her eyes for a moment, feeling the clean air pass over her face and body. When she opened them again, she saw Cooper's truck pull into the lot. She drew in a breath. All the muscles in her body tensed when he stepped out. His tight black tee shirt outlined the strength of his chest, and as he lowered the tailgate, she could see cases of his home brew, Satan's Satin, neatly stacked there. She sat in the shadow of the tall trees, so he didn't know that she was there, giving her the advantage of watching him work. She had been tough on him the night before, but she hadn't changed her mind. If he couldn't come clean about his involvement with his mentor or give her a better explanation than a lack of readily available Wi-Fi, well, then they were done.

He pulled out a hand truck and loaded it to capacity with the boxes of beer and walked into the restaurant. Once he was out of sight, Ruby sat back and looked up, almost praying for a sign from the heavens, for something or someone to tell her what to do next. Should she confront him? Should she wait until he offered up an excuse for his absence? As the breeze ruffled through the budding leaves, she saw a series of brown cocoons that she hadn't noticed before. They looked almost like alien beings, simple and silent up in the highest branches of the trees. It was an eerie sight, more befitting of Halloween than Memorial Day. She made a mental note to point them out to CeCe when she arrived, but for now, she shrank back and watched for Cooper to come back out and reload his hand truck one more time.

She didn't have long to wait. He walked back to his vehicle, stacked the remaining boxes on the hand truck, and brought them into the restaurant.

Ruby was unaccustomed to the way she felt. She was usually more decisive, knowing her mind and what she wanted to say in any given situation. This time was different. She measured each and every word over and over again in her head. She would confront him, she decided, once he came back to his truck. She would ask him to tell her about his relationship with his mentor and would carefully listen to his answer. Maybe it was innocent after all. Social media channels were unreliable sources of the truth, she knew that, and just one picture shouldn't make her as uneasy as this one did. *So why,* she wondered, *is this one photo affecting me in this way?*

And then it dawned on her. It was the look Cooper shared with this woman in the photograph. She recognized it. She'd been on the receiving end of that very same gaze. Those deep blue eyes were asking for a deeper level of intimacy without a word ever being spoken. A knowing glance.

They'd either slept together already or he was planning on getting that woman into his bed. The realization made Ruby's stomach turn, and she felt waves of nausea rise in her throat.

She sat stock-still until CeCe drove up with Carl, gave her new boyfriend a showy kiss, and jumped out with a bagged lunch in one hand and a cardboard tray with two iced coffees in the other. At the very same time, Cooper walked back to his truck. Carl drove toward him and honked, stopping in the middle of the parking lot to shout out a greeting. Ruby watched as CeCe closed the distance between them, all the while keeping an eye on the two men. She saw when Carl nodded in her direction, causing

Cooper to lift his head and lock eyes on her. It was almost like it was all happening in slow motion on a movie screen, and Ruby was just sitting in a theater watching it unravel.

CeCe sat down and dropped the bag on the table with a flourish. Cooper started to walk toward them. There was nothing Ruby could do to stop any of it; there was no place to run and hide. She drew in a deep breath and prayed that the answer he would give her would be the truth.

About the Author

Hilari T. Cohen is an award-winning editor who has worked and consulted in the publishing field for over thirty years. She built brands for Berkley, Harlequin and Zebra Books as well as edited many New York Times bestselling authors and titles in both fiction and nonfiction categories. However, she always harbored a secret ambition to write a novel of her own, and she did, successfully publishing eleven novels to date.

Hilari lives with her husband in suburban New York.